# The Pleasure Protocols

# The Pleasure Protocols

## Special Underbedcover Agent

## Max Pleasure

*thepleasureprotocols@gmail.com*

**To order additional copies of this book, contact:**
Xlibris Corporation
1-888-795-4274
www.Xlibris.com
Orders@Xlibris.com
66968

# Contents

# Proto-Logue

From: **Brother Pleasure** (brople@hotmail.com)
Sent: Wednesday, September 17 1:11:39 PM
To: Max Pleasure (maxple@hotmail.com)

Max! Hey, big bro, just back from skiing in Italy – wanna meet 4 beer tmrw? Show u pix. Usual place?

From: **Max Pleasure** (maxple@hotmail.com)
Sent: Wednesday, September 17 1:12:35 PM
To: Brother Pleasure (brople@hotmail.com)

Yeah, fine. Listen, I'm writing a book, it's magic. I'm using my life's experiences to help other people. Putting something back into society, you know? Well, putting even more back – just paid some bloody crippling taxes.

U? Hlpng other pple? Dn't mke me larf. Who the crap do u thnk u r? JC Superstar? Tht rhymes.

Doesn't scan, though. I helped you, you spineless old plonker. Where would you be without me?

**Sod off you arrogant berk!**

Yep, it's really going to make a difference. Everyone's so damn' unhappy these days, like you. I just don't get it. Always peering up their own arses for the answers, and I suddenly thought, I lead a really effective life and I can show them how to do it too! I'm calling it 'The Pleasure Protocols', you know, help people learn how to get pleasure out of life. Not like self-help, and none of that religious crap, just some excellent stories with a good, crisp point to them, and a few practical tips. Sort of natural anti-depressant.

Christ, ur so obnoxious.

Oh, and the new Testarossa arrived yesterday. Pick you up at 7pm?

D'u get the charcoal finish?

Charcoal! You're so . . . Armani, aren't you? So, dated. Two weeks in Italy and I bet you still . . . Got to go, someone's . . . just coming . . .

Arrogant wanker

# Protocol No. 1 – Openness

## THE ANTI-PROTOCOL – DULLNESS

Openness: Now, what I want to do with these Protocols is give
you a few pointers, just mark the moral of each tale as I tell it
with one word defined by the dictionary, so that by the end of
the book, you've got the Seven Golden Rules of Pleasuring at
your fingertips. But, turns out there's no definition of 'openness'
in my Collins dictionary. Sorry about that, I must've just made
the word up, so read the first Protocol story and work it out for
yourself mate, okay?

**NB: Dictionary definitions of the Protocol and
anti-Protocol words *appear in italics*.**

Dullness: Who do you think of when you see that word? If it's
you, you're in shit, but no worries, I'm here to help – just read on.

D O YOU REMEMBER when
Experience's creeping stiletto
punctured the vein of your everyday life for the first time, coaxing out a
trickle of awareness? I do.

I was 14 and on holiday with my parents and brother at a resort in Spain.
There were palm trees swaying overhead, the pool was the bluest blue I'd
ever seen and her velvety eyes were the brownest brown I'd ever seen. Her
tits were the brownest I'd ever seen, too. In the flesh, that is.

Sun, sea, sand. Surrounded by a sea of bodies, massive boner and, of course, no idea what to do about it. In public, I mean. Had a fairly good, five-times-a-day idea of what to do with it in general.

I'd met the girl at the poolside bar when I was buying a Coke, and we'd got chatting. Well, kind of chatting. Mainly it was me gawping and then letting out a bellow of overloud, senseless laughter every time she said it was hot, or the Coke was nice or something.

But there we were, lying side by side by the pool, balancing cold drinks on our stomachs. I'd put a towel over my groin, just in case anything got spilt. Was wondering if I should offer to smear her back with suntan lotion; ease that yellowy, coconut-smelling greasiness down over her shoulders past the flimsy straps and flowered scraps nuzzling her nipples, down on to the single triangle tucked so tight against her unseen pubes, protecting her dainty wound from penetrating . . . eyes. Her stomach muscles tensed suddenly, she crossed and re-crossed her legs, dislodging the bead of sweat whose progress further and further into her crotch I'd been enviously watching. I looked up and saw that her lips were moving.

"I ask, what ees your name?" she repeated, smiling.

How unbelievable to think that she could be *entered*. Literally broken into. If she would just part her thighs, I could push past the petalled triangle with my fingers, *enter* her. I'd been told it would be warm and wet, which sounded like a weather forecast but dazzled me nonetheless. How could it not hurt her to be *entered*? I ached to cause such pain, again and again, with my fingers and my bursting cock.

"It's, um, I . . ." I stuttered and the girl giggled.

On the other side of the pool, my mother sat up and glanced over at us, shading her eyes with her hand. I adjusted the towel and waved. She nudged my father and he looked across, then shrugged and went back to his paper. Surely they couldn't see the woodie from that distance?

"Max," I told the girl. "My name's Max."

She looked puzzled.

"Max? Oh, Maximilian?"

Silly chica, silly chica! I smirked and said,

"No, Max is short for Maximum."

She threw her head back and laughed, setting her little tits jiggling. Suddenly I was standing over her, pulling down my bathing trunks and unloading all over her, watching the cum trickle over her tits, off her cheeks and into her hair, all over, all over her smooth brown body . . . .

When she stopped laughing, she looked me straight in the eyes and said,

"It's a nice name."

Now or never.

"It's a good name for me," I agreed, edging a little closer and turning on my side towards her.

"Why?" Again that little puzzled frown. If only I could kiss it away with butterfly lips.

"Well, you know, Maximum means the biggest, the best."

The towel was making a tent from my groin to the ground. I gave my 'paquete' a pat and the girl a complacent smirk. She stared.

"Maximum," I whispered, and lifted the towel a bit more so she could get a better view. "The biggest, the best."

She looked down, got up, shouted,

"Papi, Papi!"

A big man about 10 yards away turned his head.

"Time for a cold dip," a familiar voice said in my ear, and Dad chucked me into the pool. It was really cool the way he caught the towel as it and I flew through the air.

Well, okay, so the line didn't go so well that time. But I held onto it and practised with it and it began to work.

Because, you see, I've worked at this. That day at the Spanish resort, I began to realise that this was not going to be a simple thing.

So bit by bit, I began to study. And I've made the pursuit of pleasuring women – and myself obviously, I'm not a fucking charity worker – my life's oeuvre.

Pleasure. My favourite word. As a verb, not as a noun. To pleasure, to be pleasured.

Mmmmmmmmmmmmm.

Mmmmmmmmmmmm is for Max.

Max is for Maximum.

Mmmmmmmmmmmmmmm.

\*     \*     \*

I don't know if you know New York? It's a great place. I've never lived there, but I've been there a lot, for work usually. I love it: it is a friendly city, yet it does not give a shit. You drop in, you make your mark, do what you have to do and leave. It is not going to pause for a split second. It's up to you to jump on the moving rollercoaster.

This time was only my second visit. The day was September 11th. Nah, not *the* September 11th, not 9/11. A different year. On *the* 9/11, I heard someone say, as the second tower sank to its knees, "Someone'll be getting pleasure out of this." Which made me turn my head. I was in a bog-standard London pub, watching it all on the box. The speaker was a bog-standard Londoner, and he'd really conjured up an image. Who knows how many people were jacking off at the sight that was holding all us suits and slobs open-mouthed in different ways. Pleasure. The purpose of my life. Giving pleasure. My favourite word, therefore. And one which, I believe, features prominently in the Koran. One of the rules is about letting the woman have her fill, so to speak, before you get your rocks off.

Odd, then, to think how people with that attitude were determined to bag women up. I mean, I like mystery more than the next man, and will often find long skirts and concealing wraps sexier than short shorts or plunging cleavages. But I don't want anyone bagged up. Not even a colour scheme! Mind you, men tend to treat themselves the same. Uniforms, suits.

I was wearing a suit myself that day in New York, in fact. So was she. It was a dress and jacket job that was just, and only just, discreet enough to be acceptable in business circles.

In front of me inside the hotel lift. She'd pressed the button of floor 29, I was going up to 35. And it was at floor 8 that it stopped.

I don't know what possessed me. Well, I do, but I don't know what led me to act on that possession, unless perhaps it was the way I'd seen her cross the foyer that morning. She'd no sooner given a sigh of irritation and muttered, "Oh jeeze!" than my hand was reaching out. As it touched the hem of her dress, she stopped pressing the emergency button; as it skimmed up over the back of her thigh, she became very still, and she was still still (not a typo, you know what I mean) when I eased aside her panties and began to finger-fuck her.

Believe me, I'd never done such a thing in my life. Her glossy head turned very slightly as I slid in the first finger. She was neither dry nor wet. I paused. For a second or two, we stayed immobile. Then she moved one foot, parting her legs just a fraction, and I brushed that glossy hair with my lips and inserted another finger.

The third one was in and I'd got into a good firm rhythm when the lift jerked back into life. Breathing hard down the side of her head, I massaged her not unwilling cunt up beyond floor 27. Then I pulled out fast and dropped back, not a moment too soon. A new gent joined us on 28. She moved her feet back together.

At 29, she turned while stepping out and flicked a sliver of plastic between her fingers.

"2901," she said clearly.

The doors closed. The other gent glanced at me, but I don't know if it was with suspicion or envy. Once we'd unloaded him, I went back down to 29 and stepped out into the cool, quiet corridor.

She opened the door with a truculent look on her unremarkable face. I didn't know why I was hard.

She gestured me in, crossed to the mini-bar.

"Scotch?"

I felt like Humphrey Bogart. I mean, Humphrey Bogart in a film. I have no idea how he felt in real life. About as good as the rest of us, probably.

"Sure," I smirked. It sounded crap in an English accent. But the smirk's international.

She came and stood foursquare to me. Nothing about her attracted me. I gave her back stare for stare.

"Did you enjoy that?" she asked.

"Not much."

Her eyebrows rose.

"I'm not fond of Scotch," I explained, and put down the empty glass.

Well, of course it would have gone better with someone who had a sense of humour. Her eyes narrowed.

"I'm a hooker," she said.

Good word. Gets it all across nice and quickly. Not too dirty, not too euphemistic. I mean, she could have said any number of mystifying things. But no, she put it in layman's terms.

"I'm a hooker. What you just had in the elevator was for free. I've got a big heart. Now, I charge $300 an hour. I have an hour before my next client. You get the next hour, I get $300."

Great. I wondered how she'd look in a shapeless black bag. But of course she was absolutely right. If you finger-fuck someone, it's because there's an agreement in place. An emotional agreement or a financial transaction, in most cases.

A hooker. Did I have my triple-strength condoms with me? New York, land of litigation. Would even a triple-skin protect me from the emasculating forces of U.S. justice? After all, I hadn't just touched up a woman in a lift, I'd touched her up her, if you get me. They could probably crucify me for it.

Jesus only got a loincloth and a crown of thorns, and he hadn't even *done* sexual harassment. No loincloth for me, I suspected, just a condom dangling from my limp cock. Except that crucifixion is agony and they say that that can provoke an erection, like pissing when you're scared. Involuntary. Hung out to dry with a permanent boner. Who would get my silver Jag? Really must make a Will, or my brother would grab it.

"Well?" she said.

I reached out slowly and took the cigarette from her fingers and ground it out even more slowly in a nearby ashtray. Then I faced her again.

"That's funny," I said. "I'm a hooker too."

There was a pause as long as my dick and then she raised an eyebrow. I carried on,

"Only I charge $500 an hour. I don't want to call you cheap, so if I just give you the next hour, we'll call it quits, okay?"

She went on staring. It suddenly occurred to me that I'd been fingering her goods in the lift but hadn't even offered her a glimpse of mine.

"Want a butcher's at my hook, hooker?" I asked.

Not a bad line, I thought. But of course she looked puzzled. I moved closer, felt the buckle of my belt and said,

"I just mean you'd probably like to see the merchandise before you buy."

She hunched one shoulder in a why-not sort of way. Frankly, I was surprised the merchandise hadn't made its own way out and displayed itself all over her suite by now. It was straining so hard against the front of my pants that I had trouble undoing the buckle. As soon as I did, it nosed out and her eyes widened a fraction and she said,

"Well, I guess that'll make a change from stumps and frankfurters."

She opened a little box standing on the dressing-table and offered a selection of condoms, like a waiter taking round the cigars or teas after a meal. Have to remember that one.

"No, please, I insist," I said, flourishing one of my own. "So, is that all you get, stumps and frankfurters?" I asked, peeling on a condom and wondering if it would be rude to pile on the next two in front of her.

She shrugged, watching the handiwork.

"Aw, it's not that bad. But yeah, a lot of stumps and sob stories, especially at conferences."

I turned away hastily. There were only a couple of hours to go before I was due to give my presentation at the conference I was in town for.

"Still, thank God for the conferences, eh?" I said. "Keeps us off the streets."

I finished heaping my clothes on a chair, turned back to her naked and said,

"Preferences?"

She smiled.

"Oh, so you *are* a pro," she drawled. "Well, I don't do kissing or oral work, I don't have preferences, and I *never* come with a client."

Well, thank God/Whatever for all that, I thought. She was fully dressed, business heels and all. So what's the fashion in New York this season, mate? Oh, business suits for the women, triple-strength condoms for the men, mate. It was clearly going to be some battle. I just hoped the protection would bear up.

"Usual rules, then," I responded in a knowing tone. "But I'm not exactly a client, am I?"

"You're less than a client," she replied. "You're not paying. Same rules."

She turned to the dressing table, shifted one foot so that her legs parted slightly, and stooped to apply fresh lipstick in front of the mirror.

Nice touch. My cock jumped. As I lifted the dress with both hands and reached for her buttocks, I suddenly realised, clear as water, why I was rock hard and burning to bang her.

Because I disliked her.

Everything she represented, the whole corporation of sex. I felt like the small-time craftsman with a shop full of handmade goods who sees a huge department store go up next door and suddenly all the punters are veering past his beautifully arranged window display and charging into the store for the quick, cheap answer. I was standing at the door of my life's work, beckoning them in with my eyes, but they didn't know the difference between what they were willing to pay for and what I could offer because they were too cheap and stupid to try.

So I pulled her knickers down roughly and slammed into her with an anger that knocked the lipstick out of her hand and almost put her face into the big modern three-way mirror. Her lipstick hand slapped down on the glossy wood to steady herself, but a classy New York hooker isn't going to be rocked by contempt for all that she stands for with her legs slightly apart.

"Careful," she hissed at the mirror.

"Yeah." I gave her a three-way smirk, got my hands on the front of her thighs, and lifted her feet just off the ground while I thrust up inside her as far as I could. Then I set her back on her heels, pressed her down so she couldn't see my face, and banged her so hard and fast that I was sweating after a minute. She didn't make a sound. That went on for some time.

Finally, dripping, I leaned forward and said into the glossy hair,

"Better than a stump?"

She straightened up slowly and met my look in the mirror. Her hand reached for the dislodged lipstick.

"Oh, have you got started?" she drawled. "I hadn't noticed."

I stared at her touching up her lips, then burst out laughing, which dislodged the lipstick again because I was still good and hard inside her.

"Okay, it's your turn. Your rules."

"You're gonna lose," she said with an icy confidence, which shows the way she was seeing it. "I've told you, I never come with a client. And certainly not with a sub-client."

I wondered if she ever came at all.

She lowered herself off my prick and gestured me over to the bed. I lay down in my sweat and surreptitiously checked the protection while she stepped out of the panties, which had been slack round her ankles, and stripped off the dress.

She approached me clothed in just her lipstick and a perfume I didn't like much. Still, she smelt better than me at that stage, I have to say.

"Ladies first is my motto," I told her. "If you don't come, neither do I."

She gave a knowing, mirthless smile that really annoyed me and hefted my balls a few times, watching my cock jump in response.

"Oh no?" she said softly, and got to work.

Well, we both tried damn' hard, I can tell you that. It was like being at a funfair where I'd no sooner got used to one ride than she dragged me off to another. I fucked her sideways, endways, forward and back, willing her to get some pleasure from my handicraft, but I could see in her eyes that all she wanted was to make me come, to prove me wrong, to class me with all the stumps and frankfurters after all.

Tell the truth, it began to feel like I was pretty much down to a stump myself. Her fanny seemed to harden along with the determined line of her jaw, and I was just beginning to worry that she was grinding my prick off at the roots and would make off with it inside her till it shrank and died so that she could pick it out with fastidious fingers and fling it down contemptuously in front of a group of laughing friends (if she had any – laughing ones I mean), saying; "He was just like all the rest," when she suddenly climbed off me, said, "You'll have to go," and disappeared into the bathroom.

"You can make me go, but you can't make me come!" I called out after her. Rubbing it in – ouch.

I checked the condom, relieved to see no scorch marks, and got dressed quickly to the sound of running water.

Laying the empty condom across her pillow, I let myself out and hurried back to my own room to soap and water my throbbing cock with the care of a father bathing his newborn baby for the first time.

After the shower, I lay slumped in a chair for ten minutes or so, staring at a haggard face in a three-way mirror.

"Where've you been?" cried a colleague in the conference hall, clapping me on the shoulder. "Get lost or something? You missed my talk."

"Hey, sorry. I needed to do some boning up for my presentation."

\*       \*       \*

There were early signs that I'd been chosen. I'm not saying I was a prodigy at four like Mozart, or anything, but by the time I hit my teens I *knew*. I was aware of a calling, and way before I fully understood what that calling was, I began to prepare for it.

As a teenager, I was dead sporty, and popular with schoolmates, but I never joined in much with their changing-room banter: knowing myself to be so much better endowed than any of them, I would've felt it was too cruel to remind them of their inadequacy by boasting of my own prowess. I was incredibly considerate for my age. Most men don't acquire that kind of sensitivity till they're about 60, if then. My schoolmates' boasts were usually pathetic; I squirmed as I listened. Was embarrassed by their loud emptiness, their lack of imagination, perhaps. I mean, I enjoyed the filth, but there was no poetry in their filth.

At 16, I stripped out my bedroom and redecorated it, so much to my parents' delight – my mother's in my exquisite taste and my father's in my constructive activity – that they asked me to do the rest of the house. So I did.

Friends – theirs – came from afar to admire. Mine trudged in and gawped, embarrassed. My 13-year-old brother scuffed his naff little shoes on the new paintwork and fabrics.

"Well, it's all marvellous, my dear," I overheard one of my parents' friends say. "But isn't it a *wee* bit strange? Unusual, rather. A teenage boy with *such* an interest in curtains and colours and so on!" She gave a metallic laugh.

"Are you trying to say my son's a poof?" asked my father. Interesting how he appropriated me to himself in the face of such a suggestion. I tried to remember if I'd ever seen his dick. Don't think so.

"Oh heavens!" exclaimed the friend. "No, I didn't mean to . . . of course that wasn't what . . . . Well! Do *you* think he is?" she said suddenly.

"I think he's done a wonderful job," said my mother simply.

And she was the one who'd seen me kissing another boy in my newly-decorated bedroom the week before. Actually, it was the same day the Tiffany lamp for their bedroom arrived – great finishing touch – so I wasn't likely to forget that day in a hurry.

The bedroom faced north so I'd kept the basic colouring – walls, floor and ceiling – light in tone, but added warmth with Spanish chestnut wardrobes and richly patterned curtains, cushions etc in jewel shades. The lamp would, I knew, bring the whole together in a glow of colourful pattern. They had proper lighting too, of course. But the most gratifying thing was that I'd placed The Tiff on the table by the armchair and after a few days I saw it had been moved to the bedside table on my mother's side, and when I carefully eased an eye round the door that night, I found out why. It was like a scene from The Arabian Nights; the soft but strong multi-coloured light throwing shots of red and gold and green up the wall, the deep, rich shades of the bedcovers, and my parents' naked bodies, quietly taking pleasure in each other on and in their bed of desire. The environment which *I* had created! I withdrew and went and whacked off in the downstairs bathroom, proud and delighted.

You're probably thinking, oh dear, Tiffany lamps – that is pants. And I know what you're saying, but they do have a place, they just need to be treated with respect. They need to be understood, not laughed at; they can't just be expected to get results on their own. Years later, in New York (no, different trip, I had a canary yellow Porsche Boxster at that point), I saw some mind-blowing examples of Tiffany's work – enormous, fabulously intricate windows depicting entire rural scenes – in the Museum of American Art, and I just stood in awe, drinking in every nuance. Then I read how the nuances were created, the care and precision that went into every glass fragment, and I stood and gaped again.

So what I'm saying here is that when, as a 16-year-old, I chose a Tiff for my parents' bedroom, I was in a state of recognition which none of my contemporaries was even remotely capable of achieving. Especially not the males. I mean, I wasn't a freak or anything, I climbed and went paintballing or skateboarding with the rest of the neds and I liked Dali too at that stage. But I had another dimension: instinctively, I knew how to create an atmosphere which would please someone else in the deepest sense, and early triumph encouraged me to pursue that skill, though I still didn't know where it was leading me or why I was letting it. But something I just *knew*.

As a matter of fact, the woman who thought it was 'unusual' for me to redecorate the house was the mother of the boy I'm sure *my* mother had seen me kissing. Well, being kissed by, to be more accurate. I didn't really have an urge to kiss other blokes. He was two years older than me and a brilliant squash player: we both played for the school team – he was the Captain and way-out-there No 1 and I usually held the No 3 slot. Occasionally No 2 if the other bloke got the squits, which he did for about half the matches. The Captain had come to see the house too, and told me in my bedroom he really liked me because I was so artistic and sensitive, then he kissed me. Which was a surprise, and quite interesting, but my mother came up to offer us tea and buns at that moment, and I just *know* she saw something through the crack, so when he suggested going to a matinee at the local fleapit at the weekend, I agreed.

We were almost the only two in there, and we sat in the back row and explored each other. His face against mine felt awkward and angular now that the kissing was more than just a quick lips-on-lips touch. Very different from what I knew of girls' faces against mine. He was tentative but forceful in his kissing and I realised that I felt defensive, as though my tongue and his were engaged in jousting, and if I dropped my guard, he'd fill my mouth with a presence that might choke me. Rather choke on my own vomit, frankly. But perhaps that's what a girl would be feeling when I kissed her, so I stopped jousting for a few minutes and sure enough, it was, like, pushy-pushy-pushy, man! Thrusting. That's what it was all about for him. It was almost as though he wanted to win something.

"Mm, oh yeah, oh yeah," he kept murmuring during the onslaught.

He seemed to be enjoying it more now I'd given up the struggle, and he probed incessantly back and forth in my mouth till I felt like I was at the dentist. My jaws were beginning to ache. He'd got my hand on his dick and was obviously expecting developments there, but I stayed passive and let him open his fly and push my hand into his underpants.

I stopped pretending to be a girl and decided to make an effort here. I felt around a bit to locate his gear and he murmured and nearly bit my earlobe off, so once I'd got hold of the thing, I gave it a couple of tugs and the poor bastard came! Major surprise to me – the guy had loads of stamina on court. Well, another major surprise: the first one, which shouldn't have been, was that it was so small and not that hard and I much preferred the feel of my own. Mine felt a lot more *alive*, a lot better *mate*, if you know what I mean. More reliable. More fun. I knew I wouldn't have to steer people's hands to my dick, but he would always have to.

By this time his head was flopping about on my shoulder and he was murmuring about how much he liked me and he wished we could stay like this forever and I nearly gagged, but thought, sad or wot? Maybe I should get up and go. But just as I was about to mutter "Sorry" and make a move, he unstudded my jeans and went down on me. And then the action on screen began to hot up, so I was actually able to get a hard-on and abandon myself to the dual sensation of visual turn-on and physical stimulation. He was down on his knees working on it for about 20 minutes before I unloaded and despite the screen distraction – excellent car chase – that gave me plenty of time to register my own reactions, and the end result was that when he finally sat up gulping and gasping, I'd decided this was not for me. Extremely useful experience, and no such thing as a bad blowjob, but it was all just a bit too, angular. Sharp. I'd been worried all through that he was going to nip it with his teeth, like a terrier, and I didn't know what to do with my hands because his skin felt too like mine. It was all too familiar, and I liked different. That was the big revelation of the afternoon – from my point of view, of course; he'd had to get his mouth round a lot bigger revelation.

I liked different. I let his head rest on my chest for the rest of the film because I'm fair and I realised he'd worked hard, but he weighed a ton. Everything about him except the one thing that should've done just felt too hard to me. Not plastic enough. The kissing bit had been the most useful aspect, I decided. It did cross my mind that if I wanted to be logical about this and find out how it feels for a girl, I should let him fuck me. And thinking that option through clarified my reaction: I'd rather use a hairbrush. Well, yeah, I *had* preferred a hairbrush. Anyway, I was under age, plus I didn't have a fanny – it wouldn't be the same.

And he smelt funny. I didn't have a whole lot of experience with girls but I liked the way they smelt and I liked the fact they were squishy and giggly and needed more convincing than this. I liked them because they were different from me.

He was murmuring something; I bent my aching neck to hear what he was saying, and it turned out to be,

"I think I love you."

Bit blood-curdling, that. It struck me that he was an ace tactician on the squash court and was surely looking for a result here. But what? He'd had all I was prepared to give. I was still puzzling over it while we walked through the quiet part of town when he stopped me, looked into my eyes and said,

"Do you?"

"Do I what?"

"Love me?"

"'Course not."

"You like me, though?"

"Yeah, 'course I like you. Just don't think we're playing for the same team, that's all." I tried to keep a straight (oh God, another pun) face, but couldn't. His face hardened – see, even his face could do better than his cock – then he got hold of me and shoved me up against the scrapyard fence.

"Hey!" I protested. "Look, I'm sorry, I shouldn't laugh, I know. All right? It's just . . . it was fine. I mean, really. I just don't, you know."

"Are you going to tell people?" he hissed, unexpectedly.

"No!" *Who* would be interested, I wondered.

He was still clutching my jacket collar. His tight face close to mine. For a nano-second we both registered the closeness we'd had in the cinema. I could see it reflected in his eyes. He might be able to get me off the squash team. If he wanted more than we'd already had, I had to play a better game than this.

"Look, I didn't mean to hurt you or anything," I said awkwardly. Good line, eh? We'd seen it in a film a couple of nights back and my mum had picked up on it and given a bit of a lecture, not sure why, but I'd been practising it with that awkward touch for sincerity and it came in handy now. "I mean, really. Okay? I just wanted to, you know, try it."

"It!" he snorted with a leering sneer. He let me go, but didn't move back. I felt intimidated – me! Suppose he wanted to be my boyfriend or something?! I scratched around for something else to say.

"Well, you did hurt me," he said suddenly.

"Yeah, well, I said sorry."

"You're so *big*!" he explained in a camp voice. "My jaws just *ache*!" He waggled his jaw expressively and I tried to laugh but the truth is he'd completely wrong-footed me. There was a tide of experience in his voice that I just wasn't prepared for, and his sneer shocked me. First set, vulnerability; second set, experience; third and winning set, total confidence. Game over.

He watched me absorb it, gave a nasty smile. Leaned forward oh so slightly and kissed my unresisting lips.

"Training on Monday at 6pm – okay?"

"You're the Captain," I responded as always, and with a short laugh he walked off.

I wiped my lips and carried on into the centre and went to the wallpaper shop to get some ideas for Dad's study. I had an almighty crush on the girl at the wallpaper shop. That day she came and stood next to me as I leafed through the huge, heavy books of samples, and I let my fingers, tracing textures on the pages, move across to explore the textures of her hand, which lay waiting alongside those pages. We both watched the slow progress of my fingertips, backwards and forwards, comparing, in silence. The contrast and similarities between passive paper and passive flesh, between soft and hard and ridged and smooth. I pondered their role in my world. It was the beginning of real exploration of someone else's flesh in that way. As substance, texture, *differentness*. At last I closed the sample book, smiled at her and left.

Of course he almost killed me at the Monday training session, but that was kind of to be expected. He was a bit of a spiteful type. I ran into him about 20 years later at a work conference in St Petersburg and he struck me as a walking bitter-bomb. I invited him for a drink in the hotel bar – panoramic view and about 100 hookers – but although he talked the talk about his great lifestyle and got together a chippy little flirtation with the gorgeous Georgian barman, I got the impression it was all just façade.

I watched his suggestive by-play (undoubtedly foreplay too) and thought back to the impact his unspoken experience had had on me when we were teenagers. Too much experience too soon, I decided, tracing my fingers across the fine gold ridges along the edge of the smooth polished bar and enjoying as always the sensation of textures under my fingertips. The idea that it takes eternity to find a pattern. Because there is none. My recognition of that, of the pleasure in constantly weaving beautiful strands towards no visible pattern, was another of those early signs of my calling.

"What are you smirking about?" he challenged, signalling for more drinks and waving away a hooker.

"Nothing," I smiled.

The drinks arrived and I raised my glass.

"To differentness," I toasted, and he, taking that to mean whatever he wanted it to, gave a reluctant smile and drank deep. I hoped never to see him again.

My Dad liked the paper I chose for his study so much he didn't change it till they moved house about 30 years later. Well, he didn't change it then either, but you know what I mean. It got tatty and I offered several times to do a revamp, a nice slick paint job, but he said no. Every time I went in to chat with him, I used to run my fingers over its ridged texture and remember the soft veins on the back of her hand yielding under my touch and the smooth, hard ridge of her gold wedding ring. Unyielding.

*     *     *

So there were all these early signs and sensations, and then I went to college and had opportunity! Tons of it! But the really big deal is that there was *time*. You know, you could leave things from one day/month/term to the next, knowing that the other person would still be around. Maybe that's a false sense of security, looking back, but I used it the right way, by carefully learning all the processes and steps that need to be gone through to build something up and get results. The idea was that with enough skill and practice, I'd be able to get the results in less and less time, thus preparing for life in the real world, where no-one has time for anything.

But I suppose what really opened my eyes to my vocation – and the fact that my brother was going to have a bald pate by 30, yeuch – was The Ferrari Challenge. It happened when I was in my final year and the bro came to stay for a week when one of my flatmates was away.

"Got an idea," he said one evening in the pub, chucking a glossy little brochure down on the table. "Whoever finds three girls in one evening – 6pm to midnight – who will have some kind of sex with him on the spot, wins a weekend driving a Ferrari and the loser pays. You on?"

"That is such a naff idea," I said, picking up the brochure.

I did intend to have a Ferrari of my own one day, but I was still at the souped-up Corsair stage, so just driving a Ferrari would be a major thrill. It was a kind of weekend package with a night at a hotel, champagne breakfast and all that stuff. I wondered who to take with me.

"Yeah, yeah. You can lay off the 'naff', Mother Superior," the bro was saying. "You and your Ford Cortina pimpmobile. Listen, here's . . ."

"Corsair, you berk."

"No better."

"No, you're right, but I might be able to get a . . ."

"Here's how it works. We both have our mobiles with us and whoever gets a bite on the line sends a message to the other one. Then the other one calls to listen in. So, for example, when you get my message and ring me, I pretend to hit the 'reject call' button but actually press the 'answer' key so you can hear me getting it on with the tottie."

Clear as a bell. It was a naff idea, but then all my brother's were, and it did fit in with me wanting to test how good I now was at getting results in a short space of time, so I accepted. It would be like finals, only more fun. And he looked so excited I couldn't bear to disappoint him, though perhaps immediate disappointment would be better than future humiliation? He struggled some notes out of his pocket while I pondered that one, and carried on,

"No friends, no professionals, no recycling old lays, no offering money to participants, okay? Just snogging and groping counts, but only for one of the strikes. At least one of the three must involve either a her-him blowjob or penetration of the female with tongue, fingers or cock. Girl-on-girl action most definitely counts as a strike in itself, and male penetration of one or both of the participating girls will score as one strike. All clear?"

"What about if the girl – a non-lesbo one – says she's up for more?"

"You mean, gasping and gagging for it?"

"Well, yes." How else? I wondered, but bowed to his inferior knowledge.

"Hm. One strike, like snogging and groping. Oh, and if it's a draw, we have a sudden death playoff, first one to get a blowjob after the end of the contest. Okay?"

"No."

"What?"

"I said no. No sudden death."

"Why not? Pussy."

"'Cos I've got finals coming up," I told him. "Can't spend more than an evening on this. Anyway, what are you talking about, a draw? Don't be daft. I mean, you might just get a snog on the scoreboard, and I hope you do, but a draw . . . Come on!"

He set his pint down a bit hard and said,

"Jesus F. Christ, you really think you're God's gift, don't you?"

I hesitated, considering my answer. I mean, the bro has no logic sometimes, just doesn't think it through. And frankly, I just couldn't see the catch here. Didn't want to nark him, though, in case he backed out. I could feel the beast throbbing under my thighs, the red mist at the edges of my vision . . . The brochure said you got to drive on a racetrack, i.e. no speed limit.

"Look, don't get me wrong," I began, picking my words carefully. "It's great that you're willing to pay for the Ferrari weekend, and I think I know who I'll take along. She . . ."

"Shut your smug face," snapped the bro, threatening me with his empty glass. See what I mean? Weird reactions.

"Just shut the fuck up! Know who you're going to take! Huh! It's your round. Get moving."

"Okay, okay," I agreed, picking up the jars. "I was going to say, I'd introduce you to her. I think you'll like her. I mean, you'll know it's money well spent."

He slung the peanuts at me.

"Knock it off!" yelled the barman. "And pick those up!"

The livid Ferrari lay and panted up at me, sharp as a scarlet tongue. I smiled down at it and said,

"My round, my Ferrari."

It was a dark and stormy night – I kid you not – but I'd made careful, weatherproof preparations, and by 6pm was sipping a pint at the all-day bar, feeling pretty smug after winning a match in the squash league earlier on. I felt in excellent shape and I'd dressed to attract a broad range and so open up the playing field as much as possible.

Because I was known in the town, I didn't plan to go to my usual haunts or where anyone might recognise me, mainly because it'd be time-consuming to shake off friends or get out of daft conversations.

I'd never been to this all-day bar, which was down the crappier end of town, and looking round, I was confident of getting one in the net to break up the bro's concentration early on in the Challenge before moving on to the classier part of the evening.

In the event, I didn't even have to chat up the barmaid – who looked pleasant enough and had already told me she finished her shift at 7pm – to get results. A solid-looking girl hefting a sports bag with a squash racquet poking out of it came in and planted herself on a barstool close to mine, and I recognised her as one of the Birmingham ladies' team.

"Hey!" I hailed her. "You're playing our lot tomorrow, aren't you?"

She looked me over, recognised me at once, and grinned.

"That's right! Did you guys cream us today?"

Not yet, I quipped to myself, but answered suitably and bought her a drink. Turned out she was staying with a friend close by, but had to kill time till 7.30pm when the friend would finish rehearsal and show up with the flat keys. Perfect.

"Tell you what," I said, inspired. "I've got the car outside – if you like, I'll run you over to the courts and you can dump your stuff in my locker for tomorrow. Save you lugging it around."

She agreed enthusiastically and by 6.50pm, we'd stashed her kit and I was showing her the vending area round the back of the courts. There were only two guys playing and they'd started at 6.45pm, so I didn't expect them to be coming off yet. So it seemed safe enough to make a move and I told her I'd be coming to see the ladies' matches next day and gave her a few tips about our own No 2, then ran a hand down her arm and said,

"You have a fabulous physique."

Pause, I apologised, she said it was okay, I pressed the 'send message' key on my phone, laid it down on top of one of the machines and ran my hands over the upper part of her body – not breasts – murmuring about tone and short twitch muscles and so on until my phone beeped and she jumped. We both chuckled as I pretended to switch it off – checking briefly that it was the bro, it'd be just typical if it was my mother or some other unsuitable female. Yep, nay problem.

"Now don't forget I'll be watching and I want to see you cream her," I murmured clearly into the space between her left ear and the mobile. She half-laughed and gave back willingly when I kissed her.

"You taste nice," I told her, hoping the bro was breaking down in tears of desperation at the other end of the line. "Mmmmm." I'd never given such noisy, sloppy kisses in my life. "I've told you what she likes and where her weak spots are, so there's no excuse for you not to cream her, is there?"

"None at all," she acknowledged, squirming against me slightly. "You've been very helpful."

More noisy kissing and murmurs and some indistinguishable stuff about 'tips' from me, knowing that the bro would only hear 'tits'. Mind you, he heard 'tits' if you said 'carrot cake'.

"And if you're good I'll be waiting for you afterwards," I promised more clearly. "Would you like that?"

She laughed quietly. Obviously not taking all this too seriously, but up for a quick snog.

"Probably not. I think my friend has plans. But thanks."

Right. No ecstatic yearnings to have me impale her being groaned into the mobile, but I had the first strike anyway, so I laughed too and drove her up to her friend's place.

Good. Only a meaningless snog, but it was only 7.25pm and I'd got one in the net while the bro had yet to break into the goal area. Probably hanging around on a street corner somewhere asking innocent passers-by if they fancied a bit of nookie, knowing him.

To make it fair – or as fair as a contest of this type was ever going to be between him and me – he'd got a car too for that day. But I confess I wasn't being entirely fair with my next move because I did use what you might call inside information.

There was a very quiet, slightly geeky girl I'd noticed a couple of times in the language lab. She seemed incredibly reserved, and I'd never actually spoken to her – wasn't that interested – but we'd kind of registered each other looking at the notice boards and so on. I knew she did archery – I mean, I ask you! – once a week and that it finished at 8pm, and I knew that her boyfriend was away for the night because the chess (!!!!) team had a couple of fixtures down south next day. And no, this is not luck, this is careful research. The information was in the public domain, on the boards in the sports centre (chess, a sport!!! Puh-lease!! What kind of effete wanker plays chess??!!), and as soon as the bro and I had agreed the Challenge date, I'd got cracking on research. If he hadn't got his own plan of campaign, that was just tough.

I waited in the car outside the main sports hall, applying a bit more deodorant, drying and rearranging my hair in the rear view and changing into the reassuring, casual look – big jumper over chinos. I thought I looked like something out of 'Love Story' – and I don't mean the girl – not to mention thick as mince, but her boyfriend was a total nerd and hopefully she'd be seeing me as a cuddly bit of not-too-rough.

And there she was, saying goodbye to a couple of the others and making her solitary – phew! – way along the road. Head bowed, she was yanking her hood up when I stopped the car alongside her, wound down the window and called out,

"Can I give you a lift? It's tipping down! I'm sorry, I don't know your name, but we've seen each other in the language lab – do you remember?"

By now she'd had time to peer in and her startled look relaxed and she hopped in.

"Thank you!" she said pleasantly. "It *is* a bit wet out there!"

Not as wet as it will be in here, I thought, but I asked where she lived and I was in luck – it was two streets from a very decent four-star hotel I'd checked out earlier specially for the Challenge. We learned each other's names and joked about the filthy weather so it was all pretty relaxed and she looked surprised but not alarmed when I drew up in the hotel's well-lit parking area and stopped the engine.

"Oh! Are you staying here? That's fine, I'm just around the corner, I can walk. Thanks so . . . ."

"No, no," I laid a hand gently on her arm and then withdrew it. The rain lashed at the windows. "Um, you're going to think I'm a complete nut, but please please hear me out. There's nothing to be scared of."

She just sat there, her lips slightly parted to show her irregular teeth, and the rim of her specs glinting. Little girl look – I didn't mind it.

"The thing is . . . ." I paused and took a deep breath. "The thing is that I really, really fancy you."

She made a noise that sounded like 'Oh God', but in the good sense.

"Um, I have a boyfriend . . . ."

"I know, I know, and that's why this may sound strange, but I would just be so grateful if you would let me take you into the hotel and invite you to a glass of champagne and just talk to you a bit more. I don't want anything else, I don't need to be your boyfriend or cause any trouble or anything, honestly, I just want to . . . . look at you. Be with you for half an hour." Which was about all I could spare without getting behind schedule. "Please?"

She was silent.

"Look, I'm sorry," I said. "I shouldn't have said anything, I'll take you home, it doesn't matter."

"No . . . ." she said hesitantly, "I'm just not sure . . . ."

"Come on," I said decisively. "Let's have a drink."

We sat by the fire in the lounge and I ordered some bubbly. She blushed and fidgeted at first, but I reasoned that archers must have a hint of steel to them somewhere, and sure enough, although she was quite boring, she wasn't as wet as I'd thought. I harped on about fancying from a distance, and after about 20 minutes I held her hand and gassed on then about how it felt to touch her. She was reassuringly stuck on the boyfriend, but when she let slip that he was away, I lunged and snogged and then said I hadn't been able to stop myself.

By this time we were back in the car, parked in a nice dark stretch near her flat. She looked stunned by the snog, but more 'cos she'd responded than because I'd lunged.

"Please let me touch you more," I begged, moving in again and pressing the 'send message' button. "Please, please. Just tonight, just now, for a moment. You don't know what it means to me." That was true enough. The phone rang and I shut up – didn't want the bro to hear me begging.

"Oh . . . ." she uttered by way of answer, and since at this stage I thought surprise was the best tactic, I leaned over, yanked at the recline lever on the passenger seat (which I'd oiled the previous day) and went down on her. It was an uncomfortable angle, but she brought her hips up to meet me and was gratifyingly noisy, emitting a nice regular bleating sound, and muttering, "There, oh yes, there, there!"

There was a more or less constant bleat going on when I sat up and let my fingers do the talking, and I grinned at her in delight when I heard the squelchy slapping sound of her cunt around my hand.

"That was wonderful!" she gasped at last, gently pushing me away. "Thank you." She gave me a questioning look, as if scared I was going to want more or ask to see her again, then reassembled her nether clothing and clambered out of the car. I waved her into the house and picked up the mobile from the dashboard with the non-sticky hand.

"Did you get all that? Two-nil to me. You do realise it's tonight, don't you?"

"No worries," he replied. "Now get off the line, I'm going for the double whammy. Two lesbos, lovely girls, just coming back from powdering their whatnots. And they are *hot*! Stand by for the equaliser."

I believed in the lesbos like I believed in my own impotence. I had the next outfit in the car – off with the cuddly old Fancier-From-a-Distance and on with Urban Stud – but I wasn't going to go for it because it looked to me as though I was away and clear and could enjoy a decent curry out while I finished my Casanova book. The Challenge was more than halfway through, and he had nothing on the scoreboard. Zip. I was just pondering whether to do the old fave curry house or try out the joint that had opened recently round the back of the cathedral when my phone buzzed.

I rang back with a sense of disbelief that only deepened when I heard him saying,

"That's it baby, take it all, you know you can take it all, I know you can do it, easy, easy . . . ."

"I . . . . I can't, I'm not used to . . . . a man," in a gasping female voice.

"Bit by bit, baby, you'll soon get used to it."

More sounds of distress from her.

"You want to warm her up a bit more, baby?"

Murmurs of assent, and a different, much lower female voice saying,

"Gonna lick you out good, honey," in an American accent.

Lots of moaning and pussy-lick noises and my brother grunting encouragingly while the two girls obviously got it on. I sat and stared and started scrambling into the Urban Stud outfit.

"You ready now, baby?" came my brother's voice. "Gonna take it all this time, hm? Here it comes . . . . Is she ready?"

"Oh, she's good 'n' ready, but you're gonna have a better ride if you just slide it in here, big boy."

*Big* boy??? Still, if she was licking out the other one, she wouldn't be able to see his dick, I reasoned.

"Oh yeah! Oh baby, so *you're* ready for me. Whoa! Yeah! You carry on cleaning her out, baby, while I'm breaking and entering your little treasure-house. Ooooooooooaaaargh!"

Semi-screams from the second girl between pussy-licks. I was getting a stiffie just listening. He must have paid them. Surely? I'd wriggled into fresh, dry trousers and was worming my feet into slick shoes while the girls' wailing crescendoed around me, punctuated by comments like, "Which one do I come on? Both? Here she blows!" from the bro, and the three-way soundtrack when he did just that.

I turned off the phone, started the engine and headed back to the hotel. I swung through the main door with confidence high and one eye on the clock, and had just locked looks with the weary but smiling receptionist, pale and worn as a Portuguese village, when I stopped dead. Sound quality. I tore my eyes away from the receptionist, and thought back to how clear and even it had been. Where would he have placed the mobile? He might have been waving it over them, but then they'd know they were on the air and that was against the rules. The receptionist glanced up, I gave her a small smile, turned on my heel (I like that expression – doesn't it just sound as though you're wearing a long sweeping cloak over a sword and spurs?) and drove over to the house I shared with three others. One of them was away for a couple of weeks and the bro had his room. The mobile buzzed as I parked up.

"Just wanna kiss you," he was whispering, and there was lots of female murmuring but nothing much else, but then, he didn't need much else after the lesbo double scorer. A simple snog would clinch the Ferrari Challenge for him. I wouldn't put it past him to be using one of the lesbos, though, for his third strike.

"C'mon, baby, just one kiss . . . ."

And then, via the mobile, I heard it – a tiny but unmistakeable belch!

Well, that did it. Not even my brother would belch when he was trying to get the first kiss. Would he? I turned the door handle as carefully as I'd squeeze a virgin's nipple and slowly inched my head round the door.

The fat fuck was slumped in an armchair facing the window with a can of beer in one hand, a ciggie in the other and empties all over the floor. I couldn't see the computer, but I didn't need to – he was tweaking the volume on something between puffs and it must've been the pre-recorded lady-moans. He leaned over towards the table where the computer and mobile were hooked up and gave the back of his own hand a big slurpy kiss!

"Oh baby!" he murmured over the table, then sat well back and took another long drag!

I'd got right up behind him by this time, so when I hissed,

"That is the most pathetic thing I've ever seen," just by his left ear, I thought for a nano-second the shock had killed him. He choked and thrashed, the computer fell on the floor with beer flowing into its keyboard, and I didn't give him a chance to recover, let alone say anything, just kicked some empties into touch and went where he couldn't find me for the rest of the week. Or preferably ever again.

\*    \*    \*

Yep, that was an eye-opener all right. It taught me a couple of painful lessons: firstly, that if you're going to be competitive, you need to set your standards high, there is absolutely no point going up against a total plonker like my brother; and secondly, I was simply different and was therefore going to have to get used to being misunderstood.

I mean, the bro just hadn't set out on this endeavour with innocence. He was being a tricky little twat as always. Cheating. Yep, he was a cheat. Well, he might be my blood brother, but all that family stuff is crap anyway. You have to go your own way in life. He sent me emails saying he'd booked me in for the Ferrari weekend, he wouldn't be there, he was sorry if I was pissed off etc etc, but I didn't reply. And didn't go near the Ferrari, of course.

Then he went off and told BM! My best mate! And the worst thing was that he made out I was sulking, and that he'd been really smart and it had all been in good spirits but I couldn't take a joke, so what I got was BM ringing me up to say, 'Stop behaving like Little Lord Fauntleroy, get your head round the fact the joke's on you, and call your brother'!!!!! 'Course I slammed the phone down on him.

The fury carried me to the top of the squash league, but I was hurt. At being misunderstood. 'Cos I *had* gone into it with innocence, you see. I undertook every challenge like a knight. I began to wonder *why* I built every sexual encounter into a beautiful experience if I could, while BM just stared at a girl's tits when he spoke to her and my brother's philosophy was, 'If it moves, shag it; if it doesn't, eat it.'

And finally, I had to acknowledge I was different. From practically everyone I ever met, ach'ly, not that I knew it then. It was really hard. Accepting what you are can be hard; I don't think most people ever do. I'm just glad I was sensitive and strong enough to realise early on that I had a calling. And embracing that, thorns and all, was the right and noble course.

Men have a huge yearning to be noble. But most of them (and I say them 'cos I am not like this) have a terrible misconception of nobility – they apply their efforts to really unworthy causes, I found later, like putting up with some ridiculous bint's emotional blackmail for years on end just out of pride in their own nobility. They think they're noble for putting up with destructive behaviour . . . . I know, I know.

Anyway, I had accepted myself and my mission, and then it was a bit like taking a vow of silence, because trying to explain it to others was just going to expose me to their stupidity and therefore cause me pain. Distract me from the Cause.

So I ignored BM and the bro and I think the bro went a bit nuts. He sent an email out to loads of my friends with a really clever little animated film making the me character out to be a humourless loser. Must have paid someone to do it for him. I was astonished that anyone that talented would associate with my brother, and perplexed by his misdirected energy/spending. Still, it gave me an opening to fire back an apology to all who'd received the 'very creative' animation, explaining that the bro's medication had been changed recently, and could they all please respect that this was a difficult time for him? Thought that closed the matter, and got on with finals.

Did well, of course – that's just the kinda guy I am – and the parents came up for graduation. They were pretty well-off, but I'd saved up from the bar jobs so I could invite them to a couple of nights at a plush hotel, and they were dead chuffed. It was all great till we went out for champagne after the ceremony and against a background of raucous celebration in a chi-chi wine bar, my mother said,

"I think you're the vainest person I've ever met."

Well, even my dad looked taken aback, and he's used to these sudden onslaughts.

"Hold on," he said. "We're celebrating."

"And I didn't say the vainest man, I said person," she continued. "You can't help but look at yourself in any reflective surface, can you? I can see the way you're gazing at yourself in the wall!"

My dad twisted round and squinted at the chrome-like surface behind him.

"You can't see yourself in that!" he protested.

"*He* can! He does nothing but adjust his hair and peer at himself to make sure he's looking good."

"Oh well, he's got better eyesight than me. I have to wear reading glasses now, you know," he added to me.

"Well, you've done pretty well so far. Most people need them well before their 40s. I used low grad ones myself a bit, for studying, but I don't really need them. It comes and goes. You can do exercises, you know, to help the eye muscles. I've got a book that . . . ."

"You're vain, vain, vain!" persisted my mother. "Vanity's a sin, you know!"

"Aren't you proud of me?" I asked, a bit hurt by all this right in the middle of what I'd tried to make the perfect day.

Disarmed, she bit her lip.

"Yes, of course I am," she admitted.

"Same again?" said my dad, getting up.

"Well, Pride's a sin too," I told her, and that shut her up.

The thing is, she was only seeing a certain trait, not all the care and style I studied that were to enhance so many women's lives and boost their rights by making them justifiably more demanding of their men because I showed them what a man could be.

It's that, it's care, not vanity. I'm not vain. I don't expect women to fall at my feet. I don't imagine I'm the best-looking guy on the block. Well, on the block I definitely always have been. In the whole of London, actually. But in a broader context, like the entire universe, I can totally see that there are other men who rate as highly as I do. I've got eyes. And here was my own mother, misunderstanding me!

Turned out my mental brother – you are not going to believe this, he was like one of those pigs invaded by demons in the Bible, was it the Bible? – had emailed our mother one of my personal home videos! You heard! The little shite must've hacked into my computer (not the one I wrecked with beer, thank God/Whatever, that was his own laptop) during the Ferrari Challenge Week.

"What video?" I asked with a dry mouth.

I mean, supposing he'd thought it'd be a laugh to send her the one where a (consenting) friend and I were practising and discussing kissing techniques? Or the Kama Sutra Tertulias, where the same friend and I each picked a different position for the evening, tried them out, then debated their merits over pizza and vino? Or the (non-consenting) one where I'd switched the camera onto a group of girls at my place while I went out for more beers, and was amazed by their locker-room take on blokes and PMT and stuff. These vids were valuable archives to me, but I could see my mother might not relate to that in the same way.

"You're sitting there making lots of faces at yourself, and then you rearrange your hair and get up and walk around and pretend to meet people and shake hands and say how pleased you are to meet them," said my mother, and I began breathing again. "And you stand in front of the mirror practising different poses, and put on several different outfits."

"Does he really?" chuckled my dad, amused for some reason. "Well, well!"

"Normal people don't do that kind of thing," pursued my mother.

"No, well, normal people are the dregs, mother, and you just have to accept that I'm not normal, if what we mean by that is lazy and mediocre. There's no harm in superiority."

"Hear hear!" put in my father, waving his empty glass and looking pleasantly surprised when a passing bargirl nipped it out of his hand with a smile and went off to fetch him another.

"Excellent service," he said happily, and hiccupped.

"If you want 'normal', ie lazy and mediocre, you've got another son who's really, really, really normal," I added. "He's not even making his own films, he's sending you mine – what does that tell you?"

"Idle git," nodded my dad.

My mother frowned.

"Yes, but . . . ."

"No pain, no gain," I continued. "How do you think people *improve*? Hm? How do you think I got this degree? By sitting on my ass? No, by studying. And yes, I work on my appearance too. Why shouldn't I? Princess Diana wasn't always beautiful, you know, she had to study her deportment and grooming and all the rest of it as well as going to the gym. She studied all the footage of herself in public, sat up every night watching video clips of herself so that she could *improve.*"

"That's right," corroborated my father, not that he knew or gave a shit what Princess Di had got up to in her spare time. "You leave him alone. He's got his degree and a job and he looks all right. He'll be all right. Let's go dancing. Any clubs round here?"

My mood-swing mother giggled suddenly and I went for a slash wondering who else the nutter brother might have sent my vids to, and which others he might have nicked. Decided to give him a call next day to re-establish diplomatic relations, so to speak.

A big bunch of us went along to this weird old music-hall one of my flatmates had recommended, and it was great 'cos there was an excellent mix of hip cats and old codgers, and everyone knew how to dance. And that was another eye-opener, but a good one, 'cos my parents were really good! Just got out there and did their thing, and when I saw them mobbed by my contemporaries, I realised that dancing needed to be part of the ongoing training for my vocation, so over the next few months I got them to teach me all they knew, then had some classes for other kinds of dance.

I really do advise it – makes it *so* easy to lift girls off other guys, not that I've ever had a problem in that department, but you might. And dance is so *sexy.* So closely related to sex. Like eating. Just go for one kind of dance if you know you're crap – it doesn't matter what it is. Fox-trot or rap, salsa or ballet – yep, did quite a bit of that at one stage, incredibly demanding but fantastic for overall tone and posture – if you're even halfway decent at one of them, you'll be beating the women off with a stick. Your own, ideally.

Dance I continued throughout the decades. Massage I discovered later on. Fragrance earlier. In my early 20s, I guess I was still more into the technicalities.

*Special Underbedcover Agent's Tip:-*

*Mechanics: this is an optional skill, but it's so cool to cut out the AA man – don't forget, rescuers always get the edge. And you can swing gratitude your way with impromptu roadside fixes for damsels in distress. Just don't try and get her into your car, you daft berk. Fix her fanbelt, making sure you get really filthy and possibly slightly cut in the process – a good tip is to wipe a weary hand over your face so that you get an endearing smudge on your forehead – hand over a business card and an admiring look and bugger off.*

# Protocol No. 2 – Faith

## THE ANTI-PROTOCOL – FEAR

Faith: *A strong or unshakeable belief in something* (like yourself or
your vocation), *especially without proof or evidence* (well, you may
need to work on providing proof, I never really had to bother
much with that, obviously).
Fear: *feeling of distress, apprehension or alarm caused by impending
danger, pain etc* (or in many cases – read on – caused by nothing,
i.e., a really horrible feeling and a total waste of time)

IT'S AMAZING HOW many girls
will let you feel their tits and peer
up their jacksies if you say you're a doctor. A friend who'd just qualified as
a gynae said he was festooned in girls every night of the week because of it.
We said, jammy cunt, but he said no, it was getting a bit much. He felt used,
he explained. Didn't know if girls liked him for what he was or for being a
doctor who'd take care of them. Didn't seem to think that maybe that *was*
what he was, if you know what I mean? But lots of people want a personality
as well as a profession.

"Dear oh dear," said BM, and belched.

"No, it's a fact. Okay, you don't believe me? Right then. That lot over
there . . . ." He nodded towards a bunch of raucous girls that BM had been
grinning and winking and belching at ever since we arrived. "We share the
cost of a round for them, and you each have to slide into the conversation that

I'm a gynae. Not in a stupid way. Just mention it, and watch their reactions, and we'll compare notes afterwards."

"Compare notes afterwards," scoffed BM, but he glanced at the rest of us and we all nodded. "All right, you're on." He hailed the barman. "Tell those birds over there the next round's on us," he said gassily. "And giss some more of those veggie crisp things, will yer?"

We all groaned, including the very slick American barman, and I stepped in quickly.

"Would you please serve all the ladies in that group with another glass of whatever they're having, and tell them, when they ask, that we're inviting."

"Sure," he said, and served the extra drinks with his own special panache. One of these people who move a lot faster than they seem to. Economy of movement or something. Anyway, he made it all look easy, and as a fellow craftsman, I appreciated that. Squeals and gasps from a couple of the girls, then they asked why they'd got extra drinks, and the barman indicated our group with a very stylish and courteous gesture of the hand, and they gave us the once-over before picking up their glasses and raising them in our direction.

"Right, we're in," exclaimed BM. "Me first."

That's the attitude that wins him the squash matches. Doesn't do him much good aside from that, as far as I can see, though. We wandered over in twos and threes, according to pack practice, and got mingling. I ended up chatting most to a sparky redhead who just screamed PR at me, but turned out to be an engineer (so she said), and you know what? The gynae was right! When she asked what I did, I included a couple of other guys in the answer, sort of showing what a mixed bunch we were professionally, and there's no denying that her gaze lingered longest on the gynae and she said, 'Really?' then asked questions about him but not about the other guy! And when we 'compared notes' afterwards, we found that no fewer than *four* of the six girls had given their cards to the gynae, while the others had only got one each and even I'd only pocketed three! Game over.

Well, everything happens for a reason, and it wasn't hard to see what my next step had to be – pose as a doctor.

Yeah yeah, I know, I know. But I hadn't had the deceit issue out with myself yet, and the whole thing just fitted in so brilliantly with the ongoing training I'd promised myself after getting out of hospital (more on that later). I reckoned I'd picked up some of the terminology and approach – not to mention the smell, I felt septic for days after leaving – so I borrowed a white jacket off the gynae (had to say it was for a fancy dress party and then he got offended he hadn't been invited) and invested in a huge pack of those finger condoms, you know, the very fine rubber gloves, and opened the 'clinic' the day after my parents flew to Canada for three weeks. Golden opportunity.

I could never have done it from a grotty little two-up, two-down, but their house shrieked professional family.

Now, don't get me wrong, I had zero intention of doing any harm. I'm not some inadequate little conman who has to pass himself off as something he's not. Wasn't about to mince into some hospital and attempt a spot of eye surgery or anything. I had my story about why my 'patients' should see another gynae as soon as possible very clear. To tell the truth, I just wanted an answer to 'What does that feel like?' that didn't involve a sexual setting or any of the usual qualifiers you'd need to take into account when asking. I wanted to know more – to *feel* more what a woman feels when she's penetrated. Well, and have a look round at the same time, yeah. It's all knowledge.

So, I had the house – complete with nice homey cats and the dog, and a recording of baby murmurs for playing upstairs – and some basic gear. I fitted out Dad's study – yep, that's right! Ridged wall paper, veined hands, wedding ring study – with a few medical books, left my dad's chartered surveyor certificates up on the walls in the conviction that people don't look at framed paper on walls, they just find its presence reassuring, and placed an open bottle of swabbing alcohol in a cabinet. You must've read all that stuff about having the smell of fresh coffee or freshly baked bread wafting through the place when you're trying to sell your house? Same principle. Then I worked a few bars. Yes, where I wasn't known, ob-vee-ouse-lee.

And one fine Saturday morning, after an abstemious Friday night, I opened the 'clinic'. Well, fucking interesting. I almost lost sight of the main point of the inquiry as I snapped the finger condoms on over pristine fingers and began the privileged probing. Because it *was* a privilege.

I don't know if you've seen that film by Cathérine Breillat about a sadist? Not 'Anatomie d'Enfer', no, another one. I am always blown away by her stuff, and then, I'd just discovered it, and it was *so* sexy and *so* helpful. So un-PC. So anti-male, yet not. Anyway, there's this older sadist who's, um, frightening? enlightening? a young woman who's entrusted herself to him for a session, and it's magic because it's dead scary but there's a weird trust and you know he's not going to get pleasure from not giving pleasure, so while she's all strung up and blindfolded etc, he's pontificating about genitalia and he says every cunt is different, while cocks are all *so* the same that if you harvested a bunch and chucked them in a basket, the owners wouldn't know which one was his.

Now, I'm not saying I agree with that, and presumably you'd've bled to death before you got to the basket anyway, so it's a tough one to prove, plus if we're talking about flaccid pricks, then yes, I admit it could be a bit more difficult, but the point is that I do whole-heartedly agree on the all-cunts-are-different issue. Aspect, odour, taste, behaviour etc.

The first 'patient' was, very: she whipped off her knickers behind the screen I'd brought in from the dining-room, lay back and opened her legs and was really polite as I probed round gently, absorbing the visual aspect of the vagina at rest, ie not engaged in sexual activity with me, and asking a series of questions designed to let me know if this was sexually exciting for her or just a bit uncomfortable. On the whole, the latter, apparently. Relaxation is the key. Since she prefaced all her replies with 'Fine' when I asked how it felt, I pushed my third finger up as far as I decently could and inquired sedately,

"Any discomfort during intercourse?"

"No, it's fine," she replied, true to pattern, but then she hesitated and, in response to my inquiring look, continued,

"Well, it is fine, but sometimes he does make me sore. Before, with his fingers."

I stopped moving my fingers, concerned.

"What, here? Are you feeling that discomfort now?"

"No," she replied. "No, what I'm feeling now is different. You see, he goes on and on at my clitoris and . . . . OH!"

This was in response to me moving my fingers again, probing deep and out towards her pubes.

"That doesn't hurt, does it?"

"No, no! It's . . . . it's . . . ."

I carried on, speaking to her reassuringly.

"You see, very often there is absolutely no malfunction, but discomfort can occur if . . . ."

"Oh, oh, oh!"

" . . . . the woman's partner is stimulating the wrong areas. Now, in your . . . ."

"Oh! Oh, oh, OH, OH!"

" . . . . case, what may be happening is that he is stimulating your clitoris, whereas what we are noticing here is that your orgasm will most probably be achieved via the G-spot."

You know, I'd only read up a bit about this – I honestly had never made the distinction. But when I felt the inner convulsions, and her hips thrusting up towards my fingers in helpless reaction, the whole G-spot thing just made sense. Her clit meant nothing to her. She had her eyes closed and her head was tilted back, spilling strands of dirty-blonde hair over the back of the chair, so I concentrated on exploring this new sensation for both of us. Her cries told me when I'd really hit the spot – I had to reassure her that my wife and baby were down at the in-laws' for the day before she gave in to her own noisiness – and I cannot describe my feelings as my condom-clad fingers, helped by her newly-knowledgeable hand, worked inexorably on that rough, responsive spot, moving oh so slightly to and fro till she oh so definitely came, letting her head hang right back when it was all over, and fair panting for breath.

I watched her melt like cheese on toast for as long as I thought was decent, then carefully withdrew and peeled off the clever little gloves while she gradually stopped panting and thought to close her legs, helplessly sprawling after those delicious moments poised on the edge of breaking tension.

She began to apologise, but I had my head down pretending to write notes at the desk while I got over it myself, and I just said prosaically,

"Absolutely normal. It's as I thought – your G-spot is the orgasm zone. Tell your partner to forget the clit – oh, and let him think he's found the G-spot for himself, not that a doctor did, during a routine examination!"

Last thing I needed was a furious boyfriend coming round to do me over or trash the parents' place. I gave her the reassuring smile over the top of my non-gradated glasses.

"As for your general gynaecological health, you do need to have a complete check-up; as you can see, I'm only just getting set up here and most of my kit is still at the clinic where I worked before. Now, you do promise me you'll do that? Good. Take your time getting dressed, there's no hurry."

I stood up and left her to it and went for an amazed wank in the upstairs bathroom. When I came back, she'd gone. Hope she hadn't nicked anything – I really ought to be more careful.

I felt a bit over-awed by that session, but the next four were all fairly standard: I gave them all the same spiel about getting a proper check-up and so on, and savoured the differentness of each one. There was one who was so flat-chested that when I said,

"I think I've found a lump . . . . no, it's . . . ."

pre-empted the punchline by chorusing,

" . . . . your nipple!" with me and bursting into fits of laughter, and another whose incredibly soft breasts flowed like music over her front, obedient as a flock of sheep to my gathering touch, and as gentle in their straying.

By No 6 I was feeling as though I'd spent the morning in Wonderland. Where's Wonderland? It's the place where ice burns and the white light is so bright it strikes darkness behind your wondering eyes. My head was full of elusive pinkish-purple folds, and the incredible discovery of that first girl's G-spot was an ever-recurring source of awe. I had pioneered her pleasure, probably changed her sex life for ever. Her life. Why hadn't she found it herself while wanking? Perhaps women were so conditioned to regard the clit as the be-all and end-all that she'd never gone in deep enough to hit the magic place. It was hard and hidden, and alighting on it had been a major discovery for me as well as for her.

So when No 6 rang the bell, I was shrouded in a haze of awed delight which quickly turned to intense irritation when she half-lay back but then kept her legs firmly closed and giggled up at me coyly,

"Pussy's very shy."

I gave her a perfunctory smile and said, 'Really?' in a dry voice that should have warned anyone with more than half a brain cell that Doctor wasn't in the mood for this. She was a plump little thing with fluffy light brown hair and lots of woolly clothes in different shades of pink. She was probably fluffy all through.

"Yes, ever so! She hardly ever comes out and she's *ever* so shy of strangers."

She had her feet and hands slightly raised and was waving them around in peculiar little imitation-helpless gestures, and she seemed to me like a grotesque, giant pink beetle that had capsized in my dad's study. Shades of Kafka and Ionesco. Would I ever get her out, or would she just lie there rotating sinister wrists until I had to have her ever-increasing, pretend-soft shell sawn up by experts and carted away on the very eve of my parents' return from Canada? The way she talked made me want to slap her – I've never been fond of coy, it's usually lodged alongside insecurity and/or deceit, both of which are inadequate responses to life's potential. And she was a betrayal of womanhood and a non-starter in the pleasure stakes if she thought of her beautiful, mysterious vagina as a dysfunctional household pet.

"How can we coax Pussy out, Doctor?" she crooned in a mournful voice, still squirming.

As if I gave a shit.

The doorbell rang. I excused myself and went out to find the bro on the doorstep.

"Home alone!" he exclaimed, at *his* most irritating. "Came to keep you company for a day or two. What's the white coat about?"

"Ssshh!" I stepped out into the elegant porchway and lowered my voice, stripping the white coat off as I spoke. "There's a nutter in the study who's meant to be letting the doctor examine her vagina, but she's just cracking on about her pussy being shy and it won't come out. She's doing my head in. Here! Take the coat, tell her whatever you want, but get rid of her. Fast."

"So you're the doctor?" He had the coat on and we were inside the house.

"That's right."

He swung into action straightaway, and I have to say that, although it is absolutely not my style and his whole approach is an insult to women and pleasure, it was a relief to hand over to a pro in his own area.

He approached the study door, opened it a crack and said,

"Hello Miss Pussy! Can Miss Pussy hear me? Are you feeling shy? Oh, naughty Miss Pussy! Mr Vet's come to stroke you – doesn't Miss Pussy need to be stroked? Nice and gently? Hm, doesn't she?"

"She might," admitted the twit inside, after a pause.

"I'm sure Miss Pussy needs stroking. But Mr Vet can't attend to that from here, can he?"

"Nooooo . . . ."

He winked at me, opened the door a bit wider and poked his head round.

"So can Mr Vet come in, please Miss Pussy? Oh, I saw you! What a pretty thing you are, Miss Pussy. No, no, please don't hide. You mustn't be shy with Mr Vet – he knows exactly what you need . . . ."

And he was in. I went and put the kettle on then nipped back for a listen, and I didn't have to put my ear to the door to hear that Miss Pussy's shyness had been quickly overcome.

"Oh Mr Vet, Mr Vet!" she was crying out between medium-sized groans, and I thought she'd have to be quick to get hers in – equality and all that – because he was already on a strong run of grunts that indicated he was fast approaching the finishing tape.

Sure enough, he joined me in the kitchen a bare eight minutes later, having shown her off the premises, and took a noisy slurp at the tea I'd made him. We didn't speak for a while. He gnawed a couple of my mum's homemade ginger biscuits, finished his tea and gave me a look.

"Doctor!" he said admiringly.

"Mr Vet!" I retorted.

And just then one of the cats burst in through the catflap and we both yelled "Miss Pussy!" and cracked up.

I was pleased he'd dealt with the problem so well, and though he couldn't believe that that kind of role play really irritated me, getting his rocks off before he'd even dumped his bags did mean that he was unusually considerate and more or less stayed out of my way for the rest of the weekend.

Which I spent mainly dwelling on the gorgeous memory of the G-spot discovery, and other newly-acquired gems of knowledge, but I couldn't help pondering a bit how my brother must have gone straight in – I mean, two quick strokes of the reluctant Miss Pussy and he must've had her legs open and his cock well up her. And I hadn't even got her to part her thighs because I despised her silly talk. But I wasn't going to change my tack here – there was nothing to be learned, from my point of view. Silly talk like that distracts from the main event and strikes me as defensive, which is a major obstacle to true pleasuring.

I was also concerned at how quickly he came: he couldn't have given her more than about three minutes' worth, and that would've been straight shagging, as I'm sure he didn't have any extras to offer. I felt twinges of embarrassment on his behalf, but next evening the doorbell rang and lo and behold, it was Miss Pussy asking for Mr Vet, and his face lit up like a Christmas tree when he saw her and off they went into the study while I rang BM to say we'd better see the match at the pub instead of at my place.

The FFs – Frank Friend 1 and Frank Friend 2, a couple of girls I'd met at college – closed me down the following Saturday. I reckon it was the bro who shopped me, but I never found out. They just appeared, confiscated the white coat and threatened to smash the espresso machine when I protested. So I put Dad's study back like it was while they took it in turns to wear the white coat and tell arriving 'patients' that I'd escaped from the loony bin where I'd been put after exposing myself to my own father in the vestry at the local church where he sang gospel, and certainly wasn't qualified to probe their privates, however good I may have looked in wine bar lighting and a designer suit.

*     *     *

This thing about the Cardinal Sins. I've always been pretty interested in that. You know how it is. You start off thinking the Roman god system is really great – this is when you're a kid, or when I was a kid – then that all seems a bit odd, having different gods in charge of different things. Bit corporate for my taste, though I have worked in a corporate environment for ages, of course. But that's probably just the gods' punishment for finding their set-up odd, or something.

Not that things had changed much from the Roman and Greek set-up by the time I was approaching the corporate pantheon. I was surprised to find, travelling around, how the system of having a different god or goddess in charge of different departments had persisted in the Catholic religion. In places like Spain and Italy, they seemed to have a Virgin for everything, from Giving Birth to Velcroing your Sneakers Properly. Not that Virgins are goddesses, but it's the same idea, isn't it? Hotline to someone, someone to gripe to, hope to, just watch go by. Someone in charge, responsible. And/or decorative.

And to tell you the truth, I don't mind the idea of departmentalisation and all that. As long as I'm the boss – Pride, you see. Which is why I started brooding on the Cardinal Sins. I've capped that up because there was a bloke who was actually called Cardinal Sin. I mean, I ask you! Your surname is Sin, and what do you do? Go off and become a cardinal! Arse. Although you can see his point. All those robes and swinging incense holders, and there you are, emerging from a cloak of sinfulness yet glorying in your own name. Out of the dimness into the spotlight. Top billing.

"Hi, the name's Sin. Cardinal Sin."

Yeah. I s'pose I'm just envious (and that's another of them, Envy) because his name is even better than mine. Let him procreate in his own name so we can get onto the Cardinal Sins.

You know the point of a Cardinal Sin, don't you? Or a regular sin? It's not just something naughty or nasty that you do, it's actually a characteristic in you that becomes a sin if it is too exaggerated. A bit of pride or envy might make you do your job better, or prod you into getting a job in the first place, but too much of either of them leads you into the bad zone.

I admit that I was in danger of straying into that zone with the New York hooker, but she was worse than me, and I don't think it was Pride she suffered from – more like bloody-mindedness. Anyway, bet you can't name them all. Here they are: **Pride, Envy, Anger, Sloth, Vanity, Lust, Greed/Gluttony**.

And yes, there is a difference between those last two. It varies according to who you ask or what you read, but as far as I can make out, the difference between Greed and Gluttony is that Gluttony is about *consuming* too much of things like food or drink, whereas Greed is about *wanting* too much of anything – it could be power, money, etc. Can't think of an etc actually – it's usually power or money, isn't it? My conscience is pretty clear on these two – Greed and Gluttony, that is. With regard to the fleshly pleasures, I've always had what I'd call plenty, which might be a glutton's nothing, but has always been a feast in my eyes. And stomach. And elsewhere. Gluttony is so passive-aggressive. Just filling yourself up with something – why? It's got to be because of an emptiness, hasn't it? Filling the void. And then some. Where's that aggression directed? I prefer filling other people up.

Since I'm not particularly passive or aggressive, the combo doesn't appeal. The most attractive thing about Gluttony, as far as I'm concerned, is steering just clear of it. Gluttony's the motorway – big and fast, boring and dangerous. I'm on the service road running alongside. Desire.

It's the only way to travel, and its curves are unexpected. They require control and intuition. Let Greed and Gluttony speed on by, eyes glazed, falling asleep at the wheel.

Does Desire ever arrive? Oh no! At its best – and hardly anyone can maintain this pace for a lifetime – it's a permanent travelling. Desire is irrational, a true journey. Desire has no destination. That wouldn't satisfy Gluttony.

But then, nothing does.

\*    \*    \*

I know what you're thinking. Lust, right? Surely that's the sin he must be most prone to. Well no, I would totally deny that. Which is not to say I don't feel lust – it's just that I honestly don't think I've ever taken it to a level where it's sinful. I personally think it's a great thing unless you let it get out of control, but that's the whole point of the cardinal sins, isn't it? They're not sins unless they are out of control.

I remember after a business meeting in Vienna once I went out with a couple of the blokes in the evening, and after downing about an entire bottle of wine, one of them suddenly went really gloomy and started going on about how disgusting sex is. The other bloke and I tried to remonstrate, but he just went on and on about how sex is nothing but taking.

"Take, take, take!" he yelled suddenly, thumping on the table. Then he gulped as though he was just about to burst into tears, and rushed off to the loo.

"Looks like he's been shagging the wrong people," said the other bloke.

"Probably hasn't been shagging anyone at all," I opined. "That's why he's angry. Probably got no knob to speak of."

"I'll go and see, shall I?" suggested my colleague, and I said good idea, and off he went.

He came back just as I was paying the bill.

"Let's go!" he hissed, grabbing his coat and rushing out.

"So, did you see it?" I asked, chasing after him.

"Oh yes, I saw it all right! Taxi!"

"What? Where are you going? We can't just walk out like that."

"For a drink. Come with me. Quick, get in. I don't want him to spot us." And he shoved me into the cab.

"Listen, the stalls were empty, so I thought I may as well take a dump while I was there. Gundèle's, on the Rundstrasse, please. So I went in and was just sitting there when the bog-roll holder fell off the wall. I bent forward to pick it up off the floor and suddenly this dick came poking through the hole in the wall and touched me on the cheek!"

The taxi driver, whose English was clearly idiomatic enough to have caught the gist of this, and I glanced at each other in the rear view. My companion wiped his hands on his trousers and stared at me pleadingly.

"His dick! He stuck his dick through the hole! There's a hole in the wall behind the bog-roll holder! They're probably doing it all the time!"

"He must have thought you were someone else," I said. "Did you say anything?"

"No, of course not, I just stuck a bog roll on it and ran."

"Well, he's going to know it was you or me now, isn't he? When he comes out and finds we've legged it."

"Oh God, I didn't think of that. I just wanted to get out of there." He wiped his arm across his forehead and then rubbed his face hard with both hands.

"And what do you mean, you stuck a bog roll on it?"

"Well, I did. Come on, what would you do? I didn't want to sit and look at it!"

"But a bog roll? They're really narrow!"

"Not that narrow," he countered.

"Yes they are! There is no way a bog roll would fit over a normal-sized dick!"

"It would!"

"Wouldn't!"

"Would!"

I suddenly realised what I often forget – that, like my mother used to tell me, I am more fortunate than most – and I shut up and got the toilet guy's business card out and called him to say my colleague had had an emergency call and I was taking him back to the hotel to phone home. He wouldn't believe it, but it took my mind off working with micro-pricks.

"Well, no wonder he thinks it's all take, take, take if that's his sex life," I commented, holstering the mobile.

"I could have been anybody," exclaimed my colleague. "I could have *done* anything!"

"I know."

We were both silent till we had drinks in our hands again, pondering the point and pointlessness of poking your most prized possession through a hole in a wall for a total stranger to act upon. I'm not too squeamish, but that did make me shiver. Take, take, take – could have had it taken off at the root with a razor blade.

"It's not that I've got anything against them," said my companion finally. "But, you know . . ."

"Well, I suppose it's not much different from going to a prostitute," I reasoned, which was a nice sly one, because I happened to know this particular bloke had accepted a 'girl gift' during a business trip earlier that year. (And we didn't get the contract – now *that's* sinful).

He stared.

"'Course it's different. That's a business arrangement."

"Well, so's what he did – just no money involved."

Pause.

"I don't think I want to do business with him if there's no money involved," he quipped at last, and I went back to my hotel and had the chambermaid.

A few hours later, and strictly speaking, she had me, because although I didn't pay her, I did hand over a very nice watch I'd picked up for my mother's birthday. Let's say it was a kind of pardon for having succumbed to temptation.

Yep, it was the old story of the morning boner, and this lady knew just how to work it. She'd come in the previous morning, when I was still in bed, and although she'd apologised and backed out, here she was back next day at exactly the same time. This time she'd come right on in and started moving round the room whilst I lifted my bleary, weary head from the pillow and wondered what it was all about. I mean, I was well used to fending off early business in the Far East, where a wake-up call meant something completely different, and it was actually really annoying not to be able to get through the morning routine without about five calls offering handjobs. But I was unprepared for action in the Viennese five-star, so I just stared when she dusted the telephone on the bedside table and said, with a big smile,

"Good morning, sir! Sometimes gentleman in morning need happy release, no?"

I carried on gawping. She carried on smiling, dusting and tidying. I watched her solid little body moving here and there, and smiled back the next time she grinned at me, which was when she found the watch box, cheerfully opened it up and said,

"Nice watch!"

Well, my smile clinched some kind of deal, and I sort of knew it at the time, but it seemed like a good idea anyway. Of course, it wasn't real pleasuring, or even good sex, it was just a 'happy release' and very pleasant too. If I do have a fault, it's that I sometimes find it hard to relax. She slid her hands under the bedcover and began to handle my balls in a practised way, like a kindly, dexterous nurse, and I unbuttoned her top and fondled her jugs while she got on with it. It was probably a lot more work than she'd bargained for – I imagine most blokes in that situation come off within the first minute – but she smiled throughout, and I like to think that when she checks the time on that expensive watch it reminds her of working her wrists and fingers on a very nice big happy release indeed.

But it wasn't Lust. At least, I don't think so. Lust, like Greed and Gluttony, seems to be desire taken to an unhealthy extreme – the extreme of damaging someone else. The thing about Lust is that because it involves indulging in fleshly pleasures, too much of it means that you neglect your spiritual side.

So what? you might be thinking. What's the point of a spiritual side anyway? Well, I've never been a religious freak or anything, but I think a bit of spirituality's okay. Necessary, even. Not sure what it is, though. For me, it's about thinking about what I've said or done, on a fairly regular basis, and wondering if I could have said or done it better. And there's no point just saying, 'Oh yeah, that was my cock-up' – you have to make an effort to do it better next time, which might mean feeling bad about yourself for more than a nano-second.

Which is spiritual. Spiritual means being prepared to feel genuinely bad about yourself because you're thinking about things beyond and bigger than yourself.

And I had a crack at yoga once. Although I wasn't really trying to be more spiritual, I'd just buggered my knee playing squash and decided I needed a more effective stretching routine. But a couple of women at work immediately told me how great it was that I wanted to do yoga, because it's so spiritual, and although I didn't fancy either of them enough to get a hard-on, I did appreciate this new source of interest from women, so I shut up about the buggered knee, put on the old soul look and asked if they knew anywhere.

Amazingly enough, it was one of the fat secretaries who came up with the goods. I wouldn't have thought, from the look of her, that she was interested in any kind of discipline, spiritual or physical, but she had a name and a number on a Post-it before you could say 'guru'. So I didn't even have to make an effort to do any market research. Sloth – more on that later.

The place itself was clean, which bothered me a bit. Don't see how you can improve your spirituality among all that cleanliness. Cleanliness is next to Godliness? Yeah, yeah, let's have the next one on the list, because although I am quite tidy, I am not a total clean freak, and there's no point being in a category where you stand no chance of excelling. Well, no point for me. Everyone's different and I have no problem with losers. Accepting they exist, not accepting them into my orbit or office or bed or anything, I mean.

So anyway, the place was all spanking clean. There were five women in the class, including the giant secretary, me, and the teacher, who turned out to be a bloke. Then another bloke, who was really small and probably had a miniscule penis but looked a lot more supple than me, meandered in, and bugger me down dead, he was Miss Fatty's boyfriend.

It didn't click until we'd done a few useful things and a bit of animal life and breathing and whatnot, which was all fine. But then Mr Guru began a spiel about exercise in pairs. I wasn't happy. There was no-one I wanted any kind of physical contact with, and I was just squinting at my watch and coming up with a convincing excuse to leave when Mr Guru crossed his legs, said something about inner thighs and improved karma, and invited someone to come and sit on his crotch.

Well, surely no-one was happy now? I glanced round. I've-got-a-tiny-one was getting a reassuring look from Miss Fatty, who would have puréed Mr Guru at one sitting; three of the other women were gazing spiritually at their kneecaps; I was well experienced at not making eye contact with nutters; but the other woman looked up at the fatal moment and the next thing we knew, she was straddling Mr Guru on the floor, facing him, while he wanked on about energy flow and muscle control (yeah!) and suggested the rest of us follow suit.

Fatty and Tiny swung into it with an enthusiasm I would forever see when she put my calls through, while two of the remaining women, though unresponsive to Mr Guru's initial invitation, seemed intriguingly keen to improve each other's karma. The poor cow sitting on Mr Guru looked pretty unhappy, but he was having a good old sway and moan. Which left me and a woman in sober loose clothes who came over, sat down opposite me and said quietly,

"Is this your first time?"

I nodded.

"Mine too. This guy is a scary wanker and I am not going to sit on your crotch to jack up my spirituality or tone my muscles."

"And now, this position!" cried the gyrating guru.

"It's nothing personal."

"No, well, that's the problem," I agreed. "It's not personal, and it sure ain't professional. Which leaves limbo, and if I'm going there, I'd rather have fun on the way."

"Shall we go for a drink, then?"

"Embrace! Embrace the sensation!"

"Yes, but not 'then'. Let's make it now."

Now *that* was Lust. And Greed. And probably all the others. Mr Guru, I mean. Because he was using others for his own gratification. Control freaks and bullies are so *lazy*. It's so much easier to control others than yourself.

The woman was quite nice. We split a bottle of South African Cabernet at a chic little bistro she knew and had a good bitch about Mr Guru's exploitation techniques.

"Do you think he does it in an all-male yoga class?" she wondered.

"No such thing," I riposted.

"I bet he would, if that's all he had. It's all about control for him."

"But blokes would just laugh at him," I said.

She gave me a wicked look and said,

"Not if he's all *they* had."

I shuddered at the thought and ordered another bottle.

\* \* \*

Anyway, back to Lust. The indulgence with the chambermaid was simply that – self-indulgence. I didn't use her. The cut-off point for me is when it starts damaging other people, and since I'd dedicated my life early on to giving pleasure, it's hardly likely I'd be guilty of that one. In the sack. The boardroom is different.

No, I felt a bit bad about the chambermaid incident because I'd been lazy. Sloth – not one I suffer from a lot. But I'd let someone else do all the work. Didn't have any nice memory afterwards, just went for a shower and an aspirin while she dealt with the drenched sheets and snapped that chic watch onto her chubby wrist. I hadn't even fulfilled any evangelical purpose of improving a woman's expectations and I didn't learn anything from it myself.

I once heard BM say, to a woman next to him at a dinner party who was giving me the eye and obviously probing my status,

"No, no, just a bit of a workaholic."

It may have made him feel better, but I think it's kinder to be upfront and explain that I've taken a vow of pleasuring and am simply not worth looking at in terms of husband/provider. But he didn't know, of course.

She made a pass later on, and I explained myself, and we ended up going back to her place for a pretty good bout – she was into non-genital stimulation and I actually learnt a lot about timing and erogenous zones. Oh, and talk. When to, when not to, the power of words. Next morning she blindfolded me naked in a chair and talked me into a hard-on without touching me or letting me look at her, or even talking particularly dirty. Educational. And delightful to find that her expectations were so compatible with my hopes. It's a pity the blindfold trick didn't really work on her – we did reverse the roles, but it is a bit frustrating not to be able to *see* when a woman's aroused. Usually you have to take her word for it. Which is dodgy – just think about how they can fake orgasm. Deceitful or wot? I've never been caught out like that, but I know my brother has, and several mates. They said it made them hurt pretty bad when they realised – well, it would, wouldn't it? – and I can totally see why it would make you mistrustful. The non-genital stimulation expert suggested I could try the talking-into-an-erection thing with another man so that I could see the results, with the reminder that a man's 'arousal path' (great expression, love it) is different, so even if my talk worked with another man, it might not with a woman.

In any case, women tend to see the whole blindfold thing as a proof of their trust, I've found. Which doesn't excite me that much, because although they may think it's a big deal, I *know* they can trust me anyway, so it's not that impressive for me. I just want to hear what they're experiencing and what I have to say to get them to slide off the chair in a rush of their own cum, not stuff about, 'I wouldn't let any other man do this, you do realise that, don't you?'

Mind you, the physical danger thing for women is just *so* different, and reminded me of when I first became aware of it. It was a kind of by-product of my Envy revelation.

\* \* \*

The Envy thing surprised me. I didn't really realise what was happening at the time, but then you look back and see things in a different light. I was aware of Envy, of course. My mother had a bit of a thing about it, which was good on the whole because she told us not to be envious when other kids had better gear than us etc, and explained why. I can't remember her reasoning actually, but the point is that it's only any good at all in very small doses, and I was pretty confident that I didn't suffer from it in extremes. I just felt sorry for other people around me, 'cos I could see really clearly how they'd be envious of me: I had massive sex appeal, a massive piece, enough dosh, a sexy car (usually), a good job, no marriage, no kids, good health. Not hard to see why Envy is something I've always felt washing around me in waves, but not rising up inside me.

But I still remember the first epiphany. I was living in a bit of a dump at the time – first job, before I bought the Pleasure Palace etc.

I'd met a girl at the office and after a few weeks of chitchat and simpers (hers) in the office caff, I'd asked her round for lunch one weekend. I was planning to play it cool over the meal, then take her out for a drive and try the old 'Do you mind if we just run the car through the car wash?' routine. See how things went while the big brushes were slapping and fumbling against the streaming wet windows.

But it didn't get as far as that. I'd told my brother he could drop by casually – I'd heard that other people being around helped reassure girls during that delicate phase before you lunge – and I had to admit, for her sake, that it's just as well I had.

I suppose I didn't pay much attention to food then. Despite realising early on that my life's work was to be pleasuring, there was a way to go on some of the external factors, and I'd just assembled some tinned soup and bread and cheese. Plenty of beer and wine, though, and since there wasn't any cooking to do, I had a couple of drinks before she arrived.

Well, then she was there, and as an attentive host I was keen to keep her glass filled so mine kept filling too, and suddenly I realised I was too pissed to drive and the cheese wasn't that great so I'd better make my move pronto, before she buggered off in disappointment. So I did, and it was all going fine. She was cool about passing wine backwards and forwards in our mouths while we kissed at the table; we moved over to the rank sofa and got a bit heavier; and her top was off and my trousers were open when she gave a shriek, pushed her little fists against my chest like an offended cat and said,

"Don't put that anywhere near me!"

"It's okay," I said, quickly, producing a condom from behind a cushion (I later had little pockets sewn onto all my underpants. Much cooler, not to mention easier – there's not always a cushion around when you need one). "It's okay."

"It is not okay," she snapped, squirming out from under me and staring at my nether regions in growing horror. "That's enormous! It's much too big, it's disgusting! I have to go."

First I'd heard that size was an issue that way. And frankly, I thought the comments were bang out of order – it would never occur to me to start criticising a girl's body at this stage in the game. Right in my face too, how rude is that? I stared, totally speechless, while she did up her top and reached for her jacket.

"It's bigger than my arm!" she carried on, sliding said member into her tasteless pale green jacket. "God, you could rupture someone with that! Brute!"

Aha, I thought. Virgin. I'd just been a bit too precipitate. I shoved the condom back behind the cushion and asked her to relax, just sit down on the sofa again.

"No way! Not with that around!" She shook her hair back, snapped it into a ponytail and looked round for her bag.

"Hey, look, I'm sorry," I said at last, wondering just how to apologise for my body parts. Not to mention why. "There's no need to be scared, I wouldn't . . . ."

"I'm not scared!" she shouted. Then she sat down hard on another chair and burst into tears.

The door burst open and my brother came prancing in brandishing a Haagen-Dazs bag.

"Hello there, hope I've missed the main course, I brought some . . . . Oh," he said, glancing from the sobbing girl to me doing up my trousers.

I made a gesture of 'she's got issues and my knob's frightened her', and was about to speak when he put down his stuff, motioned to me to leave the room, and sat down on the arm of the chair where she was bawling.

"Hey, hey," he crooned very gently. "Hey, it's all okay."

Well, I'd tried that line and it hadn't gone well for me, but next thing I knew he had his arm around her shoulders, and bugger me if she didn't turn towards him and bury her head against his torso, just above the danger line.

"It's all okay now," he murmured, stroking her hair.

And as I crouched halfway up the stairs watching through the banisters, she sat up and wiped her tears away.

"There's a nice café on the corner," he told her, still in that gentle, crooning voice. "I'll take you down and we'll have some tea together, okay? It'll all be okay."

I mean, I ask you! Tannin is the answer! What a line!

But she sniffed and nodded, let him put his arm round her, and went out gazing up at him with dewy eyes and saying,

"I'm sorry, I'm sorry for being so silly."

His "It's okay, everything's fine" wafted back to me through the closing door.

I sat on the smelly stairs for another 20 minutes, puzzling it out. *I* hadn't got laid, *I'd* apologised to her just for being built the way I am, then *she'd* walked out with my sodding brother, *apologising* to *him*!

Well, you tell me. Just how had he done that? I know it was partly just circumstance, but I decided, though it hurt to be fair, that it might also be to do with his technique.

And that was my first tinge of real Envy. Because he'd made *her* apologise.

No envy involved when I heard that he'd taken full advantage of the situation, for obvious reasons: if she'd opened her legs to him it was because he had nothing scary between his. Even he seemed to realise that.

Apart from making me determined to try and copy his crooning, however much against the grain it went to copy him in anything, that incident did open my eyes to women's fear. And the whole thing of penises as weapons. Penises at dawn.

En garde! Would you think of yours more as a pistol or a sword?

**BANG!**

Could be quite fun, striding bravely across the damp, unresisting grass in the sullen light of dawn, your magnificent long cloak sweeping about your ankles.

The brief, hard warmth of your opponent's back against yours, the endless 20 paces, turn, reveal, aim your piece . . . .

*BANG!*

Or, hands tied behind backs, dancing and thrusting with artificially erected members (or maybe naturally, if you were scared enough), grunting, skewing, eyes fixed on his every move as you parry for the stroke that will . . . . what? Wound him? With my weapon, it might be a case of instant death for the foe.

And that's another thing . . . . I'd feel terrible laying some poor sod low with one blow from my mighty member after seeing at the start of the duel that he was poorly endowed. Maybe the seconds could take care of all that beforehand – decide the fairness of the match and perhaps establish some handicaps. But then, I'd always be handicapped to the max., and some of these small blokes can be quite nippy, not to mention nasty when roused, so maybe it wouldn't be fair after all.

It would be nice to think the whole thing could be settled through admiration, wouldn't it? You know, isolated spot, damp grass, sullen dawn, pursed lips of the doctor, worried frowns of your friends and all that – but all the dread dispersed when you cop a whack of each other as the swishing cloaks are flung aside and one of you goes,

"Oh nice one, mate, I wouldn't want to go up against that, let's go and grab some breakfast instead."

Or just swooned with desire instead of fear. But I suppose if the insult was mortal and enough to challenge someone to a duel over, that wouldn't really happen.

Anyway, when it's something you've got which brings you immense pleasure, and you're expecting everyone else to be equally thrilled by its possibilities, it's a real shock to find that there's genuine fear out there.

Now, some people might say men – not me obviously – are frightened of women, and they'd be right. Emotionally, financially, practically, verbally. But not scared in that physical, 'she might rupture my privates' kind of way in a sexual context.

So I could relate to the blindfolding fear, but I really got into being blindfolded myself. I just loved fumbling to undo her clothes, finding out with my fingertips whether or not she was smiling, and exploring that soft, warm body without any visual distractions. Usually warm body, anyway – it's a useful tip to remember that most women just don't work in bed if they're cold, it totally distracts them and makes them pretty ratty. Get the feet warm before you go for the fanny, is my advice. I had quite a phase of blindfolding until one woman I'd been with a few times – which is more than the average, so she was one of the lucky ones – said one night would I just pack it in 'cos she needed a shag, not a gynaecological examination, and she was sick of feeling she was banging a reversed-out Zorro, and ripped the blindfold off, drenching me in unaccustomed embarrassment.

There was some kind of delusion going on there – well, there usually is with human workings, isn't there? I mean with regard to the embarrassment. I was on a different sensual plane, being blindfolded. Manual work. Working blind. A universe trembling at my filigree fingertips – and occasionally threatening, I have to admit. It's a major challenge, to pleasure blind.

I had an aunt who made a comment about me pleasuring myself blind when I was a teenager. I went a bit haughty and said my mission was to bring pleasure to others, not myself (so much). She let out a big fat horse-laugh, stood up, leaving my mother and her tea at the kitchen table, and said,

"Blind already! You must be at it day and night."

Even my mother thought that was vulgar, and said so as soon as the door closed. Didn't stop her giving me a funny look, though. Speculative.

I worried about why the Zorro woman had got tetchy. I knew I'd been doing a cracking good job, exploring more and more nooks and crannies every night and taking longer and longer to do it, but that wasn't the worst thing. The embarrassment really flooded over me and into my crimson cheeks at the moment the blindfold was untimely ripped from me because she'd said 'banging'. "Someone I'm banging," she'd said, contemptuously. As if I was just anyone!

Stupid, impatient cow, I thought suddenly. All my gentle fingerwork, exploratory tongueing, caressing words, all blown up in a single BANG. Her treacherous groans and libellous moans had all been just for show – she hadn't *understood*. Or even tried to. Because, come to think of it, I didn't feel as though I'd had much pleasuring myself. So I told her I wanted to try clitoral stimulation with a razor blade next, would she trust me? and she left and I never heard from her again. I did think of contacting her to pass her onto my brother so that he'd have a change from the sofa cushions, but never got around to it, somehow. But they deserved each other. No need for a blindfold.

*Special Underbedcover Agent's Tip:-*

*Eloquence: of word and body. Get a few good quotes from the poets or pop songs to back up your chat-up lines (and get those into some kind of shape first). Passion has a silver tongue. And a golden dick.*

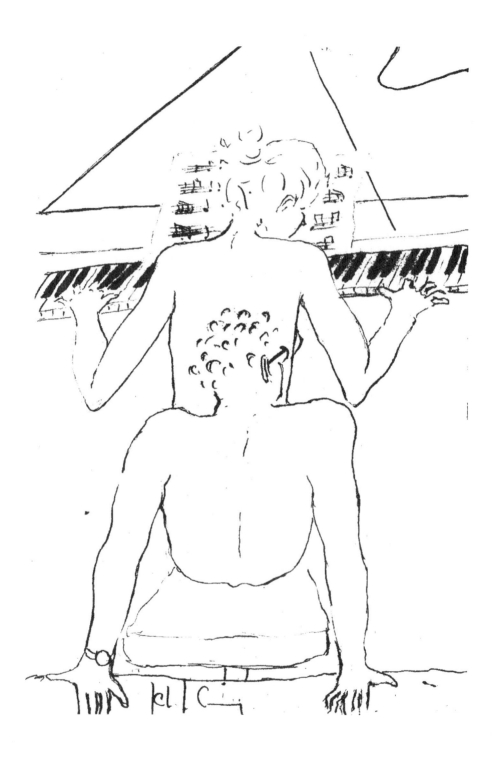

# Protocol No. 3 – Fun

## THE ANTI-PROTOCOL – IMPATIENCE

Fun: we're talking about the second definition for this one 'cos
it sounds so much more . . . gorgeous and light – *pleasure, gaiety,
merriment.* Some people say I take myself too seriously, but I
disagree. Anyway, the point is, fun is vital in pleasuring, and that
takes the form it takes – I can't define that for you.
Impatience: well we all know what that means, don't we? *Restless
desire for change or excitement* is one definition. Unforgiveable in
pleasuring – if you're doing it right, you'll be getting plenty of
change and excitement anyway. 'But in the initial stage, getting
to first base, if you don't ask you don't get . . .' – I hear you, mate.
But really, patience is the key.

I N   T H E   C O U R S E   of my
studies – the study of pleasuring,
that is – I decided once to take a week off work and impose some tasks on
myself. You know, like the Labours of Hercules. Not that I'm muscular or
anything. At least, I wouldn't say so. Not a pipe-cleaner either, I mean, I work
out. Anyway, I'd been out with the FFs one night and we'd got talking about
chat-up lines. I thought I was pretty strong in that field. None of the 'So, do
you come here often?' crap for me. I'm original.

"I'll ask the girl her name," I began explaining to them. "Nice and simple. Then, when she asks mine, I say it's Max. Mmmmm is for Max, Max is for Maximum. Mmmmmmmmmm."

One of the girls went a bit pink in the face when I said this. Yeah, she's feeling it, I thought. Probably undressing me with her eyes – or would be if she was looking at me – and wondering why she hasn't made a move on me all these years. The other FF was staring at me, all attention.

"Go on," she urged.

I felt triumphant. These two were just friends, but even so, look at the impact I was having.

"Well, another really good one – probably my best – is this." I cleared my throat, raised my eyebrows and said in my best James Bond voice,

"The name's Prong. *The* Prong."

Well, I thought we were going to get chucked out of the bar, they screamed so loudly.

"You *didn't!* You *don't!* You *can't!*" squealed FF2, while FF1 lay back with tears pouring down her cheeks.

I was pretty pissed off. It was quite a posh bar on the King's Road and I was a regular. I glanced at the barman and was relieved to see that he was grinning himself. Not because he'd heard what we'd said (had he?) but at the sight of a couple of girlie-wirlies squealing their heads off. It was a quiet time and he came over to get a slice of the action.

"More wine, ladies?" he inquired, still grinning to see them clutching each other in fits of laughter.

"Oh, let's see. Whose round is it? I think it's time our friend the, the P . . . . P . . . . Pr . . . ."

Oh Christ, I thought, but it all ended in tee-hee-hee and more tears.

"Just bring us another bottle of the same, would you?" I told him.

"Nice to see the ladies enjoying themselves," he said admiringly. "I don't know how you do it, man."

Well, that really cheered me up.

"I work at it, amigo, I work at it."

And that's the whole point – it *is* nice to see the ladies enjoying themselves, isn't it?

When the girls had sobered up enough to tackle the next bottle of wine, they made me recite all my chat-up lines. I didn't enjoy that session at the time, and in fact, there was a scrap over the bill because I refused to pay anything since they'd been such shits. They went serious then and one of them quietly paid while the other one said,

"We didn't mean to upset you. We just don't want you to embarrass yourself. You know, we want you to get girls. We're your friends."

"Yeah, well, fuck off," I said, and disappeared into the night.

*   *   *

Not good, I know, not good. I had to grovel. Dinner at expensive restaurant, all that. We talked it all through, I'd had time to think, we were still friends.

But from all that came my idea for a week's intensive study. To try out the new chat-up approaches, to get to know the greatest possible variety of women in the shortest possible time so as to learn more about what women want in the way of pleasure. And get my end away, of course.

So I booked my leave and asked the cleaning lady to do extra hours so the flat would look good and all my clothes would be clean, then I got the FFs round for a drink one evening to see their reaction to the environment. I didn't really want to hear their comments, but if you sign up for courses, you may as well listen to what the teachers say.

I was wearing a dark rollneck with a casual jacket. I'd shaved to within an inch of my life, and I was sparkling clean and lightly perfumed.

Opening the door, I was pleased to see that they'd dressed up a bit and were proffering champagne.

"Oh look, it's the Milk Tray man!"

"Nah, not enough stubble."

"No, you're right. He shouldn't have shaved if he was going for that look."

"I don't think he knows what look he's going for."

"Oh the flat looks great!"

"Wow!"

"It is a cool pad, you must admit."

"Real little fuckpad."

"And it's clean."

"Only looks clean because it's big."

This was an interesting thought. Did dirt show up more on small/medium-sized cocks than on mine? I poured champagne into the waiting glasses.

"Look, he had the champagne glasses waiting. How did you know we'd be bringing champagne?"

"What else would ladies like you bring?"

There was a pause. They looked at each other.

"Oh, that was good."

"What are you saying? That was disgusting! What a creep! Ugh!!"

"Well, I think it worked."

"It was absolute shit."

This wasn't helping me.

"Look, I've got plenty of champagne in the fridge – I wasn't relying on you."

"Oh."

"Of course not."

Abatement of giggles and – or was it just my imagination? – slightly hurt looks. Which told me more than all their smart comments and would help women in my future to climax into their own, not that any of us knew it then.

"What do you think of the flowers?" I inquired, more gently.

Ask a vulnerable question, put your prick on the chopping-block.

Six huge white lilies and one splash of blood, a blazing fireflower, amongst them.

They looked, they drew in their breath, they parted their poison-pout lips and said,

"Oh, just gorgeous."

Aha! I had made them come, and they knew it. Surprised them with one thrust of gentle boldness. Casanova the Musketeer, in and out with his naughty point.

Silence. We all lipped uncertainly at the bowl of concord.

"You don't think they'll think he's gay?"

"What! No-one's going to think he's gay! Look at him!"

We all looked, I resignedly, in the huge, matt-gold mirror. It was going to be shit if women thought I was because I put flowers in my flat because of them. For their sake, for God/Whatever's sake!

Okay, okay, I'd been surprised at the thrill I'd got from buying the flowers for myself. The old lady at the market had been so thrilled too, so complicitous, so knowing in her toothless grin. Mind you, she probably grinned because she knew something that wasn't true – probably thought I was buying them for someone else. Or maybe she didn't have much business that day. But the point for me was to experience the companionship of flowers as a woman might.

I carried them home in my arms, secretly drinking in their fragrance as we made our way through the busy streets. Yes, it was the first time. I carried them over the threshold murmuring into the petals, with a stamen caressing my cheek, and once I'd set them tenderly in the tall, square new vase, I carried them round the flat, patiently seeking the perfect place.

When I'd found it, I made myself a cup of espresso and sat gazing at them with new sensations.

And yes, then I did have a bit of a wank. And if you think that's over-sentimental, it's because you've never opened your mind. It means you're like my brother. No, that's not fair. It just means you're more like my brother than I am.

Where was I? Oh yes, the Tasks. The Labours.

Well, I decided I had to bed a different woman every day for five days. And not just a different woman, but a different *kind* of woman every day. As a treat, I could repeat the one I'd liked best on the Saturday night. The other five days/nights were pure study – work, work, work.

I spent the weekend prior to the five-day plan buffing up. Cut back on the booze, spent an hour at the gym instead of 45 minutes, went to bed by midnight with a good book, and didn't have a single wank. Oh well, the flowers encounter on Saturday morning. But that was it for the weekend.

Monday morning I awoke with an indefinable sense of well-being and a nice big boner that augured well for the coursework. Daytime excursions, evening activities, it was all planned. On Monday evening, I was due to go to the theatre. Something traditional but trendy – 'Othello' with an all-black cast and a white man in the title role – where I could expect to find the kind of person I'd be looking for. Imaginative, sensitive, open, female – the opposite of my brother, basically.

But now for the daytime. Boat trip to Greenwich: single mothers, frustrated housewives, unemployed singers, the idle rich, and all kinds of people on the edge of suicide. The outfit was cool – mainly because of the shades – although I suspected I was going to freeze my nuts off.

So it's spring? Well, nobody had told my gonads, and frankly I thought they were about to detach and float off down the river like a couple of undersized buoys. Wrong colour, of course. It was grizzly and drizzly and I didn't fancy a thing. I told myself that was the whole point. Crouching inside the dreary old floating hulk with smeary windows and a funny smell that didn't make me laugh, I told myself that not fancying people was sheer prejudice. A prejudice I needed to overcome for the good of the human race. Or women at least.

I have nothing against older, younger, thinner or thicker women. Nothing whatsoever. But I began to realise that they do have to look a bit welcoming, not furious or depressed or wiped out. And the only single mother I could spot looked a real bruiser.

"D'ya wanna smack?" she kept shrilling at her kid, who was about eight and incredibly eager to please, rushing off to fetch her a floppy sandwich, running around painting faces on the windows with his finger, asking her how the boat went, how it knew where it was going, why it was going there, what you had to know to drive it.

"D'ya wanna smack?" was her response to practically everything. The sandwich wasn't right, and he shouldn't mess up the windows, and he was making too much noise, and she didn't thank him for anything he brought her or did for her or told her about.

My cock felt as limp as the soggy sandwich she'd decided, after all, to push into her fat pink gob. Next time the poor kid came my way and looked up at me, I told him how the boat knew where it was going, what you needed to know to drive it etc.

"I'm going to tell my Mum!" he cried excitedly, and bounded over to her. How many years would it be, I wondered, before he realised that it wasn't worth offering her anything?

"Mum, Mum! That man knows all about it, the boat, and he says . . . ."

Mum looked over at me and I realised with a stab of horror that she fancied me. No mistaking that look – I'd thrown it often enough to recognise it when it slapped me in the face.

"So can we, can we?" and I just sort of nodded.

Oh God, tea in this dump, did I really say yes?

Her repulsive fat face was smirking into mine. The kid was messing around with his Gameboy. I glanced at my watch. Time was getting on.

"I ought to be making a move," I said. "Don't want to miss my 'plane."

"Ooh, you haven't seen upstairs yet," she said, taking the cup out of my hand and replacing it with her own soft pink trotter.

The house (her sister's) was awful, the staircase was disgusting, but most disgusting was the creature leading me upstairs by the hand.

Well, I nipped into the bathroom, which had an avocado suite – I kid you not – and worked feverishly to get a stiffie, for the boy's sake. His evening would be a whole lot better if Mum was happy. Mum soon came knocking at the door. Now or never. I opened up and dragged her in, laying a finger on my lips. She didn't need to be encouraged. As soon as she saw my cock, she was locking the door with one hand and reaching out to grab with the other. Since I didn't know how long I could keep it up in these conditions, I didn't waste any time but yanked up her skirt and began to tug at the sofa cover that was her knickers.

"Oooooh, you really can't wait, can you?" she exclaimed, delighted with herself.

It was as she struggled out of her top and released her massive tits into my face that I felt a rush of guilt. But I had undertaken the week's study, and there was no guarantee I'd be able to find someone else to bed that day. And actually, I've always been a tit man, and now I'd got in amongst those big fleshy jugs, there was no problem maintaining the boner.

So that was fine. I was going to, um, pleasure her just fine.

"D'ya wanna shag, then?" she said in a fond voice, exactly as she said to the kid, 'D'ya wanna smack?' when she wasn't even angry but just didn't have any other way of talking to him.

"Well, you be a good boy and I'll give you a shag," she crooned, stroking my hair. "Gonna have a good shag, aren't we, for a good boy?"

"Mmmm," I mumbled, too busy getting around nipples the size of saucers to think about what she was saying. Could do the analysis later.

There was only one way to have this fleshy creature, and that was with my face buried amid her pillowy tits. Snag. The bathroom wasn't big enough for us to lie down. Lifting her for a wall shag without machinery was not an option – there would be no more coursework that week or possibly for ever.

"Ooh, you're like a terrier after a rabbit," she giggled, thrusting me back onto the loo lid. "You won't get anywhere like that now, will you? Can't wait to shag me, can you?"

"Take your skirt off," I gasped. "Want to see all of you."

I think for a split second she thought I was taking the piss, but I really wasn't. There are experiences in life which are worth noting at the time 'cos you sure as hell won't want to repeat them. The bulk loomed over me.

"Please," I whispered, and I swear that word was her orgasm.

"Oh, you don't need to beg, big boy," she said softly. "You can see all you want. You can have all you want."

And the folds settled over my prick and my face was engulfed in glory.

\*     \*     \*

I didn't get a lot of the first half of 'Othello'. I mean, I automatically clocked the woman as I was standing at the bar having a drink beforehand. But once we were in and the lights went off, I just drifted into my own thoughts. Some people pass out as soon as the lights go down. I don't know how they afford it. Others immerse themselves in what's going on on stage – at least for as long as they can. If the acting's crap or something, you can't, can you? You can stack it all up in your mind, or have a fit of laughter, or get indignant that you've paid for this, but you can't really maintain much interest. Unless it's *really* crap, then it acquires a sort of cult interest. Like Monty Python or Mr Bean or something that people quote at each other in pubs 20 years later, though they're good cult rather than bad cult. That's all easier with film or TV than theatre, anyway. 'Oh yeah, do you remember that bit where . . . ?' 'Oh God yeah, that was classic!' Everyone cracks up over his/her own and the shared vignettes. How many people do you know who do that with a theatre performance? Well, of course, the mathematical probabilities come into it then.

Anyway, I'm normally one of the people who concentrate on the job in hand, and if that's a theatre performance, fine.

But this time I just let them get on with it and pondered my own performance that afternoon instead. The thing is, I couldn't work out if I could call what had happened pleasuring. Nasty feeling it might just have been shagging. But whatever, I was supposed to have learnt from it. To have brought away something that would be of service in future, um, exploits. And I couldn't work out what it was.

The good thing was, she'd definitely enjoyed it. She'd bounced up and down on my prong till I thought I was going to need a hip replacement, and although she wasn't the sort who has orgasms, she was flushed and triumphant when I finally surrendered and came softly inside her, like a champagne cork popping in the room next door.

"There!" she exclaimed, panting as I leaned back exhausted against the cistern and thought I must get the name of the loo manufacturer because I needed to do up my bathroom and the old bog had stood up to a lot of punishment that day – I was impressed. "There! Told you we'd have a nice shag, didn't I? Eh?" Suddenly her eyes went watery; she pressed her heaving flesh against my front and whispered tearfully, "You've been so good to me, that was lovely, it really really was."

When I left, she was bright-eyed and still triumphant, and though she said it was a pity I lived in New Zealand, I suspect that shagging a foreign diplomat (which is what the story amounted to) on her sister's avocado bog was most valued by her as a wonderful thing to be able to tell all her friends in little trickling instalments, and much best left that way than expected to 'lead to something'.

Which actually gave me a faint sensation of having been used.

"You're very pensive," a voice said, and as in the cliché, I realised it was mine.

The woman I'd said it to was standing nearby on her own, thoughtfully sipping a glass of wine. She'd divided her time between gazing into space and gazing at me. She was neither young nor old, she looked calm and intelligent, and just at that time, she was back to gazing at me with a complete lack of embarrassment or intent. When I spoke, she smiled faintly and said,

"Oh well, nice face."

"What, me? Mine?"

She nodded, her uncomplicated smile deepening.

Well, instant hard-on. Which I wouldn't have thought possible, considering the pounding I'd taken on the loo seat a few hours earlier. I tried to dredge up one of the new chat-up lines, but they'd all buggered off somewhere, so I just drank some more wine.

"Anyway, you're very pensive yourself," she said.

My turn to smile.

"Oh well, nice face."

"No, no, that's my line!" she laughed. "And you were thinking of something outside here."

"Can I buy you a drink?" I suggested, with quite a graceful forward movement and willing look. The body language seemed to be way ahead of the lines, though perhaps that was to be expected from someone as physically eloquent as myself. The problem is that most people don't speak body language. I thought she probably did, but just then the bells went. The bells, the bells . . . .

"Thank you," she replied, putting her glass down. "Maybe another time." She began to move off.

"Wait!" I cried. "Just a minute! I mean, we don't *have* to go back. We could stay out here and talk."

The same faint smile, and she kept moving.

"Look, I know how it ends! We don't need to go back! I can tell you the ending! How about tomorrow? I know a great bar. Or dinner? We could do dinner. Here, here's my card! Please call me! I'm not a psycho or anything! I just want to talk to you!"

Somehow the card had slid from my hand to hers. There was a touch on my arm – or was it just my imagination? – a ghost of a smile, and with the low-pitched words, "I don't talk much," she melted into the crowd.

Well, I do like Shakespeare, and it was a good performance, but again, my mind was on my own recent performance, so I turned against the tide and made my way back to the bar for another drink and a bit of a think. Finally, I went down to the cloakroom to get my jacket. There was only one girl behind the counter. I handed her my ticket and carried on pondering why my chat-up lines were so lousy. It had been fine with the enigmatic woman – okay, so I'd nicked one of her lines – until I'd got an inkling she might be interested, and then I'd just started babbling at her like a complete nerd. Desperate or wot? But why?

"I can't find it," said the cloakroom girl.

"What?"

"I can't find your coat." She looked apologetic but not devastated. "I looked all through the rack, but there's only a lady's scarf on the hanger for that number. Are you sure that's tonight's ticket?"

Still a bit out of it, I fumbled through my pockets.

"Yes, it must be, I haven't been here for months. It must be this one. It's a plain black jacket."

"Well, I'll look again."

"Yes, please."

She disappeared again but was back in no time.

"I'm sorry, I just can't see it." She gazed at me passively. She wasn't bad-looking, and there was an almost bovine quality about that passive look that wasn't unappealing, in an odd way.

"Shall I come and have a look, see if I can see it?" I suggested.

She let me through the little gate thing and went ahead of me into the warm, musty jungle of coats.

It takes you a while to catch on sometimes, doesn't it? I mean, there's such a huge grey area between the tart who gets slaughtered and propositions you in a nightclub bog and the indignant girl who knees you in the balls when you try and kiss her, just when you thought everything was going pretty well, that it's really hard to tell sometimes. Pleasuring does involve cottoning on fast to what is and isn't welcome, but maybe my senses had been a bit dulled by the day's events, because it was only when we reached the innermost recesses of the cloakroom and she turned and stopped very close in front of me that I began to think anything at all.

"I couldn't find it," she repeated.

But instead of searching again, she just stood there looking at me with that disconcertingly bovine gaze. She obviously expected me to do something. I turned hastily towards the racks and said jumpily,

"Right, let's see, must be here somewhere."

I reached up to the rail and found that we were in the 400 range – about 200 numbers away from where my jacket should be. I turned back to the girl.

"I think we're in the wrong section."

She was standing ridiculously close to me. Someone was clattering crockery in the kitchen. I hoped briefly that it wouldn't be audible inside the auditorium. I mean, this was the National Theatre. You'd think anyone clattering crockery during a performance would be sacked. I'd sack anyone who clattered plates during mine. She was a tall girl and I didn't have to look far down into her eyes.

"Maybe you need glasses," I croaked, dimly aware that the FFs wouldn't have much truck with that as a chat-up line, either.

"Maybe," she agreed, very softly. She gave me a bit more of the passive stare, then suddenly muttered, "Maybe I'm just stupid," and turned away.

I caught at her arm.

"No! No, of course you're not."

I pulled her round towards me. The coat jungle, warm and protective, was folded around us. Cautiously, I touched her cheek. No knee in the balls, just more passive staring. It was beginning to excite me. I nuzzled her neck and worked my way up to her lips. She wasn't a very good kisser. Inexperienced, I diagnosed. But willing! Therefore a perfect subject for the exploration of pleasure. My spirits, etc, rose. After a few minutes, she disengaged her tongue and whispered,

"The others will be back soon."

I don't know if it was a warning or a reproach, but it affected me. Others! Probably a herd of giggling girls with a battleaxe of a manager who'd castrate me with a coat hanger in front of the theatre crowd. That would make the papers. Front page or review section? The girl put her tongue back in my mouth and I continued to run my hands over her back, shoulders, arms and waist while we kissed. Speeding it up slightly in view of her comment, I began to caress her breasts. She murmured responsively. The kissing was improving, thanks to my techniques.

Suddenly, she guided my hands down the front of her shirt, which had somehow come undone. Things were hotting up. Quickly I unfastened her bra and pushed it up out of the way of my exploring hands. Her little moans were louder now. I shushed her gently and sat her down on the bench that ran along under the dark, sheltering coats. My crotch was on a level with her face now, and of course I paused, hoping she'd tear open my fly and suck feverishly at my knob. But she didn't. So I knelt in front of her and cupped her tits in my hands and slowly (but not *too* slowly, in case the rest of them were coming back) leaned forwards and licked her nipples. She gave a shudder and eased herself back, splaying her hands behind her on the bench, and her legs so that I could move in closer.

Her tits were a lot more manageable than the ones I'd been immersed in earlier that day, and just as pleasurable. I licked and sucked the cherries on her cream cakes while she delivered constant little moans into the woolly undergrowth and reached a hand up every few seconds to run it through my hair. Soon, she just collapsed backwards, and that was amazing. I pulled the coats above her together so that her top half disappeared altogether, and then I was working by feel alone. I slid my hand up over the nylon skirt and over her half-bared belly. By now, she was quivering all over, and when I finally stopped caressing her stomach and inner arms and ran the flat of my palms over both nipples she gave an almost convulsive shudder. I played in the dark a bit longer, relishing the feel of her flesh relinquishing again and again in my fingers, then lowered myself down through the undergrowth and paid lip service.

"The others will be coming soon," she whispered aeons later, pushing me off.

Lucky others, I quipped, but she was right. I stood up. She pulled her bra back into place and did up her shirt while I nipped round the racks and found my jacket. As we had a final snog and feel – I did the feeling, since she didn't seem to want any more than she'd had – I reached down and pulled up her skirt.

"Don't!" she exclaimed in alarm. "What are you doing?"

"Sh! It's okay, I just want to check something."

She stood patiently as I slid my hand up her skirt, down her tights and into her knickers, which felt nylony and scratchy like the rest of her clothes. I ran a finger along her gully and was pleased to find it was warm and very damp.

Outside, I waited till the show was over and watched the people coming out, but I couldn't see the enigmatic woman. But on the whole, I went to bed a happy man. There'd been one far-off climax out of the day's encounters, but the cloakroom incident still stands out as an excellent piece of non-penetrative pleasuring, and I drifted off to sleep trusting that the two women I'd dealt with were happily rubbing their clits and thinking of me.

\*     \*     \*

By lunchtime next day (Tuesday) I was well ahead of schedule thanks to one of the girls who worked in a local café. I'd often suspected she fancied me but my frank friends had put me right off by saying that she looked a bit calculating and was probably on the catch for a rich husband.

"Rich?" I squeaked in horror. "Husband!? But I'm not either!"

"Yes, but you look clean and wholesome and rich enough for her to get away with having babies and not having to work in a caff at her age."

"Her age! She only looks about 30!"

"Hm. But she doesn't look happy, does she? So if she's not a student and she's not the sort who's going to be running the place in a year's time, why's she here?"

"Well for God's sake, maybe she's just trying to earn a living like the rest of us!" I exclaimed. "Maybe she wants to buy a flat or has a sick mother or a kid to maintain!"

They both stared at me.

"Exactly."

"Oh."

I never did find out. All that happened was that that morning I went down to the local bakers to get some croissants for breakfast as a special treat and ran into this woman on her way to work. She was a bit early, the caff still looked dead as a doornail, so I did the civil thing and invited her to come up and wait in my flat over a cup of coffee and a croissant. She was a shade too eager to accept, I decided.

Anyway, you know how it is with croissants. You get crumbs on your crotch, if you're sitting down. Get them everywhere if you're not. About the third time I went to brush them off, she reached over and said,

"Let me do that for you."

She seemed to think the crumbs were pretty ubiquitous because the next thing I knew, she'd got my trousers undone and was cleaning the end of my knob with her tongue.

Great way to start the day, I have to say. After the initial shock, which nearly made me come straight in her face, I got a grip and settled down to make it last. This was most definitely pleasuring. I leaned back and gazed at the gorgeous flowers, slightly mistily reflected in the mirror because of the way the morning sunshine was coming in through the bay windows, and, in front of them, the gratifying sight of a woman on her knees busily sucking me off, and I gave a sigh of aesthetic pleasure even as my hips pushed my cock up to meet her.

She couldn't get it all in, of course, but hey, it was very nice licks, and the combination of the sight of my glorious flowers and the feel of her assiduous tongue meant that it wasn't so long before she was standing up, dabbing at the front of her wet shirt and asking where the bathroom was.

Once she'd gone I sat down to make some notes on the course so far, feeling smug. It was 10am and I'd had three bouts of pleasuring in the past 18 hours.

What? No, of course it was pleasuring. It did count for the coursework. I hadn't used her. I'm sure she was trying to catch a rich man – I could tell by the way she kept glancing up at me as she sucked. If she wasn't, if she did it for pure pleasure, then she'd had plenty of pleasure – there'd probably be little flakes of it dropping off into the customers' coffee all day. And if your argument is that I used her, then my argument is that the cloakroom girl had used me, because I'd spent 20 minutes working on her tits, and there was cum in her knickers when I stopped, and if that's not pleasure, what is? And I'd enjoyed that, ergo the waitress must've enjoyed the suckjob.

It did cross my mind that I'd cheated on the task I'd set myself of pleasuring a different kind of woman each day, because I already knew her. But she was a different *kind* of woman, and we'd never had any physical contact before.

I had a rest and some lunch, then got a bit complacent and went to the flicks before meeting my mother for tea. She was late, so I had time to go over my notes, and I came to the conclusion that although the functional side seemed to be coming along well, the initial approach was still not as good as it could be. I didn't have a proper system emerging here. So far, I'd pulled by a) telling an eight-year-old kid about boats; b) checking my coat at the National; and c) offering coffee and croissants in my flat. Well, that last one was valid. I tried to remember exactly what I'd said so that I could use it again, and decided I'd been quite natural. Non-threatening, of course. Reassuring.

"Oh, you don't want to wait down here on the street. Why don't you come up to my flat? It's that bay window just up there. You can even have one of my croissants."

Opening the bag to show her my buns had seemed to clinch the deal. Right. Food, then, helped. But was it the food per se or the fact that it was in my hand and the female had a clear view? Was food, like a baby, something that acquired magical properties when seen on a bloke? I know, I know, she was dying to get into my pants anyway as part of the rich husband campaign, so my coffee and croissants may have been irrelevant. I probably could've got the same results with someone like her by asking if she'd like to come and check the engine oil in my car. Flat, car . . . . whatever. You can't rely on a bag of buns. Probably it was just my indefinable aura and I was worrying unnecessarily about perfecting the chat-up lines.

"Sorry I'm late," said my mother.

I watched in admiration while she charmed the miserable git of a waiter who'd served me, and said,

"Like mother, like son."

"What?"

"The waiter. He fancies you."

She looked puzzled.

"Um . . . . Oh! You mean you're gay?"

"No! Don't be stupid!"

"Oh sorry."

"I just meant that you have members of the opposite sex crawling all over you wherever you go."

"So you've found a girlfriend at last?"

"No!" Although I'd never explained my vocation to her, I was always irritated by her failure to grasp that my mission in life was not to pander to and hinder one woman over a period of years, but to bring to many the blindingly magical moments they would remember on their deathbeds.

"Are you crying?" inquired my mother. "I only asked if you'd found a . . . ."

"I'm fine. No, I haven't got a girlfriend, yes, I'm perfectly happy, and no, of course I am not crying. Stop being stupid."

"Well, it looked like it. Maybe you've got weepy eye, or leaky eye or whatever it's called. That's not very attractive. It would put girls off. But I think it's quite easy to put right. Do you want me to ask our doctor about it?"

"Look, are you trying to wind me up or have you gone completely ga-ga? Because if it's the former, you can back off, and if it's the latter, you can forget any idea of sympathy from me."

"Oh look, here she comes."

'She' was this really attractive friend of my mother's. She lived in London, so round that time she and I used to meet occasionally for a drink or to go to the flicks, and I must admit that if it was the flicks, I very often had urgent thoughts about the woman sitting next to me in the intimate darkness. Never done anything about it, of course.

But today, when my senile mother buggered off to the loo, I took the bull by the horns and invited the friend round to the flat next afternoon, ostensibly to help me re-design my bathroom. She gave me a slightly quizzical look, but it wasn't actually the first time she'd been round, and she agreed without making much of it, just changing the time I'd suggested, like women always do.

I spent the evening at a pub in Kilburn, where I chatted up an initially morose girl who loosened up amazingly and giggled at everything I said. This was new to me. I probably could've had her that night, but I decided to go home instead. I was feeling a bit knacked – more because of my mother's stupid conversation than because of the pleasure bouts, I think – so I made some dumb crack about, "Maybe we'll run into each other again some day, like the day after today?" and left. The girl was standing with her mouth open when I glanced back and I wondered if she'd got it. Oh well. All that vapid giggling had done my head in. I went home and flung myself on the sofa.

\*    \*    \*

I spent most of the following afternoon on it, too.

"I haven't really asked you round to help with the bathroom," I admitted almost as soon as my mother's friend had got in the door. "Although that would be nice. If that's what you want to do, fine."

She put her bag down and said,

"What do you want to do?"

You just can't find the words sometimes, can you? I sort of shrugged.

"Life's too short for embarrassment," she said, and very kindly took two steps towards me.

Well, no lack of experience there. It was pretty sensational. First we had quite a fun bout – first time I'd done anyone over the back of a sofa – then we lay on the sofa to recover, then after a while she began to kiss me all over my chest and stomach and thighs, coming close, very close, but never quite getting to my point, till I was practically begging. In fact, I did groan, "Oh please, please," and do you know what she did? She breathed on it! Doesn't sound much? Try it, mate, try it. When she moved up and breathed in my ear, I was about ready to have at my own dick, but that would obviously have been absurd – what's the point in having a gorgeous woman breathing you off if you're going to butt in yourself with a hand like a bunch of bananas halfway through?

The word 'please' was trembling on my lips again when she moved back down, sliding her tits over my chest, and came down on me with a breathy tongue that felt like all the wings of the angels of fuck.

I'd had the main room done when I bought the flat – and this is the Pleasure Palace we're talking about at this stage, my real flat – so it was a nice big, new sofa we were operating on. As she swung herself round and fitted her fanny over my eager lips, I fingered the cushions and thanked God/Whatever I'd gone for the more expensive fabric combined with small silken roll pillows in between the big cushions. No, I mean it. There was just something about the textures – the rough, rich fabric with flashes of silk, her soft, bony clit, the powerful grit of her liquid tongue. If I'd gone for the cheaper, fine cord stuff the bloke in one shop had tried to sell me, that beautiful 69-er would not have lasted forever.

As she kissed and licked, her hands were running over my legs. I wondered if she was feeling the textures like I was. Maybe it was visual for her. I couldn't have seen a lot even if I'd wanted to at that stage, so textures marvelled my world, but she didn't see my sofa every day like I did, so maybe she was wondering why I'd gone for a dark shade with a small fleck instead of light with stripes or something. Not floral, she wasn't any more floral than I was. I was happy to think of her seeing the rest of the room from her flesh bed. Like I say, I'd had it done up. The light was good, the window was open, the flowers were nodding in gentle agreement with our activities.

Neither of us came, it wasn't that sort of thing. It was just infinitely delicious. After a long, luscious time we lay slumped, half-entwined, with our heads at opposite ends of the sofa, and slumbered.

When the light outside began to fade, I stood up to pull down the blinds. She lit candles, I made tea (yes, it was herbal – so what? Women like that). I slipped in a DVD and somehow we stayed upright for an hour or two, but then I was pushing her down onto the expansive cushions and parting her thighs and forgetting about the film.

Four bouts in total, 'cos she stayed the night. Ten orgasms between us, 7-3 to the visiting team. We had croissants for breakfast.

*   *   *

So that was Wednesday, and here I was on Thursday morning, well on schedule but, I have to admit, feeling a little bit knacked. Giving in to it, I scrapped the morning programme and just lay around reading a book on Casanova.

After lunch I tried to broaden my horizons by riding around on the top of a tourist bus for hours. Thought I was doing well with a couple of Italian girls till I realised they were just that – a couple. That gave the old confidence a bit of a knock. I mean, I can accept that a girl doesn't fancy me – no, really, I can – but it does freak me out to think she's rejected all of us. *All blokes!* And half the time they're ramming imitation dicks up each other anyway. Aren't they? I mean half the time they're engaged in sexual activity, not half the real time. Well, if it's that and licks, I can do it for them. I don't get it. Why go for something the same as what you are yourself? Vive la différence! Maybe for women the differences are all negative. I can see this point, ach'ly, but only because I've been eavesdropping on female conversations for years. Farting, ball-scratching, boringness, the incredible ugliness of the male genitalia etc etc.

All these thoughts took a while to sublimate. I'd been home, changed, and got to the pub in Kilburn by the time I was pondering on negative differences, but the trusty old smile was fixed in place, and so was the girl.

"So, shall we move on?" I said in my smoothest tone, and she giggled. Picked up her coat and slung her bag, but giggled. I wondered if she was going to giggle all the way through.

Well, almost. She was tall but quite skinny, and definitely wall-bang material, so although she'd suggested going back to her place, I followed my own plan. I mean, why go back to what might be some crummy dump where the shower doesn't work and the neighbours thump on the wall when you come? Anyway, I wanted to get home. So we stopped up some back alley, where I suddenly realised she was wearing jeans. I was a bit stumped, but while she was giggling like a hyena and saying, "I've never done this before," she manoeuvred her jeans down and somehow it was easy to hoist her up and settle her down on the rod.

I was a bit scared of scraping her naked arse or my hands against the brick wall, but it was fine, and I pumped away carefully till she stopped giggling and began to look over my shoulder. Closing time. I must admit I'd been feeling a bit more limited than I liked because of the position, but even so, it seemed a bit ungrateful of her. Unfeeling. I gave her a good fast run till I came fairly satisfactorily, and she dismounted and pulled her jeans up, saying I'd made her sore. I apologised – it was probably the cold air up her bits that had done the damage, so that was a useful lesson for me – but she walked off okay. And at least it had stopped her giggling.

Friday morning I went through my notes over an enormous breakfast. Eggs and bacon, tons of coffee, the whole deal. I was *starving*. I was feeling pretty smug: coursework completed in four days not five. Pretty good. I could do some clothes shopping, take myself out for lunch, and perhaps start looking for bathroom tiles and taps later on, all with no pressure. Magic.

It was then, looking at the notes and pouring myself more coffee, that I remembered I could repeat the best experience as a reward if I'd completed the coursework on schedule. And – this is the spooky bit – I didn't want to!

'Mum'? No way. Anyway, she thought I was in New Zealand. National Theatre cloakroom attendant? No, no. Like I say, excellent non-penetrative pleasuring, just too much nylon. The coffee shop schemer? Aaargh! Thanks for the blowjob, but a croissant and a gush of cum was all she'd ever get out of me. My mother's friend? Hm. Gorgeous, and definitely the most complete and satisfying pleasuring/being pleasured experience. Lots more to explore there, I felt, and sheer repetition would be no hardship whatsoever either. But somehow, not yet. I didn't pause long over the Kilburn giggler. Washout. I felt ashamed of that one. Neither of us had enjoyed it enough. I felt like my brother. Except that he would have enjoyed it, of course. Because he has low, not to say no, expectations. Just eternal hope.

Just as I was reaching hesitantly for the phone to call my mother's friend, the bro himself rang.

"Line up a couple of totties for tomorrow night," he yelled. "I'll pay. It's my birthday."

"Oh shit. I'm not here."

"Bollocks. Come on, it's only once a year, and anyway, I haven't seen you for eight months. Got your bathroom sorted yet?"

"No!" I snapped. "Come round at seven, then, if you must. I'll think of something to do."

"Told you what I want to do," he bellowed, but I rang off.

The phone rang again almost instantly.

"Look, I've never had to pay and I don't intend to," I told him.

"Me neither," said a throaty voice, and by some weird leaping convergence of senses (or maybe I just recognised her voice) I realised it was the enigmatic woman from the National. "Since we've got that aspect out of the way," she continued, "are you busy?"

\*     \*     \*

It was lush, louche, all of those words that slip thickly off your tongue like the end of a kiss. Deep red walls, the colour of crushed raspberries, with decadent swathes of rich fabric falling from modern gold rods. There was some kind of insidious music oozing from an invisible wound, and the cats – there were two – gazed at me with deep shining eyes.

Good thing I'm not American, I reflected. They all seem to be allergic to cats, and what a complete pain in the arse that must be, when you think about the number of women who like them. Not a problem for me. Had a couple myself, in fact, and I could have sat and watched them for hours. Well yes, I *did* sit and watch them for hours.

The enigmatic one wasn't sentimental about hers, but there was a definite fur-skin thing going on. Which was great. Augured well for me and my hairy legs. Not too cool at the time, hairy legs, but I refuse to wax, and electrolysis – I mean, what is all that about? Might as well have your clit snipped off or whatever they do to little girls in Africa – and what is *that* about? How the hell is a bloke supposed to gauge his performance if the machine's broke? Not that most women, to be fair and ensorrowed at the same time, would know the difference between coming and finishing. Most women if we look at the global population, I mean. Bagged-up ones and deeply uneducated ones and ones who've gone frigid from trying to be perfect, and all the rest.

It's what I was saying before about not many being willing/able to pleasure/be pleasured.

I'm not some kind of raving feminist, I just think it's illogical. Blokes have got nothing much to aim for under these circumstances, have they? The really sad thing is listening to guys who rate themselves, even when they're talking about societies where a Pepsi bottle would be a lot more use to a woman, especially if she'd had the contents first. Pathetic.

"More wine?"

"Yes please."

Of course yes please, it was a very decent bottle indeed I'd taken round – she wasn't the sort you could fob off with the local supermarket special. And I had been glad, when she opened the door with all that harmony of modern and comfortable backing her up, that I had a bottle of something fine to thrust forward as my own personal ramparts.

In fact, it wasn't that intimidating after the first ten minutes. She told me to make myself at home while she carried on cooking, so I had a good poke round and met the cats and checked myself out in the bathroom before going back to the kitchen.

I don't know if you do that – check yourself out in the bathroom, I mean – but it really is worth it. Just a tiny bogey in the wrong place at the wrong time, for example, can mean you don't get laid. It's that simple. Check nostrils prior to a date, don't finger your nose *at all* during a date, don't belch, except, possibly, for one profound but inoffensive burp of appreciation after a good meal for which you apologise, safe in the knowledge that the explanation makes a compliment of the offence, and never, never, *never* fart. Ever. For the rest of your life.

Although everything is a question of taste. You do hear about couples who think it's a real gas to try and blow each other out of bed, but all I can say is, no woman has ever started that kind of thing with me any more than she's suggested getting a couple of lesbos in as a warm-up act. These are bloke initiatives which may or may not be accepted, but should not be attempted on the first date unless you're paying or have reliable inside information. And be prudent: 'reliable' is not the same as someone like my brother saying something like, 'Oh I'm sure she'd be all right with it, mate – it's only a bit of warm air in her face, isn't it?'

Anyway, the main thing was the piano. A proper concert piano, and there was an upright, too. Turns out she was a concert pianist.

Now, I don't know about you, but I found this a massive turn-on. Something so incredibly solitary, with all the work going on unseen. All the rest of us would register would be the result. And nothing, no clue, until she actually sat down and played. No canvases, discarded tubes of paint, manuscripts or curtains or ceramics. It struck me, as she unfolded this aspect in the huge (and sound-proofed) red room, that musicians, ironically, are in this sense the silent artists.

Of course I asked her to play. She laughed and went back to the kitchen, and I think it was at that moment that I had the idea.

Don't remember much about dinner, I have to say, except that it was nice and light, and she didn't keep urging me to eat more, as lots of people seem to. It brought her closer to me: one really handy tip is to serve a light dinner if you're wanting to get laid. More than once I've had a cross girl fend me off when I've moved in after the coffee. "Ooh, don't, ooh leave me alone. Not now, not yet, no."

No. Not the word you've spent the day leading up to, what with planning the menu, getting the shopping in, tidying up the flat, showering and scouring yourself and then setting the table and cooking all the bloody stuff. 'No' is the last bloody word you want to hear. And don't tell me that 'no' doesn't always mean no, because I'm talking about the times when it definitely does. I only really cottoned on after a conversation with the FFs when one of them said she'd been to some geezer's for dinner and he'd given her spaghetti.

"Which is fine," she said, "because I really like spaghetti and he'd done a great sauce, but I had two platefuls and then, *then* he plunked himself down on the sofa beside me and started feeling up my thigh!"

It sounded good to me. The guy can cook and he wants to shag. But the other FF immediately covered her face and said,

"Oh, he didn't! What, straight after dinner?"

"Yes."

There was a pause while they both shook their heads and sighed and I waited for enlightenment.

"And the other thing," resumed the first one, "is that we'd had ice-cream for dessert and of course I'd left some in the dish because I didn't want it all at once, then when I went to sit on the sofa, he . . . ."

"He cleared it away?" breathed the other.

"No," she said in a low voice. "No, it was worse than that. He said that since I didn't want it . . . ."

"Aaaaaaaargh! He ate it himself!"

"Yep."

Silence.

"And then he had the nerve to make a pass at you?"

Head-nodding, head-shaking, more silence.

"Well, what's wrong with that?" I asked finally. "He cooks you a great meal, he lets you leave the table without finishing dessert, he *eats* your germ-infested leftovers, and he's planning to finish off the evening by banging you arseless on the sofa – what exactly is the problem?"

I mean, it is bewildering, isn't it? This is not just me, is it?

They went on at me for about 20 minutes. The ice-cream came into it a lot, but I have my own ideas about what to do with semi-melted ice-cream after a lush dinner, so I didn't pay much attention to that. But, the thing I did take away with me – and you might want to remember this – is that the guy didn't get laid because he served spaghetti and he let her eat too much of it.

Now, I did my own testing on this, and the results were startling.

Got a couple of women round (on separate nights, obviously) and gave them both exactly the same menu. Tons of pasta with a shrimp/orange/ginger sauce – sounds disgusting, but it does work – and ice-cream. Haagen-Dazs. Yes, I can do my own, but this was only a test, for heaven's sake – why would I spend an hour making something that might not get the results? Same ambiental music, same vino, same outfit for both ladies.

Night One: gave her a very modest helping and began stroking her thigh almost before she'd finished it. She responded for about six seconds, then pulled away and said,

"This pasta's delicious – can I have some more?"

Naturally, I gave her what she wanted – that's just the kind of guy I am – and she choffed down two and a half platefuls, let me kiss her for about another six seconds, then went for the ice-cream.

No shag, no licks, just a bit of tongue work and assorted gropings before she said she had to be up early and pushed off. Proved the FFs' point, I thought: guinea pig too stuffed to be stuffed.

Night Two: I let her eat all she wanted – about two and a half platefuls – of the spaghetti, gave her a bit of a rest while we listened to a few tracks I'd lined up specially, then fed her the ice-cream. She had two helpings of that, we listened to a couple more tracks, then she went to sit on the sofa.

Now, you may call it a bit of a macho thing, but I'd felt obliged to keep pace with her. And it has to be said that when I flumped down on the sofa beside her I felt about twice my usual size and more in need of a brandy and a long walk than sex on a narrow sofa ('cos it was a narrow one at that time – one of the things I learnt early was the value of a good broad, firm sofa).

Hand on her thigh, just going through the motions really. Any second now, I was expecting – possibly even hoping for – the indignant or just sated, 'No! Not now!' in line with the FFs' analysis and the previous night's experiment.

Well, I swear, she had my hand halfway up the creek before I well knew what was happening. She'd got the gates of Paradise open and there was the weediest-looking erection I had ever produced, but of course she thought it was huge – that's just the kind of guy I am – and I barely had time to snap on a rubber before she'd spread her legs over it and was bumping up and down like a kid at its first gymkhana.

She wasn't huge or anything, but I'd got the angle of my sprawl wrong, so that every bump seemed to come down harder on my bulging gut than on my half-flaccid prick, and I was feeling a bit queasy when she suddenly stopped and I thought, 'Oh great, maybe she's had enough.'

I know, sounds pathetic, doesn't it? Especially from me. But the ice-cream was Banoffee Pudding or something really sicky, and it was just being jerked around on top of all that ginger/orange/prawn stuff. I felt like a blender.

But instead of rearranging her knickers and looking round for her bag, she leaned right into my face and said,

"Come on, bang me, bang me hard."

Maybe if I'd had a decent hard-on I could've finished her off quickly. As it was, she moaned and thrashed but mainly just bullied me for more.

'Well, this is it,' I thought, dutifully plugging away while she slapped my arse and cried, 'Fuck me!' in my ear. 'I'm going to have a heart attack shagging, and it's all because of that bloody pasta.'

Nice situation down at the morgue or wherever, when they cut me open to find out what struck down such a perfect specimen of manhood, and the police pathologist gets drenched in half-digested pasta.

"It wasn't a heart attack at all, chief," I heard him say to a grim-faced, balding police inspector. "He'd just eaten so much spaghetti that when he tried to shag, his organs burst."

And I knew which would be the first organ to go. ('Fuck me! Oh fuck me hard!'). No, not the one you're thinking. First one to go would most definitely be my stomach. After that, toss-up between the over-stretched prick and the disappointed heart.

I don't think she came, but I just couldn't finish. I withdrew and went to the bathroom, where my climax took the form of several minutes' uninhibited puking. When I came out, she'd left.

So, the moral of the story is, that whatever your potential partner's appetite, you can't go wrong by serving light dinners if you want to have a decent shag, let alone enjoy some serious pleasuring.

And the concert pianist (CP) had the right idea.

And, since we seemed to be so much in tune (pardon the pun) over that, I didn't lose much time in suggesting my idea to her. She was lying back on this purple and red chaise longue at the time – either there was more money in piano playing than I'd suspected, or she was bloody good – and I was caressing her already naked body.

"Are you serious?" she said, gazing at me from those deep brown eyes.

"Of course. I think it would be incredible."

"And distracting!"

"I'll be very still. Well, as still as I can be."

There was a pause, then she lifted her pale torso from those rich draperies and said,

"Okay, let's try it."

She played Albeniz's 'Asturias'. They say it's a village lament for miners trapped underground, but to me it was swift and compelling, exquisitely paced, and filled with an urgency that surged alongside my desire for life.

And I kept very still, as still as I could. We'd placed another stool behind us so that I could splay my hands on it for support and keep slightly back from her. The music isn't full of flourishes or anything, but even so, you wouldn't want your face to be in the way of her elbows as she played.

I'd never been inside someone who was totally absorbed in a completely different activity. It was humbling and inspiring. For once I was more focussed on someone else's performance than my own, and being able to trust someone else in that way was in itself a revelation and relief. We repeated the idea several times over the coming years, often with me thrusting from underneath and trying to make her miss a note while she hammered out the latest hits and finally gave up, giggling, but that first night was pure, pure intensity.

When the final chord died in the warm, candlelit air, and I sat with teeth still gritted and knots in my arms, she stood swiftly, turned around and reinstated herself on me with a passion born of beauty and triumph. You might not want to hear this, but I actually wept when she came. Or maybe that was her. Anyway, it was pure magic.

*     *     *

One of the things that's always annoyed me about my brother is his taste. Lack of. You've seen what he's like with women, but it's everything. Crap hair, shitty clothes, just no *style* – you know? But some people think he's cool. Maybe he's got something. Apart from the clap. I dunno, longish hair and bald spots and striped shirts over jeans at all ages are not my bag, that's all.

And that's exactly how he insisted on going to her place. She'd invited me back for the Saturday night and it was so obviously the right thing to do that I'd said I'd love to come again, but that my brother was in town. "He can come too," she smiled.

She didn't seem to mind the way he looked, just said it was nice to meet him, and she'd got a present for him.

We didn't find out what the present was till after dinner. I went for a waz and when I came back he was sitting back in the armchair where I'd left him, but with a glazed look in his eyes. He made half an attempt to move when he saw me, and his lips almost managed to say something, but all that came out was a groan, and it was really only then that I clocked her head moving rhythmically over his groin.

Hands and knees. Gets me every time. She was wearing a skirt that evening, and if she hadn't done that on purpose, I'm the Pope. I moved swiftly round to her back end, went down on my knees and began to stroke the backs of her thighs, up under the skirt.

"Hey, look . . ." croaked my brother, his head rolling a bit now and the eyes still glazed. "I . . . I . . . Sorry, I . . ."

"It's all right mate, it's fine," I told him. I'd just discovered she was wearing stockings. "Oh Christ," I muttered – which is not necessarily blasphemous, as I do believe that the moments of most intense pleasuring bring us into contact with the higher power, whatever its name is – and she wiggled her ass appreciatively, so I slipped her knickers down and my tongue in.

It was a little strange, maybe, to be tongue-teasing a woman whose own tongue was busy on my brother's piece, but it didn't distract me too much. It did occur to me suddenly that I hadn't seen my brother's dick in years, and I must confess that part of the reason I stopped licking her out and prepared to enter was that I thought I'd be able to see it if I was kneeling.

And you know what? From what I could see, it wasn't a bad size at all. Anyway, by now he was leaning well back among the cushions, his hands clutching the arms of the chair, and now his eyes were closed. I was a bit surprised that he didn't touch her at all – it seemed detached and ungrateful, somehow. He said afterwards it wouldn't have seemed right, because he thought she was with me, so the hands-off approach seemed most appropriate. I understood. Blowjobs can be pretty mechanical.

It wasn't as if I wasn't prepared to make up for any lack of gratitude or enthusiasm on his part. I'd got her top and bra off and was enjoying her tits when I slid the old rod in, and very quickly after that, I'm ashamed to say that I'd completely taken her attention off my brother's dick. Sure, part of it was still in her mouth, but she was gasping and moaning so much that she simply couldn't draw breath and be sucking him at the same time.

"Hey!" He opened his eyes and realised. Tried to press her back down, but she was collapsing sideways onto his lap, and it wouldn't be long before she was face down on the floor with just me in the arena. "Oh come on, guys! Wait! Please wait!" he cried. "I'm nearly there! Oh come on!"

"Sorry," she whispered as she sank right down onto the floor. I was nearly there too, as it turned out, but she'd given a kind of triumphant shriek and subsided into little moans by the time I released.

The bro was not amused. "You selfish bastard!" he hissed at me as I withdrew.

She began to laugh. Rolling over onto her back, she ran her hands over her breasts and said,

"Come on me."

Well, at the look on his face it was my turn to laugh. He glanced at me as if to get the go-ahead, but she'd reached up a helping hand and while I peeled off the condom and sat back for a breather – well-deserved if I do say so myself – he took her up on her offer and quickly unloaded over her pearly tits.

It was strange to see him then. He knelt on the floor in a kind of stupor, staring at her in awe – it was me who helped her spread his wetness over her, and me who soon slid back inside to enjoy a second and even more powerful arousal. He just sat there. I remember that at some point he got up and wandered away, hitching up his trousers and still giving me awed looks over his shoulder. Probably thought I spent every Saturday night spit-roasting, when in fact I'd never had that particular experience. I kissed her all over and wondered aloud, "What the hell are you going to give me for *my* birthday?"

*　　*　　*

"Marry her!" he exclaimed next day in my kitchen.

I was pleased with that kitchen. It was the second bit of the flat I'd had renovated and it struck just the right note of urban chic. There were some small Italian detail tiles scattered round the otherwise white walls which I'd had to wait weeks for and I was just gazing at them appreciatively, waking up gradually over an espresso while the bro supped his tea when he said this thing.

"*Marry* her! What on earth for?"

"You mean, you don't want to? Too much of a slag? Be shagging all your friends when your back's turned?"

"My back wasn't turned last night, was it?" I pointed out.

"No, right enough. Mega-slag, then. She must be a pro. But you know what? It's worth the risk, isn't it? Fucking hell! I'd take the risk!"

"You sound like Mother." I reached up to put the kettle on for his fourth cup.

"*Mother* knows about her? You're kidding!"

"No, of course she doesn't. I just mean, you're obsessed."

"What do you mean, obsessed? It's what everyone wants, isn't it? To settle down. And God, imagine settling down with a bird like that!"

I shivered and got the biscuits out.

Gratitude's a funny thing, isn't it?

### *Special Underbedcover Agent's Tip:-*

*Cooking: (or possibly gardening, I reluctantly add after the incident of BM's wife – more on that later – if it suits your lifestyle better). You need to know enough so you can rustle something up without getting stressed – and therefore distracted from the main point of the dinner – and remember not to let her stuff herself so much that then she won't let you.*

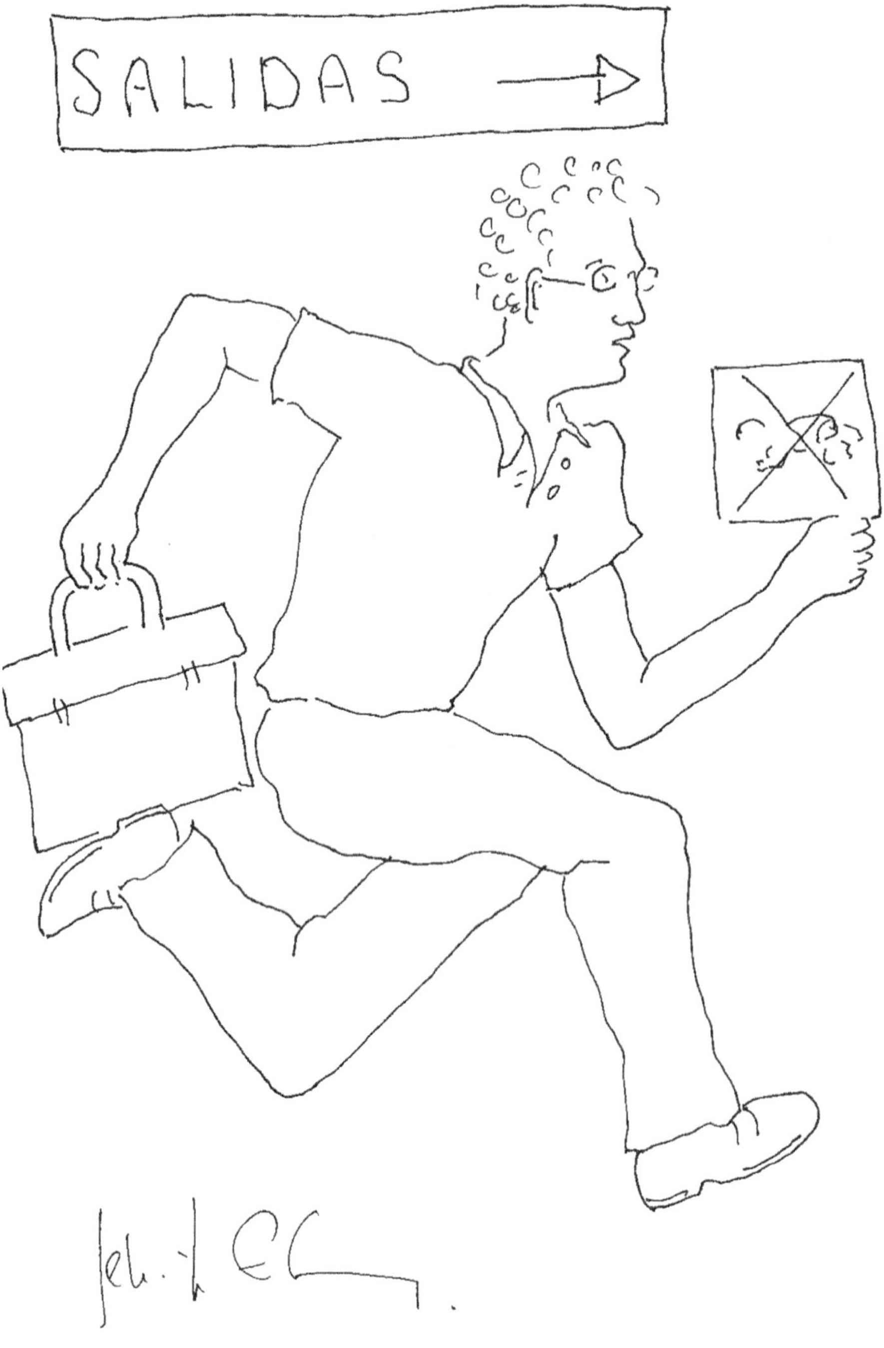
SALIDAS

# Protocol No. 4 – Judgment

## THE ANTI-PROTOCOL – DISHONESTY

Judgment: *the faculty of being able to make critical distinctions and achieve a balanced viewpoint; discernment.* Well, there you go – discernment, a closed book to the bro. And balanced viewpoints are harder to come by than Miss Tiny Cunt (that story coming up now).
Dishonesty: Miss Tiny Cunt is the definition. It's only physically that she was a tiny one.

GRATITUDE. NOW, I'M not saying I haven't felt it. In fact, it sometimes seems as though I've spent most of my life wallowing in it. But you do wonder whether a quality with so much capacity to corrupt its object is more of a sin or a virtue. That's why I say it's a bit dodgy.

Anyway, you can generally swing the Virtues both ways, like the Sins. Like capitalism and communism, they're very akin. **Prudence, Temperance, Justice** and **Fortitude** were the original Virtues. Then the Christians – incredibly competitive types, just look at all the colonising they did – added **Faith, Hope** and **Charity** to balance out the concept and provide a foil to the Seven Deadly Sins.

Which automatically excluded anyone who's a depressive. You must know a few, probably got one in the family. Probably you. Anyway, Hope, that four-letter word forgotten by all those who creep through the valley of depression. Or run and then crawl, if they/you are the manic depressive type. Bipolar disorder. Sounds so exciting, reminiscent of the days when you set off with your huskies for the unexplored geographical areas, and now that those barely exist, all we can do is explore the 95% of our brains that we apparently don't use. Don't use the huskies either for that, so there's a saving.

Not a bad boundary, almost the entire brain. And the advantage is that wherever you wander, no-one can really tell you they've already been there (though psycho disorders are becoming quite a competitive field too, have you noticed that?). But not always fun. No, not always fun, which is why I don't really do it. More of a physical bloke, really, though you can see from things like me opening a gynae clinic that I do exercise my brain in a way most people don't, i.e. by trying to imagine what it's like for the other person.

But I started on Hope because it occurred to me once that my brother has it whereas I have Faith, which is a lot more confident and, um, muscular. And I found this incident in my diaries and thought, well, there you go, that exemplifies the old Hope/Faith thing. Could be useful. Yertiz:

＊　　＊　　＊

You might be thinking I'm at it hammer and tongs the whole time. Totally not true. That would be my brother. 'If it moves, fuck it; if it doesn't, eat it', is his slogan. I once tentatively mentioned my Ladies First philosophy and he snorted and said, "Hey, I believe in equality – she's got exactly the same amount of time to come as I have."

Which is the kind of comment I can't disagree with, but absolutely don't agree with, if you know what I mean.

I suppose he's okay, and I have to admire his enthusiasm, but it's so misdirected. He's a real trollop. Just to give you one example, we were in this club in Dundee once with some of his college friends. I was the big bro who'd blown in for the weekend, and he was kind of showing me off and showing off to me, I guess. We'd had some eats and were onto the third club when it happened.

I was enjoying myself. I wasn't so much older that I felt out of place, and I was suited up and just that much slicker than the rest of them. They were slightly in awe of me 'cos I had a job and a flat in London and so on – I mean, none of it was any great shakes but I was clearly on my way to success so these college kids were impressed. Plus I was getting a kick out of eye-flirting with the girlfriend of one of the group. And no, I didn't feel bad about that. She was up for it, and the boyfriend could see what was going on, which hopefully meant she'd get a better bang out of him that night, if they were into banging yet.

Wasn't sure about that. He seemed to have the nervous attentiveness blokes get when they're with a new girl. Anyway, he'd sunk a few pints like the rest of us, and he was obviously desperate for a waz but I could see he was afraid to go and leave her at the same table as me, so he just hung on in there, clutching her hand and shooting me nasty looks and just about peeing in his pants.

Eventually the girl said something in his ear and he nodded and leapt to his feet and, putting a protective arm round her, escorted her over to the ladies' loo. I got up myself and pushed through the swaying drunken bodies to the men's. He was in there, so I took the stall next to him and of course he was trying to get a glimpse of my cock. Well, I guess I'd do the same if I felt threatened that way. Just never have.

He'd finished and was on his way out, and I was washing my hands when the door was slung open and a girl staggered in. The bloke took a step back to avoid her and just stood there staring while she backed me up against a mirror and breathed in my face,

"You're gorgeous, you are."

She fumbled at my zip and began to try and get her tongue down my throat. I pushed her off but then she sank to her knees and started mumbling at the front of my trousers. Guys were coming in and out, more or less unfazed by the floor show, and over their heads I could see the boyfriend still staring, all his worst fears confirmed.

"Mistake!" I called out above her head, trying to get her to stand up again. "I don't know her!"

He gave me a filthy look and left and I got her to her feet, shoved her into a cubicle and sat her down on the loo.

"You're gorgeous," she slurred again. "You gonna shag me?"

She was pretty slaughtered. Well, I don't need the admiration, and shagging some drunken tart in the men's loo of a stinky nightclub is not my idea of pleasure. Never was, never will be.

"You really want to shag?" I asked her. She nodded emphatically. "Hold on, stay here. You're going to have a great shag."

Her eyes brightened and she grabbed at me, but I slipped out and went back to the group, straightening my jacket as I went.

"There's a girl asking for you," I shouted in my brother's ear.

His eyes brightened just like hers had. He had Hope!

"Where?"

"Men's loo, first cubicle as you go in."

And he just plunged across the dance floor to get there.

The bloke with the new girlfriend was hustling her away and the rest of the gang were dancing or getting more drinks etc. I sidled off home and pleasured myself contemplatively over a glass of whisky. Well, with a glass of whisky beside me. You know what I mean.

About half an hour after that, while I was sitting wondering how he could have been so enthusiastic without even knowing which girl I was talking about, he came bounding in.

"Sorry 'bout that. Got held up, arf arf. God I'm thirsty. D'you want some tea? Thanks for the tip-off."

"Did you have a good time?" I asked.

"Oh yeah," he called, clattering about in the kitchen. "Banged her dry, bought her a drink, put her in a taxi. What do you want to do tomorrow?"

And that's it. That's the fundamental difference between us. He's not looking to pleasure or be pleasured. He's not looking for someone with the capacity for total abandonment and unhurried enjoyment – he doesn't have that much Faith in himself, let alone anyone else. He's just hoping for someone who'll let him get his end away. Probably shags the sofa cushions when there's nothing else around, I thought, taking the tea he was handing me.

"Aaaaah! Nothing like a bit of unexpected nookie on a Friday night," he said, taking a gulp. Which is another thing I've never understood, how he can drink tea so hot; I always have to wait for mine to cool down. Better for the food pipe or whatever it's called, anyway. "Why did she ask for me, by the way?"

There was a hint of suspicion in the way he looked at me as he asked and just a trace – or it may have been my imagination – of appeal.

"Saw you across a crowded room," I said at once. "Collared me 'cos she'd seen us talking and said, you're gorgeous."

\*     \*     \*

Despite being a tit man, there was a time when I began to travel more for my pleasures because lots of the women in the UK seemed to be getting so enormous it was a turn-off.

Like I say, not particularly fussy age or size or anywise really, but I'm not big on fat. It just seems to imply a lack of effort in a lot of cases, and if someone can't be bothered about herself, why would I think she's going to bother about me? Of course yes, then you get the other extreme, where a woman's so obsessed with staying stick thin or trying to stop her face getting a wrinkle that she just doesn't give a shit about you either. Non-starter in the pleasure stakes.

S'pose it all comes down to confidence, dunnit? Nothing so attractive as, if it's genuine, and if the tits aren't, how can the confidence be, is how I see it.

Anyway, the point I was going to make is that Britain had taken the game to a new level on the flab front, so I went on some non-business trips abroad to check out other markets at my leisure.

And it might have been something to do with revenge and the young girl who'd set her dad on me when I was 14 – except that she didn't, because my mother, probably prudently in that case, I have to admit, had already set my own on me – that one of my first ports of call was Spain.

Don't know if you noticed, but that paragraph was one sentence? Which is something they did a lot in Spain at the time I'm talking of – couple of decades after the end of a 40-year dictatorship, rampant materialism, everyone dying to be different now that they could be, excess, excess excetera.

But in some ways the literary and journalistic world was still anchored in the Franco era: the longer a sentence was, the more abstruse the words used, the more respected the writer.

In a way, you can understand it. It happens/happened in transitions from Communism. Technique, training, professions, excellence, suffering for excellence – these were all valued and, in fact, expected in a way that was, at the time when I was researching my own profession, incomprehensible in the increasingly decadent UK. Celeb-based, flippant, no individual responsibility – fat, really. Flabby. Not as obese as the USA, but heading that way.

Perhaps I was eager to explore different values, but I'm not convinced by that. I had a big dick, a fast car, good health and enough money to travel – these were my values. Nah, it was more a dread of mediocrity – because lazy fat is *so* mediocre – that drove me away.

You're probably wondering what all this has got to do with Prudence? (Virtue, therefore capped up).

Easy. Condoms. Protection. Prudence. I can't say I've ever been inactive in the pleasuring stakes, but one of my most frantic periods was at the height of the AIDS pandemic. Suddenly it was cool to wear condoms. The fact that I'd been doing it for ever highlights the depth of my commitment to pleasuring (not to mention being cool before anyone else) – I mean, I never have had any interest in exploring someone who's scared shitless of getting pregnant. I'd be just the same. Plus *I* was scared shitless of getting her pregnant. Relaxation is key. And what about all the diseases? Puh-lease. I didn't have time for them.

So what caused me to waver from the principles of a lifetime and abandon my natural Prudence?

Well, I admit I was probably a bit desperate because I'd been in the country (Spain) for 36 hours, and still no action. Spaniards tend to do things in clusters, and although I'd've been more than happy to service several señoritas in the same session, it was pretty obvious that the clumps were protective rather than sexually adventurous. I suppose they were just being prudent in their own way, but it was getting on my nerves a bit that I couldn't even chat up a waitress without six of her chums appearing out of nowhere to listen in.

Perhaps I looked too predatory – I was on my own on that trip. Anyway, the long and short of it is that I went to this nightclub where, lo and behold, a girl in a cluster detached herself after I'd given her the eye a few times, and went to stand by the bar.

She was very petite and I'd selected her specifically because I needed to do some research into the whole pain/pleasure thing, and I was curious to know how to pleasure a tiny cunt and what there would be in it for me.

She was wearing a really vulgar gold belt slung round the mini-skirt, and foundation an inch thick, but she'd left the herd and she looked at least willing to give me a chance, so I moved in and got started.

My Spanish is hardly strong and her English was non-existent, but over the course of the next 24 hours, I'd made enough progress to get her into my hotel room, perched nervously on an upright chair whilst I made her a cup of tea.

It can be tough finding women who are happy about casual pleasuring, especially in Catholic countries, and I certainly never raise any false hopes – learnt that lesson from the squash captain at school – so the first move was to show her a picture of a baby and draw a big red cross through it, then open the condom packet and look politely hopeful.

It's amazing what looking politely hopeful will do for you. She closed the condom packet but smiled, so of course I went down on my knees and gave her lots of ultra-gentle kisses and touches and reassuring murmurs, and it all progressed pretty well. She was a competent kisser but seemed fairly distant from the whole procedure, and though I'd assumed she wouldn't be up for intercourse so soon after meeting me, I began to feel more and more curiosity as to what would get her going.

Of course, an important part of pleasuring is having compatible vulnerability levels, and equally obviously, she'd be feeling incredibly vulnerable with someone like me, so I didn't try to grope her or undress her or anything. I just got up, went to the bathroom, stripped off (and did the routine checks), slipped on the hotel bathrobe and went back so that she could decide how much more she wanted to see.

It worked well. She was clearly delighted to be in charge, and did lots of kissing and caressing, then smiled when I reached for the condom packet and opened it, raising my eyebrows in inquiry.

The smile meant yes, I was well ready, I didn't need her naked, just wanted to know how far things would stretch before she thrust me away. So I manoeuvred her little buttocks forward onto the very edge of the chair and kept my tongue moving round her mouth while I eased her tights and knickers down round her ankles.

This gave limited access, but judging from her size, access was going to be limited anyway. Except for having her underwear hanging round her ankles, my little señorita looked almost exactly as she had before, perched neatly on the edge of an upright hair with her smooth dark hair still in place, her little matching skirt and jacket totally unruffled, and not a blink of emotion in her velvety brown eyes. There was no passion but no fear either, and to avoid her suspecting that we were about to attempt the equivalent of passing a camel through the eye of a needle, I carried on with the kissing while I came up to meet her and began to rub my tip against her clit.

She still hadn't uttered a sound, so I slipped a finger up to make sure she was ready. I think she thought that was it, as she stopped kissing me long enough to say "Ees good" in an approving voice.

"Thees ees better," I assured her, parting her lips with my fingers and inserting the tip as far as I thought would be fair.

She gave a gasp and bit my bottom lip as she disengaged from the kissing again and turned a wide-eyed stare on me, clutching her chair with both hands.

"Okay, it's okay," I told her, gently moving within the two-inch range permitted.

She just stared. I had visions of pushing it another six inches and not needing to move at all within those desperately tight, moist walls – just see her perched motionless and startled on the pain/pleasure pinnacle for an eternity while I simply throbbed and swelled and burst inside her.

But a couple of inches is fine if you're helping yourself out at the same time, and eventually, after aeons of surprised silence from her, I succumbed to my own temptation and sat back on my heels, sweating from the discipline of it.

"Ees good," she repeated with a smile, and decorously pulled up her underwear before disappearing into the bathroom whilst I pondered on the two-inch range, and whether such an intense focussing of sensation was conducive to pleasure or an affront to it. Had just decided that it had been interesting but that the best pleasure is to do with uniting the broadest possible range of simultaneous sensations, when she emerged freshly-lipsticked, picked up her gold-chained handbag and told me I was a very nice man before leaving. Patronising or wot?

But we stayed in touch and after a few weeks I went back for a weekend, safe in the knowledge that she lived with her parents – I know, but Spaniards never leave the nest, apparently – so I could have her at my hotel in the afternoons and find someone a bit less trammelled for the late night action. A weekend was plenty – it's not as though I wanted to spend any non-naked time with her. Nice enough, but heavy going language-wise, and I suspected she wasn't big on humour, which is always a major turn-on for me, especially if it's sly and I'm the only one who gets it. To be quite honest, I haven't met many women who do that for me, but I suspect perhaps they're better at it in a female-only situation.

So here I was, swinging out into the Arrivals area at Barajas with a really nice leather holdall I'd picked up in Rio de Janeiro slung over my shoulder, a packet of soon-to-be-amply-filled Maxi condoms in one of its pockets, and a carefree whistle on my lips, when I saw . . . . her! Come to meet me! Over-emotional over-reaction or wot?

I stopped and stopped whistling and was trying to get my head around it when she advanced on me with that approving smile and suddenly I found myself being clapped heartily on the shoulder by some youngish bloke while a beaming older woman reached up to give me a couple of pecks on the cheek and I realised she'd brought the whole fucking family!

I know what you're thinking – this man has the reflexes of a retarded snail. Why wasn't he back through those one-way doors into the baggage area again *at once*? And yeah, you're absolutely right, I was way too slow. Allowed precious seconds trying to get my head around it, and I just didn't have those seconds. But in my own defence, these people were the ultimate pros. They had me sat down with a glass of tinto in my hand at one of the city's best roast meat joints, surrounded by a sea of grinning relatives, before I could say, 'No way José'.

At the end of a convivial evening – the brother and one of the female cousins spoke some English – they accompanied me back to my hotel in a pack and disappeared in a laughing, kissing clump, leaving me to sort my head out and rest my jaws, which were aching from the permanent false smile.

Apparently she and I had arranged to meet next day for lunch, and again, I was too slow off the mark, or else just too curious to know if she'd be able to take another couple of inches if I gave her good tongue first. Be that as it may, I turned up half-expecting to meet the whole troupe again – and let's be fair, these were very pleasant, hospitable people so I would've accepted that as best I could except I didn't have to 'cos it was just her – and managed to get her back to my hotel room for more sodding tea after a fairly silent lunch.

This time she was the one to pick up the condom packet and raise her eyebrows, but when I reached out eagerly to grab it, she smiled, put it down and produced a pack of birth control pills from her handbag.

"Okay, ees okay!" she beamed, and you know what? I thought oh fine, let's go for it. She hadn't been a virgin – even in Spain at that time I wouldn't have expected someone of her age to be – but I couldn't imagine she'd had more than one or two boyfriends. And the whole pleasuring aspect was too strong to be ignored. After all, she was fairly passive, and if there's nothing going on in the way of added stimulation and you can't fit even half the piece in, then all your pleasure focus is restricted to a pretty reduced area, so I reasoned that the more exposed that reduced area was to any heightened sensation going, the better.

By the time I'd reached this conclusion, she'd got all her clothes and most of mine off and had actually touched my balls! And – but this may have been my imagination – given a little gasp when she saw the pinnacle rising before her.

She wasn't scrawny, just very petite. Felt like I was searching for errogenous zones on a doll. But ear-licking seemed to please her to the extent that my fingers were rewarded with some welcoming moisture when I prised her thighs apart. I reckon we did about three inches – breadth is obviously an issue too – and again, she was pretty silent and passive, though she did smile a lot. One or two more sessions and our time would be up, I reckoned, particularly if the family was going to start wanting in on the action. That said, I wouldn't have minded getting to work on the cousin who spoke some English. Looked pretty rough and bossy – could do with some English discipline.

In fact, we only had one more session that weekend and it was fine. I perched her ass on the washbasin and did her there, dipping my fingers into the warm water underneath and using a touch of soap to tease her tiny anus. That shocked her hugely, which excited me, so though she wriggled and protested, I gently persisted and had about half a centimetre of my little finger up her arse when I came. While she was still wearing her startled look, I carried her over to the bed and gave her nice gentle licks and that really went down well – she definitely moaned a couple of times before whispering, 'Enough, enough.'

Good girl, I thought, and, wondering if I'd ever be able to surprise a shriek of real pleasure from her, I booked another flight for the following month.

Maybe it's because I'd been playing a lot of squash, which tends to sharpen my reactions, or maybe it was because I'd had time to realise that I do like to be able to ram in the whole item and get some audible proof of pleasuring, but my response when she met me at the airport and told me with gestures and a politely hopeful look that she was pregnant, was swift. (Another whole paragraph that's one sentence, did you spot that?)

"Baby," she repeated, smiling, but by the time she'd started to get out the unbelievable words, "You, daddy!" we were at the BA desk and I had a seat booked in Business Class on the next flight home before she'd got to the stage of trying to put my hand on her belly.

"Girl, boy?" she was saying as I hurried back towards Departures with her trotting at my heels. "You want boy? You want girl?"

I got out my passport and a card showing a baby that I'd asked my mother, who was pretty good at drawing, to do for me.

"Are you trying to tell me something?" inquired my mother when I'd asked her to do it over tea at Selfridges a couple of weeks earlier.

"No, I'm trying to tell other people things," I responded, getting my big red marker pen out and putting a decisive red cross through her handiwork.

She poured me another cup and said,

"Are you seeing a shrink yet?"

The card was just what I wanted and a great improvement on the picture I'd initially shown TC (tiny cunt), though that one had been more than adequate for getting the point across. She stared at my mother's effort and the politely hopeful look began to fade, a storm gathering about her beaklike nose and those velvety brown eyes darkening menacingly.

"Me no daddy," I said emphatically, showed her my ticket, and went through to Passport Control without a backward glance.

Yeah, yeah, I know what you're thinking. Looking politely hopeful hadn't got *her* very far, had it?

*　　*　　*

"Well, that was unfair!" exclaimed the FF1 when I was telling them about it in some new bar that had sprung up round the corner from their house.

The place wasn't that great – they'd gone for the school canteen look that was in at the time. You know, orange plakky chairs and thick glasses. You could see it wasn't going to wear well. But I was chuffed by the FF1's sympathy.

"I know! Thanks. Okay, so I'd been really . . . . imprudent" (first time I've ever used that word, I think), "but I didn't deserve to be abused like that."

The FFs looked at each other.

"I meant it was unfair on her," said the FF1.

I stared.

"What? What do you mean? This nasty little tart plays the oldest trick in the book on me . . . ."

"And it probably wasn't even true," put in the FF2.

" . . . . and it probably wasn't even true," I agreed, then paused. "If it wasn't true, that makes it even worse. Doesn't it? I mean, that would mean – well, what *would* it mean?"

"Might mean she was calling your bluff," said the FF2, swishing her gluey little cocktail round its too-thick glass.

"Is that any good?" I asked her.

"Not really. Bit of a dump, this. Can we go somewhere else?"

"Okay, not yet. Why call my bluff? What bluff? What are you talking about?"

"Oh come on, it's obvious. You're popping over to see her every couple of weeks, you're well in with the family . . . ."

"Hey, that was kidnap, not a normal introduction!"

" . . . . and she probably just wanted to know if you were a realistic prospect."

"A realistic prospect! We had zero to say to each other!"

"Maybe she thought you'd be a good family man."

"She couldn't have done! I'd shown her a picture of a baby with a red cross drawn through it the first day we met, for God's sake!"

The FF1, who'd picked up her bag to go, paused.

"You'd shown her what?"

"Something like this, but this one's better. I got my mother to do it." I pulled out the improved baby card and handed it to them. "It's the easiest way to get the point across."

"All you did manage to get across with TC," tittered the FF2.

"Shut up, it was the best sex she'd ever had."

"Told you so, did she? In her fluent English or your fluent Spanish?"

"Shut up! Some things don't need to be said in words."

"So she drew you a picture, did she? Or did she get your mum to do it for her?"

"Come on, we're leaving."

The FF1 handed back the baby warning card and gave me a wondering look.

"Shouldn't you be seeing a shrink?" she asked.

Out in the street, I told her she sounded like my mother, which didn't disturb her the way I'd expected it to.

"So your mother thinks you should see a shrink too? Do you see a pattern emerging here?"

"No! What I see is you women having a ridiculous urge to sit around yakking with some sexless berk called a shrink when you could be out running a business or a marathon or having a decent shag."

"Or running a family," remarked the FF1. "So if TC really is pregnant, don't you think your reaction was unfair?"

The injustice and total lack of logic of this stopped me in my tracks. It also recalled my wandering attention – I had been wondering if it might be worthwhile doing a spot of shrinkage just to flesh out the pleasuring techniques (ongoing training), since women seemed to think it was such a big deal. Expensive, but I need only do a few sessions to be able to understand their point of view. And get sympathy. Which, although I don't go for it 'cos I don't need to, has been a bonus on a couple of occasions.

"How can you say that?" I demanded, rounding on the FF1. "You're talking as though I inflicted something on her . . . ."

"Only a couple of inches."

"Shut *up*! . . . . whereas in fact she was the one who persuaded me to, to . . . . unprotected."

"Why on earth?" sighed the FF1.

"I know, I know. I lost the plot. I just thought there was no way she'd be diseased, and she showed me the pill she was on, and I told you, I thought it might give me heightened sensation."

"Well it did – you're all flushed. How about this place?"

We trooped in. Much better. Excellent lighting – makes all the difference – and the FFs liked the way the wall textures had been reflected in the chair fabrics.

"Whether it was calling my bluff or not, the point is, she lied and I don't like it, and that's why I got the next flight home. It absolutely ruined the whole thing, and there wasn't much to it anyway. Nasty, nasty thing to do. Enough to put a bloke off women for life."

"Not you?"

"No, obviously not me. But if one treats you like that, it is hard not to remember it and who knows? I might take it out on someone nice."

"I doubt that." / "Oh no! You wouldn't!" they chorused, and again, I felt chuffed for a nano-second before the FF2 said,

"You never shag anyone nice, do you?"

"It depends what you mean by nice," I responded after a dignified pause. Was actually quite interested to know her definition. If she thought I was never with anyone nice, what would she think of my brother's activities? He got my rejects when I felt like adding some Charity to the Faith/Hope mix.

"Yes, I can accept that," she admitted. "But I suppose 'nice' women would usually have objectives in life, like having a good job, or getting married, or being with someone, or running a business or a family."

"Or a marathon."

"Or a marathon. And you're not up for any of it, are you? I mean, sharing it on a long-term basis. So, although you didn't like her methods, TC flushed you out pretty efficiently, didn't she?"

We were all silent for a while, eyeing up the bar staff and other clientele. Not much in that night.

"Wouldn't you be curious?" asked the FF1 finally.

"About what?"

"About the child."

"What child? It was all a lie."

"But she may really be pregnant."

"Then she should pay me for the sperm. Thieving cow."

"Oh for heaven's sake!" muttered the FF1.

"No, I mean it. And she should pay for my therapy to get over the trauma."

This definitely sounded appealing to me. Free fleshing-out of my pleasuring techniques.

"You're nuts!"

"No, hold on, let's think about this. If I'd gone over there, identified her as a suitable mother of my children, but she told me she didn't want kids, then I'd told her I was using a condom and deliberately split it before sex and therefore got her pregnant, would you think *she'd* been unfair?"

Awkward silence.

"It's different."

"It is *not* different! Your brain is not working! By accusing me, you're putting the victim in the dock. I was clear and I was respectful. I think it would be criminal to trick any woman and put her in the situation of expecting a child she had clearly said she didn't want. It might be a minor physical inconvenience if she found she was pregnant, but it could be major decision-making anguish, and it could be severe physical trauma, not to say danger, not to say death sentence in certain circumstances. How can you be so careless of another woman's life or feelings? And why can't I have the same feelings? The physical danger doesn't come into it in the same way, thank God/Whatever, but an abusive intention is still an abusive intention and it can do great damage and it's evil. I'm getting another drink – do you want anything?"

"Suppose she is pregnant and, given your reaction, wants an abortion?"

"Her choice."

"Shouldn't you pay for it?"

"No way! It was her choice to try it on in the first place."

We ordered more drinks and some food and I took a look round at the hidden lighting they'd used because I was thinking of something like that for the main room at home. I do like reading, and it's not easy to get the right combo of discreet lighting and good focussed reading lamps. Aesthetic challenge, it can go horribly wrong, know what I mean? One is so integrated and the other can't help but intrude. I'd been considering insets in the wall to house small, angled wall lamps as reading lights, but it's still limited – you can't pick them up and carry them with you if you feel like reading on the floor, for example. And you can't shift the furniture around, ever again.

"Surely you'd feel curiosity?" resumed the FF1. "Wouldn't you wonder, just a teeny bit, ever, what your child might be like?"

I took a few sips of wine to give the impression I was thinking about it while I jettisoned the wall insets idea once and for all, and then said,

"No. No way. I have no interest whatsoever in creating more people, I don't want to see TC ever again, I think the whole kids/family thing is way over-rated and I have plenty of curiosity and interest in my own life – I don't need to pile on unnecessary responsibilities. No. No. The answer is no."

I wasn't at all vehement about it and I think they began to get the message.

"In any case, the whole thing is based on deceit," I continued. "That kid – if there is one – could be carrying its mother's deceit genes. Gross!"

"He's probably worried it'll have a tiny dick," said the FF2, and they both started giggling helplessly.

I put down some cash and left them to it: I had a long-haul flight next day and needed an early night.

I spent quite a lot of the flight pondering that comment about, 'You never shag anyone nice, do you?' Getting over the fact that she'd used the word 'shag', which is what my brother does, not me, I was still puzzled and disturbed by her possible idea of a nice woman and my relation to that.

Because it was long haul, the company had put me in Business Class, which helped, and I was with an older, mid-fifties colleague who wasn't such a bad guy but really fancied himself and always moaned about flying. Well, about everything, really. But he was a genius with the clients – point and click. A brilliantly straight-talking, positive sales type who could also turn on the gentle persuasiveness and who knew how to look as though he was processing every word the other guy was saying, when in fact he'd worked out how to handle him within the first 30 seconds and was now wondering where to go for dinner. He was the sort who always knew the best restaurants in town, always had contacts, radiated bonhomie, yet moaned like hell in his off-duty moments. Always having a plan was his way of dealing with life and he just moaned at times when he wasn't in control because he thought it wasn't going to be any good if he hadn't organised it. I usually let him have his head and just ignored the moaning, which is why we got sent out quite a lot together. Nobody else could stand him, but money's money and this guy attracted it like a magnet.

"What's your definition of a nice woman?" I asked him over the coffees.

He glanced at me but did give it some genuine – I think – thought. And shortly before he passed out from all the booze, he gave his pronouncement.

"I'd say a nice woman is one who keeps her fanny clean."

Just before landing I came back from the loo to find him inspecting a miniature box of two champagne truffles which he said the stewardess had just given him.

"Oh, nice!" he exclaimed, passing it across to me, and I saw that she'd written her phone number and 'Feel free to call me' on the inside of the lid.

"It must have been for me!" I said at once. "She put this on my seat for me and you've picked it up and you're trying to wind me up!"

"Don't talk bollocks," he said, trying to snatch the box back. "Why would I do that? Why would she do that? She gave it to me, you twat. Waited till you'd gone off to the john and then came and gave it to me. What's the matter with you? Give it back!"

I mean, did you ever hear such a thin story? I glared at him and held on to the truffles.

"You've lost it, man," he said. "See a fucking shrink."

"They were for me!" I hissed, and tipped the two truffles straight into my gob.

He stared at me open-mouthed – not many people would've sussed him, let alone challenged him – and then burst out laughing.

"All right, all right, they were for you. Have it your own way. But the 'phone number was meant for me." He twitched the little box out of my hand, popped it into his top pocket and turned to gaze out of the window, muttering something that sounded suspiciously like, 'Christ, thinks he's God's gift.'

I could've hit him. But since I didn't fancy the stewardess for any kind of pleasuring, I refrained. It just seemed a bit sad that the poor bastard had to nick another guy's credits, so to speak, to pretend he had some kind of appeal. Thinking it over later, I realised I felt sorry for him.

*     *     *

Watching the five-star TV that night, I wondered if the FF2 considered herself a nice woman. It was off of her to say I didn't shag anyone nice. They were probably all nice in their own way, even creatures like 'Mum', and anyway, it was unfair of her to judge what she hadn't even met. Presumptuous, too – it's not as though I told the FFs about all my encounters. Perhaps I only mentioned the off ones because the good ones were too intimate to be laid out on the table for their crass inspection.

Pondering unfairness took me on to contemplation of one of the great injustices of life – women who never come. Possible causes, manifestations, possible cures, and my role in the latter. Pleasurers Sans Frontières.

So it was ironic or timely, or just part of the universal harmony, that on the way back from the Tokyo trip – and I know what you're wondering, but no, it was a packed schedule and I barely had time to wank – I met the Good Conversationalist (GC).

The truffle-snitcher had gone on to Singapore for another conference, so I had an excellent trip reading my Casanova book and thinking out which techniques to apply to one of the stewardesses, even though I wouldn't have done if I'd got the chance 'cos I didn't remotely fancy her, and fantasy-snoozing, which means closing my eyes and indulging in pleasuring fantasies. Usually gives me a hard-on. It was only towards the end of the flight that I became aware of the woman in the opposite row and we got chatting – there was no-one in between us and I could see she wasn't enjoying the turbulence on the descent. We exchanged cards and a few days later I rang her and we met for lunch.

Well, you know what? It was really good, because from the word go she was all-out friendly, but in a totally relaxed, I'm-not-after-you kind of way. She made me laugh, which, like I said, is rare. We got on absolutely great and it turned out she'd been promoted to just the kind of job I was after myself in my company, so we had plenty to talk about. And since we shared a taste for trashy films, we fixed up to go to the flicks that weekend.

"Fantastic," she agreed enthusiastically. "I'm between blokes and I've been dying to see that film, but it's just so much more *fun* with someone, but none of my other friends will go and see that kind of trash."

She put a hand up to my shoulder, gave me a completely natural peck on the cheek, and disappeared off down the street, leaving me weirdly flattered by that phrase 'my other friends'.

In the pub after a game of squash that night, BM pursed his lips.

"Hm, I dunno, mate," he said. "A lot of birds use that line, you know. Pretend they just want to be friends but all the time they're eyeing your wallet or wondering what kind of car you drive."

"Oh, she's not one of those. Makes more than I do."

"What does she drive, then?"

"BMW Z4."

He made a grudging thumbs-up face and stood up to order a couple more pints.

"Well, time will tell," he remarked. "What I can't get over is that you're not going on about how to get her into bed if she's so great." (Point of order: I never 'go on' about such things because it's never a problem for me). "Not sickening for something, are you?"

"Give it a rest. I wasn't thinking about her like that. Really. She's just good company."

But he was right, it was odd. I think we were both puzzling over it during the first half of the match, and when he said at half-time,

"You want to be careful – I reckon you could be falling in love," I actually wondered if he might be right.

*Special Underbedcover Agent's Tip:-*

*Massage: this one's also a definite. Never say 'I'm not very good at that' – just get on with it. If she's asked for/accepted a massage, she's up for sex, no matter how much she gasses on about how it's just that she's got a neckache from sitting in a draughty caff. Any mention of an ache or pain, get in there. Bone up on a few basic moves and make sure you've always got oil around – almond and vanilla are both scents that girls tend to go for. Oh, and make sure your hands are warm before you touch her, or you don't stand a chance.*

# Protocol No. 5 – Generosity

## THE ANTI-PROTOCOL – WASTE

Generosity: well, the main definition is fairly obvious, and there is
a story of staggering generosity of time and effort on my part just
coming up, but I particularly like these two definitions for myself.
1) *freedom from pettiness in character and mind* (think my Dad's
pretty free in that sense, ach'ly); and 2) *abundance, plenty* (which
has obviously been bestowed upon me and I'm bloody grateful).
Waste: This is an evocative one, isn't it? Effluents and all that.
Nah, but what I really had in mind was the definition, *to fail
to take advantage of.* Always stay alert for the opening – and
that means opening yourself up sometimes, tackling your
own fears and prejudices, taking advantage of qualities you
didn't even know you had. Otherwise they turn into effluent.
EFFLUENT – how much of that do you need in your life?

I T'S NOT THAT I'd set my mind
against any of those things – falling
in love, marriage etc – it's just that I realised very young that they were
probably incompatible with my vocation, and there was no doubt in my
mind about what had priority.

I use the word 'vocation' advisedly. I liked climbing the career ladder, I
enjoyed being out with my mates, had no problems with my parents etc etc,
but the focus and main stimulation/satisfaction of my life has always been

the path of pleasuring which I chose at an early age. Or, to put it better, that chose me. You do know when you have a purpose in life, and that conviction can strike very young, and I personally think it's a sin to ignore it, even if you know it's going to involve work or suffering, because so few people are given a purpose. Most people just fill up time with jobs and kids and relationships and money, and half of them moan about what they've got even if it's what they set out to get.

"But everyone has to find something to do," my mother challenged me one day when we were gassing about the meaning of life over tea and buns at . . . . no, caught you that time, it was Fortnum and Mason's. "What does it matter what route one takes?"

"I know what you mean," I replied (straight out of the Management Techniques Handbook, but I have to say, those techniques have stood me in very good stead over the years, particularly when dealing with intensely irritating people like my mother). "But I do want to feel, when I'm on my deathbed, that I used myself to the full, that I didn't *waste* anything."

Waste, incidentally, was one of the 21st-century sins voted for in that radio search for new sins I talked about before. I agree with that one.

"Well, you've always done well at work," said my mother, which surprised me because I didn't know she'd realised just how good I was even though I did keep explaining, "but is that your main focus in life? You don't have a family of your own, so what is your chief focus?"

I hesitated.

"You don't need to answer," she said in a kinder tone than she generally used to me. "But I genuinely am curious. After all, you are my son. You are a part of *my* life's focus, achievement, whatever you want to call it. A huge part, you and your brother. I liked working too, but I didn't miss it. Running the household was my real vocation and I'm not ashamed to admit it. Watching you two grow up. So yes, I'm curious."

I gawped back at her, unsure how to respond to her unexpected sincerity. She'd always been a down-to-earth, unfussy parent and we never went into emotional discussions. I mean, what was I supposed to *say?*

'Well Mother, it's like this. Haven't you ever wondered why I bought a musician's flat and had the soundproofed studio converted into the master bedroom? That was so that whenever I have some lucky lady speared on my mighty prong and she is literally screaming with the ecstasy of that exquisite piercing, we don't disturb the neighbours.'

'Well Mother, it's like this. I love loads of things about life, but if you're asking about focus, I know that I am unique in my desire and ability to make a woman quiver helplessly under my careful fingers, take fire at the touch of my tongue, melt under my potency.'

'Well Mother, it's like this. You are so right to be proud of me – and thanks for that, good call – because not many blokes open a woman up like I do. Take the trouble to do it properly. In fact, probably no-one else.'

'Well Mother, it's like this. My true vocation in life, and I'm not ashamed to admit it even though I know I'll get shit for it, is pleasuring. What coarse-minded people could call shagging because they don't know the difference and never will, which is really sad and against my personal commandments.'

What I in fact said was,

"Oh well, I dunno. I think there's a lot to be said for being a jack-of-all-trades if you enjoy it and are pretty good at most of them. I mean, it's not as though I was born into times or a situation like a war that would've demanded something specific of me, is it? What is wrong with being in step with your surroundings, well-rounded, a complete and pacific person? I actually think that's pretty radical."

It came out as a bit of an unconvincing mumble, but to my amazement it went down really well. She looked at me with astonishing – for her – gentleness and reached over to touch my cheek in a gesture she probably hadn't used since I was about ten. Overcome by that blatant show of tenderness, she picked up a bun and shoved it onto my plate.

"Round yourself a bit more," she quipped. "I like your chosen path."

I had a bite of it to please her, but I'm not fond of those kind of buns and I do keep in shape, so there's no point eating stuff you don't like. Which is a good moment to bring in a few words on Temperance. Yes, I've got it. No, really, nothing more to say – I've never done much in the way of drugs, drink plenty but not too much since I was about 19 and did the usual stomach-pump thing at college etc etc. Of course, they came up with these virtues at a time when there was no electricity and after 3.30pm on a winter's afternoon there was bugger all to do except get intemperate. Or go off your trolley. I have absolutely no idea how the women managed if it was frowned on for them to drink. No wonder they're pragmatic. Still no excuse for TC, though.

Anyway, back to Justice.

It was weeks and weeks after we met that the GC revealed her secret. We'd got together several times and the whole thing just carried on as it had started – great. Fun. Straightforward.

"I don't know," the voice of doom, i.e. BM, was still saying. "Seems to me you could be wading in deep here without realising. You're out with her practically every night of the week . . . ."

"Oh bollocks! I see her about once a week, if that, and then it's usually lunch."

"Lunch? Lunch, is it? 'Scuse me, love, got anything with a bit more bite to it than this Beamish crap? All right, giss a pint of that. Lunch? Come off it! Are you honestly trying to tell me you've never thought about shagging her?"

"It's crossed my mind . . . ." I began.

"Told you so!"

"It's crossed my mind what it would be like to kiss her," I continued with the kind of dignity that's wasted on BM and the brother – well, everyone I know, actually, bar one, and no, that's not the GC, then or now. "But it's just idle curiosity. I think I wonder more because I'm not going to do it and don't really want to than because I want to and am going to do it, if you know what I mean?"

"Nice tits on that one," he said, winking at the barmaid and suppressing a belch.

"How's the beer?"

"Gassy. Get her along for a game."

"What do you mean, a game?"

"Game of squash," he replied, looking surprised. "Come on mate, what else would I mean? Get her to come and watch a game and we'll take her out for a drink after. Here. Nice place. Nice tits. You don't need to worry, I won't put the moves on her. Wouldn't do that. She's yours."

"She's not mine," I snapped. "And you're married."

"No, not *yours*, but she's your . . . . friend."

"Sister," I said in the same instant.

There was a pause while he dragged his eyes off the barmaid and looked at me.

"All right, all right. Hoy! Love! You with the nice . . . . hairdo. Two more pints of gas over here, please. Get her along next week. I'll soon suss her out."

It was two or three weeks later before she could make it, and she'd asked if she could bring along some bloke she fancied who also played squash. I said of course, and felt pretty smug when I told BM she was bringing someone.

"Clever," he said, irritatingly. "Very clever. Probably her brother. Trying to make you jealous now."

"I'm going to wipe the court with you," I promised him. "I could give you ten points and still wipe the court with you. She hasn't *got* a brother, you fat berk, she's . . . ."

"She's got you, hasn't she?" he cut in, and hung up.

\*     \*     \*

The truth is, he was better than me. At squash. And, since I'm not particularly competitive – no, really – and he's been my BM for ever, I was just happy for him that he was better than me at something.

Now, by the time the GC had got her act and the bloke together, it was me and BM playing off in the local club league semi-finals the night she came to watch. Fairly major stuff. He'd won the championship for the past two years and was all out for the hat trick, but I was narked about his attitude to the GC, so we were all set for a pretty sharp match.

As usual in competitive situations, we didn't talk beforehand, but I did have a brief word with the GC when she joined the other punters at the No 1 glass-backed court with the bloke. Bloke looked all right, actually. Firm handshake, in good shape, thin on top and very fair, but saved from mediocrity by very piercing, intense grey eyes. He wished me luck in a businesslike way which indicated he knew the pressure was on and we could save the small talk for later, and I liked the way he found the best space for the GC about halfway back in the raked seating.

And in the pub afterwards, I have to say he did an excellent job of congratulating BM on going through to the final without pissing me off. Good handling of a delicate situation. I wondered how he performed in bed – on the GC's account, obviously. So when he and BM went up to the bar for the next round, I asked her.

"Oh fine," she said, watching them go.

"You mean, nothing special?"

"What's special?"

"Well, you know, special is when the whole world melts like red-hot ice-cream and you come all up the wall."

She was gazing after him – lawyer, conservative but good clothes – and smiled when he glanced back at her.

"Oh, I never come," she said casually.

Significant pause while I let my eyes bulge. The woman was round the 40 mark, for God's/Whatever's sake – she should've been coming for years.

"What?" she said, reacting to the unaccustomed silence. "Why are you looking at me like that?"

"Are you having me on?"

Bloke's Guinness was almost there.

"About never coming? No. Why, what's wrong with that? I don't think I have, anyway. I don't know. Maybe I have without realising."

"You'd know if you had," I assured her. "You mean, you don't even come when you masturbate?"

Bloke picked up his Guinness and her G&T and turned for the return journey. She wrinkled her nose at me in a fleeting expression of disgust and suddenly the whole thing fell into place. She obviously didn't wank. She wasn't sexual. That's why I didn't imagine being in bed with her, because she simply didn't, ever, at all, respond to the tiny sexual feelers we all throw out via a look, a comment, a question. She could've been sexy if she'd acknowledged that part of herself, but she just didn't. I gazed at her so intently during this silent revelation that Bloke must've got a bit narked, 'cos suddenly BM moved stools so that I had to turn away from her to talk to him.

"She's lovely, mate," he said as soon as they'd driven off. "But you're right, she's not after your wads – either of 'em. Nice girl, just not very sexy, is she?"

So he'd spotted it the first time he met her! Sometimes we just complicate the issues too much, don't we? It was a relief to realise, but inevitably I began to worry about why she was like that, what she was missing etc, and yes, I think it was natural that after a while I thought the least I could do was try and help out. After all, she was my . . . . sister.

*　　*　　*

"Don't you like sex?" I asked her whilst we were buying Maltesers and Coke for the matinée session at the cinema a couple of Saturdays later. She nudged me crossly and the kid at the till gave me a funny look and giggled. I didn't realise I'd spoken loudly enough for him to have heard. Have to watch that – discretion is alluring, and the word sex should not be squandered by bellowing it all the time.

"Sorry," I muttered to her, giving the kid a 'don't waste your pity on me, you have no idea how hot my sex life is' look.

"Of course I do," she said on the escalator.

"But if you never come . . . ."

"Oh so what?! You can't miss what you've never had. What does it matter?"

"So what do you like best about sex?" I asked, shifting my ground slightly as she seemed to be a bit edgy about it. And you'll never guess what she said! Well, you might, everyone's life experience is different, but it totally blew me away.

"The cuddling and kissing afterwards."

Good job the film was starting as we fumbled into our seats, 'cos there's no way I could've let that go without comment, and maybe comment was not appropriate.

By the time we came out, I'd got a grip, and though I was still convinced it was a tragedy that she never came, I had also acknowledged to myself that if that's what she found the best bit, maybe I needed to incorporate more of it into my pleasure procedures – not that I think I'd ever stinted in that aspect either.

Trawling through underwear with her at Selfridges, I asked how things were going with Bloke and she said fine. I wandered over to Agent Provocateur whilst she went to try on what she called 'comfy cottons' and was enjoying myself immensely among the latest fantastical creations, trying to find something the CP hadn't already got, when the GC came back with her purchases and said,

"If I buy you a coffee, will you tell me why it's such a big deal?"

Bloke's not happy with the sex, I diagnosed to myself immediately, and off we went to tuck ourselves into a corner of a backstreet caff where I was able to practise my new discreet volume voice. At first she kept saying 'What?', 'Why are you whispering?', 'I didn't catch that', but when I explained what I was trying to do, she got right into that and we worked for a while on adjusting the volume and tone for sexy conversations in crowded places before getting to the nub. Bloke's nub. Which was not, of course, the nub of the problem. As I'd expected. He'd looked normally lusty to me, and from everything she said, he was in good working order. Obviously, and she herself said it, she was the less enthusiastic one, and she was beginning to worry that it bothered him.

"Don't you ever fake it?" I inquired, not that I have ever been an advocate for such dishonesty.

"No," she said defensively, and I realised that it's tricky to fake something you've never experienced.

"Do you watch porn?"

"No!" Definite disgust this time.

Pause.

"He wanted me to, but I said no."

"Who? Bloke?"

"No, another one."

"Why did you say no?"

At this point, you're probably wondering why I wasn't a paid and qualified sex therapist. I was beginning to wonder myself. But her total indifference to the keynote of my life was fascinating, and I was happy with just a coffee in payment.

"Oh, it all just seems a bit . . . ."

"Disgusting?" I suggested gently.

"Well of course it's disgusting," she shot back, staggering me yet again.

"Why?" I leapt in at once.

"Oh, you know, just the whole thing." She looked round at neighbouring tables then brought her eyes back to mine. "Not just disgusting. I don't know. Ridiculous, I suppose is the word."

"More coffees," I said, standing up. I needed one; I was overcome by a glorious flood of memories of intimacy, vulnerability, joy, true nakedness, raucousness, the whole damn' thing, and not one of them was ridiculous in the condescending way she'd meant it. Caffeine. The sensitive man's best friend at times like this. "Do you want another bun?"

The glint in her eye said yes, so I didn't wait for the hesitation, just dived off and got her the sexiest-looking hunk of cheesecake on the counter, totally counter to her preference for homely old apple tart. This effort had red fruit on top and oozing down its edges; she might be questioning the foundation stones of my existence, but I was the pleasure warrior, holding fast to velvet and lush.

"Oh!" she exclaimed when she saw it, in exactly the tone so many women use on beholding the Prong for the first time. Or the second, or the third – which is, on average, the last.

"Dig in," I urged, then observed how she politely carved a tiny piece off the big end and pushed the rest towards me. But she got through it all, bit by bit, during the conversation, and that told me a lot.

"It's like any deal," I said finally. "You've both got to feel you've got something out of it."

"Oh he seems to enjoy it," she assured me anxiously.

Hm. I let that one pass, but in my experience, unless he's saying it's the best he's ever had, he's just keeping his hand in, so to speak, until something better comes along. Okay, lots of times nothing better does, or more usually, the guy's a lazy sod (Sloth) who can't be bothered going out looking or making himself attractive. But Bloke struck me as the sort who would fix malfunctions in his life as soon as he spotted them.

"Yes, but what about you? I know, don't tell me – the cuddles afterwards. But do you always get all you want?"

She gave me a surprised look, as though realising something for the first time.

"Well . . . ."

"Yes?"

"No, not always. He's tired after, after . . . ."

"After getting his rocks off, yeah, normal. But have you told him that you need the cuddling in the same way he needs to come?"

"No, but it's not the same, is it?"

"Everyone's orgasm is different," I said sententiously. Must have got the volume control a bit wrong 'cos the girls at the next table glanced over. "I think you need some techniques," I said more quietly. "You need to get this on the right track now. If you're happy with Bloke shagging away more or less on his own as long as he's affectionate afterwards, and you can respond enough to stop him feeling he's under-performing or being selfish, you've both got it made. But you need to get across to him exactly what he has to do to keep you satisfied, right?"

She nodded and carefully speared the remaining tip of the cheesecake. "Do you trust me?" I asked as she put it neatly into her mouth.

She nodded again, and I leaned over and kissed her, parting her lips and running my tongue round her creamy-filled mouth. "Then let's meet one evening this week," I said, ignoring her wide-eyed stare. "We can work on techniques."

She swallowed.

\*　　\*　　\*

The bro was around more than usual at that time. A few years before, he'd married someone out of gratitude again – just over-excited, really, by the fact she'd gone to bed with him more than once – and it was all going completely pear-shaped, so I got to hear most of the details. I did think about passing the GC task over to him, but only for about a nano-second: he was bitter, confused and under-confident, and the GC was expecting a sexual revelation, not the poke'n'snore approach my brother no doubt specialised in. No, I'd thought it might cheer him up, but it would only set everyone back. Might even, if she found out, give his wife more grounds for bleeding him dry. He'd been doing very nicely thank you for the past ten years, and she'd spotted him a mile off. Fact. I'd not taken to her, but there's not much you can do, is there? People choose their own path to hell, if that's their destination, and they can get narky if you tell it them like it is.

I did mention the GC project – without naming her, because he'd met her once – and it roused a bit of a laugh, but then he went all mopey again and said he was glad to hear I was getting some because he probably never would again, wouldn't even be able to *pay* for nookie after another divorce, blah, blah, blah. It was like watching a cartoon character being victimised, it was so . . . . seen that.

And you see what I mean about crass? Nookie! Here was me planning how to ease open the gates of fear so that true abandonment and pleasure could flow sweetly into someone's life, allowing them to engage in a unique sexual and spiritual communion, and he was still cracking on as though I'd struck lucky at the school disco. Still talking as though I was like him, in other words. It completely weirded me out. It's partly why he was never going to get anywhere interesting with relationships – he just didn't get that they needed constant . . . . re-decoration. He's the sort who buys a lamp 'cos he needs it, not 'cos he loves it, sticks it on a table and never moves it again, then grumbles when it gets smashed and trundles straight out to look for another one the same and stick it in the same place.

Now me, I like experimenting with several lamps, it's true, but I thoroughly enjoy the sensation of trying each one in different positions till I find out where it works best – in other words, I pay attention to it for its own sake, learn about it and where it should be, no matter how temporary our relationship. Like the Tiff: I sensed an effect and my mother perfected it and I learnt from that. Yet the bro doesn't even take that care over the one lamp he can afford. Weird.

"Can't you introduce him to anyone?" our mother had said accusingly a few days before.

"I'm not his . . . ."

"Mother. I know, but . . . ."

"No, I was going to say pimp."

"I see. But you must know people. Women."

"So does he!"

"Hm, but not very nice ones."

"Mother!"

"But I'm right, aren't I? His first wife wasn't too bad . . . ." (I didn't comment, the woman was psycho; seemed to think he was her personal slave as well as her private bank. Threw the entire breakfast tray at him one morning 'cos he'd taken it up late. Funnily enough, I'd introduced her to him . . . .) " . . . . but he's suffering another divorce and I don't understand it. I know I'm his mother, but I do think he's a nice man, don't you? He's too easily taken in. His selection technique doesn't seem to be right."

"It never will be," I said. Then, because she looked so upset, I added, "Not unless he gets some self-confidence going."

"He's a salesman!" she exclaimed faintly.

"Yep, and a good one. Don't mean a thing. Can't sell himself because he doesn't believe in the product. And he pays no attention to himself, he's always looking for solutions outside, someone to validate him, reassure him. Quite appealing at 25, loser-ville at 45. Do you want some more tea?" This, because she'd gone quite pale and she was knocking on a bit.

"Yes. I never realised. You're probably right. Maybe I should have . . . ."

"Don't you start," I cut in. "For God's sake don't start to think it's your fault or you should've noticed or something. Excuse me, can we have another pot of Earl Grey for two, please? Thanks. It's just the disease of the times. One of them. Here. Have another bun. Practically everyone I know is under-confident."

"Why? What does it mean?" she half-whispered.

"Means they're no bloody fun," I said firmly, and she laughed till she cried – well, till my dad came back to pick her up – so I didn't add that it also means that people like myself are isolated by our self-confidence. The neurotics simply can't handle it. Ho-hum, no fun.

The point is that I had the bro staying at my pad for a few days and Bloke had buggered off to some cousin's wedding in the south of France, so we set the date for Operation GC.

"Didn't he invite you too?" I said indignantly, when the GC told me. "Serve him right to come home unexpectedly and find you in bed with someone else."

"Oh no, it's fine," she laughed. "He accepted the invitation ages before he met me, it's all some friends of the family event, and we didn't want to make a big thing of me, us, till we knew if it was more than a one-night stand and all that. It's fine."

Well, not my business. As long as he didn't come home and catch us at it – "You shouldn't have given him his own keys." "I know." – good luck to him.

Her place, then. I went to pick out two or three DVDs with the bro, settled him in with a good dinner and a fridge full of beer, and set off for the GC's.

"I thought you said you were only going for one night," he said accusingly as I edged my suitcase past him to the front door. "What the hell's all that? Looks like you're off to the Bahamas for a month."

"I told you, it's a major project and this is probably our only chance. It needs some preparation."

"Gawd," he said, and cracked open another beer.

"Don't top yourself," I advised. "She's not worth it, there'll be somebody else, and you're in my flat."

"Yeah, yeah. Fuck off. I'll be here when you get back."

Which was, and at the same time absolutely was not, what I wanted to hear. If you twig my lay.

\*       \*       \*

"Wow," she said, her eyes going straight to the suitcase when she opened the door. "Moving in? Sorry," she added immediately.

"If this is going to work, you've got to be in it with me," I reminded her, and she apologised again and led me through to the main room.

I'd known that untimely jokes and giggles might come into the proceedings, because we were Chums so I could understand her feeling a bit of embarrassment, but I hadn't anticipated to what extent. Or how distracting they'd be. It was quite teeth-grinding at times, but I had my mind focussed on the job and tried to keep the irritation capped. For me, pleasure can be fun but not funny, but she treated the whole situation as a joke. The challenge was really on to wipe that silly smile off her face.

First move was to send her out for a decent takeaway whilst I prepared her flat. Her taste was okay – bit mumsy and flowery, and I wondered how Bloke was coping with that, but some people just don't notice décor, and it's not as though he lived there – so I didn't have to do anything radical. And I wouldn't have wanted to anyway, because it was vital for her to feel relaxed, and what we had on the agenda was plenty radical enough already.

So I just cleared the surfaces I thought I might be needing, replaced some of the over-stuffed sofa cushions with my own softer versions, set out the glasses (which needed cleaning – isn't it amazing how few people can clean glasses properly? I worked in loads of bars when I was a kid, got the technique down pretty well), lit lots of small candles, the sort that can't get knocked over and set fire to your date's hair in mid-snog too easily, and wafted a Czech and Speake Frankincense and Myrrh incense stick around. It's a fabulously langurous, heavy perfume, and a little goes a long way. I've had faith in it ever since the time I walked into the shop and said to the attendant,

"Hello, I'm trying to seduce someone. I need the most erotic fragrance you have,"

and without a blink he replied,

"I see, sir," whipped the F&M off the gleaming glass shelf behind us and said, "This should do the trick."

And it did! Has done ever since. Best in winter situations and climates. I use their Citrus collection for the heat – fragrance and incense sticks.

So there we were, all set, when she came back with the nosh. Hearing the key jiggle in the lock, I scanned the room and felt smug. Right temperature, soothing background music, faint but sensual fragrance, and beautiful, romantic light from the dozens of tiny candles set out at different heights all round the room. Nice work.

She clattered about in the kitchen and I just sat sipping the excellent wine I'd brought to give her time to get over the fluster of getting the food in. Nobody wants those just-in-the-door irritations: 'What took you so long?', 'Did you remember the poppadums?', 'Your bloody mother rang again', 'Shall I help you?', 'Haven't we got any more beer?' etc. Guaranteed to break up relationships, I'd've thought. Well, it does, I've seen it.

Organise your own side of things as best you can and don't criticise the other person's efforts, is my motto. Yeah, I know, that works for my lifestyle, maybe not for long-term situations. But it's a civilised theory to start from, isn't it?

After a few minutes she came through to the main room, stopped in the doorway, peered around and said, with one of those bloody giggles,

"What have you done? It's like a morgue in here."

!!!!!!!!!!!!!!!!!!!!!!!!!!!!!!!!!!!!!!!!!!!!!!!!!!!!!!!!!!!!!!!!!!!!!!!!!!!!!!!!!!!!!!!!!!!!!!

I know. How did she ever get laid at all with that attitude? And then women complain that men aren't romantic! Well, just don't give up on her, mate, if it happens to you. Give it another try. *Then* give up on her.

"Sorry," she said almost immediately. "I'm just not used to seeing it like this."

She was obviously uncomfortable with it, but that was understandable. I'd invaded her space, taken control, and created a different environment. It's what we were there to achieve, to get her to enjoy that. Another technique of mine is not to get distracted by silly remarks or nervous outbursts from anyone, but just to stick my tongue down their throat whenever something like that happens, and that's what I did now. She was incredibly tense, but I worked away at it and got her to the point where she was wanting more when I pulled away and went to get the food onto plates.

I didn't want her getting too 'chummy' again, so I kept the conversation over dinner fairly Bloke and sex-based. Better to have her defensive for the right reasons than feeling guilty about kissing her brother, and kicking me out. Also made sure she didn't eat much by clearing away dishes and distracting her with not-quite-enough kisses that made her giggle each time, but only to start with. Irritating, though.

Bearing in mind the cuddling fetish, I steered her over to the sofa after dinner and pulled her into my arms whilst I used the remote to put on the film we'd agreed on, and sure enough, she loved it! The cuddling, I mean.

"Oh this is so nice," she kept murmuring, and I think it was the fact she had her back to me and so couldn't *see* that I was her chum/brother that helped dry up the giggling eventually.

I let this go on for about half an hour – us cuddled up, watching the film and drinking wine – then moved my left arm up a bit and began exploring her breasts. I'd been fondling her hands, arms, neck etc before hand. No cold calls. I felt her stiffen slightly. She must have felt me stiffen quite a bit – I'd been more or less ready since the first kiss, and handling her tits was having its inevitable effect.

"Sh, sh," I whispered into her hair. "It's all okay, it's okay, just let it happen." (Remember this? The bro's technique, soothing nonsense).

She gave a kind of half-giggle, then squirmed with what I recognised as the first tremors of true pleasure, and after a few minutes, she actually turned her head to kiss me! It wasn't that she was frigid or anything, but it seemed she was almost entirely passive, and so her turning for a kiss was a breakthrough. She regretted it quickly and turned away again, but it paved the way for the next move, which was to manoeuvre down so that we were both lying full-out on the sofa (not as broad as mine, but adequate), semi-spoon style, and I had access to her whole body whilst she carried on watching the film.

By the time the film finished, her skirt was bunched up round her hips, her top was askew and her bra unfastened, and her tights were rucked up just below her knees. It was an immensely pleasurable sight. Full nakedness is delicious, but I sensed that half-hidden would suit her better, and I have to say that to see her in such disarray, her hair all over the place and a worried look in her eyes, was almost orgasmic in itself.

"You look gorgeous," I told her, smoothing the flat of my hand rhythmically over her thighs – no, absolutely no attempt at pussy-penetration during the film, no way – and kissing her neck. She gave a – yep, you guessed it – nervous giggle, and said,

"I'm a mess!"

"That's the way I like you."

I propped myself up on one elbow and gazed into her eyes whilst I teased her pubes with my fingers and studied her reactions. Was she, I wondered, feeling a strange, almost violent delight coursing along her nerve endings at being so intimately touched by a friend who was not her lover? I was. I let my middle finger work its way down to find her clit. She gazed back at me, biting her bottom lip.

"Doesn't Bloke do this?"

"Not . . . . the same, way," she uttered, struggling to get the words out now that it was my hand at the controls. "You're more . . . . intense."

"You okay?"

She nodded, still biting her lip. She closed her eyes when my fingers probed deeper, and I just watched, wondering when her thighs would relax and part naturally, but it didn't happen. Her eyes stayed closed, her thighs stayed tense, her lip stayed bitten. She was moist but not wet. Essentially, she was waiting for me to finish.

After a while, I got up and took off my shirt, unfastened my trousers, since she obviously wasn't going to volunteer to do it, and peeled off her tights and knickers, which made her give a little gasp and open her eyes.

"Oh God, what am I doing?" she said suddenly, putting a hand across her eyes. "I don't know if this is right."

"It's all fine," I assured her, lying down and cuddling her till the worried look disappeared. And you know, when my fingers entered her again, she was more welcoming than before – the cuddling really won out against lust/technique for her! Okay. Each to her own. I was learning a lot. I was also suffering quite a lot.

"You can . . . . you know, if you want," she whispered. "I don't mind."

'I don't mind' is hardly effusive, but I just added it to the mental notes I was making to pass on later for her and Bloke's benefit, and moved on.

Since she'd explained that part of finding sex ridiculous was seeing someone bounce up and down above her with an intent look on his face, I'd decided that from behind would be best. So I hauled her onto her hands and knees – not without difficulty, since she didn't seem to know what I was up to and kept trying to 'right' herself – pushed the long gipsy skirt up to her waist and without more ado, penetrated the fleshy orbs of her arse firmly from the rear. A couple of gasps and 'Oh no!'s emerged from under her dangling hair as I slid the rod in, but I paid no attention, just went right up to the ¾ mark before enveloping her in a hug, kissing her neck and cheeks and teasing her nipples.

"Are you alright?" I said then.

"Yes, I think so," she said hesitantly. "But no more, oh, no more . . . . oh!"

The final oh! was only because I'd started to pump her, not because I'd inserted up to the hilt or anything. She felt reasonably moist, not uncomfortably tight, so I persisted with gentle but firm thrusts – nothing jerky or rough – whilst running my hands all over her still-clothed upper body and naked buttocks. Standard stuff, yet I got the feeling she'd never been done from behind and was still apprehensive instead of submitting to the sensations. It was very pleasurable indeed for me, and I could keep it up more or less indefinitely whilst she loosened up a bit – and I needed to, because it took ages before she made even the slightest accompanying movement.

I gathered her hair back into a ponytail and gave her buttocks a couple of very light, experimental slaps, but the turned head and 'no, no,' indicated that rodeo was not her scene, so I went back to stroking and kissing. I wondered, as I thrust rhythmically – and carefully, as I still didn't have the whole piece in – backwards and forwards if her anus had ever been penetrated at all. Gripping her buttocks not too hard, I manoeuvred my thumbs down to open it up a wee bit, but though just that gave me visual and sensual pleasure, she turned her head again in the beginnings of anxiety and I relaxed my grip, allowing the tight pink aperture to retire, blushing, into its fold.

Perhaps to take my mind off rimming her with a large wet thumb and hearing some gasps of real anxiety – no, am not into inflicting pain, but a wee bit is sometimes the true pathway to pleasure – I withdrew, slid under her and let her collapse onto my chest for more cuddling and breath-catching. Then I realised she thought it was all over!

"That was nice," she murmured, settling down for a prolonged embrace.

I hoisted her slightly so that my erection carved a furrow up her front, and she opened her eyes and said,

"Oh! Didn't you . . . . ?"

"No, nowhere near. And you neither, so don't even think about going to sleep yet!"

"Oh but this is so nice!" she repeated, gently stroking my chest.

Which it was, and I'm not into rough stuff, but this was too twee for words.

"Come on," I urged, lifting her up and poising her on the tip of the Prong. "Sit on it, sister. Time you did some work. Pleasure me!"

I smiled as I said it, and the hint of humour seemed to reassure her.

"Oh God," she said, squirming down a tiny bit. "This is so stupid. Am I doing it right? I've never been on top before."

"Anything you do is right," I assured her, though the shock of hearing she'd never been on top before had nearly finished off the erection. Maybe she was a 40-year-old virgin, and Bloke was just her brother, like BM had suggested. But no, she was experienced enough, just extraordinarily passive and unexploring. Maybe that was a turn-on for some men. Or a relief – no matter how useless they were, she wouldn't challenge them. She was messing around with the Prong as though it was an awkward bicycle she was trying to mount.

"Here, here, like this." I moved her hand round to my balls. "Now, gently, touch them gently . . . ."

And she did and my cock jumped and so did she, from the shock of it, apparently – what *were* she and Bloke up to, missionary-style once a week on a Saturday night? Whilst she was coping with the new sensation of being obliged to undertake some action, I seized her buttocks and moved her down partway onto the Prong.

"Aaaaaaaaaaaaagh!" she gurgled unexpectedly, her head tipping back as I pushed her down. "Oh no! Oh, oh!"

"Now move! Come on, move up and down!" I cried, thrusting as best I could. Seemed to me we only had about half the meat in the can, but she was moaning something awful and rolling her head, so I didn't force any more in, just tried to thrust, and reached up to massage her tits. That worked a treat – she fell forward eagerly so that I could suck as we fucked, and now she began to move! Finally!

She was still crying 'Oh no! Oh no!', but her feet were in the air as she balanced entirely on her knees and hands to get the best purchase for easing more and more of me inside her. I remembered how long she'd taken to eat the cheesecake and gritted my teeth, but she'd got it all in finally, I reminded myself bravely.

When we passed the ¾ mark, she was rocking back and forth with her tits in my mouth and her hair all over my face, and she was making a strange, suppressed screaming noise in my ear which was exciting me so much I really had to concentrate to keep it all going. As opposed to coming. I felt as though my cock had a buzzsaw touching its tip each time she brought me in a little bit further, the whole piece was about to explode, and I was sweating and moaning myself as she forced me through the pain barrier when she suddenly changed her pace, lifting herself off my chest and hesitating on my tip for a moment. The suppressed scream died between her clenched teeth; she stared into my eyes with the intentness of someone who's just been shot but doesn't know why, gave a long, snarling growl, and forced herself down hard onto the full length of what must have been the longest, hardest cock in operation in the galaxy at that moment in time.

"Oh God! Oh good girl, oh good girl!" I yelled, bursting through the pain barrier and anticipating in almost unbearably intense pleasure the almost unbearably intense pleasure I knew was the sequel to that exquisite suffering. "Oh yeah! Oh yeah!"

And it was at this supreme moment that I realised the intent look was now simply blank and she was motionless and silent.

"Baby?" I said, heaving myself up onto my elbows to look more closely, and she gave a long, choking rattle in her throat and pitched forward, face first, onto my chest!

"Aaaaaaaaaaaaaarrrgh!" I cried, flinging myself back onto the cushions as if there was a way out there. Her torso slumped messily over one side of mine, disconcertingly heavy now that all muscle control had ceased so abruptly, but her lower body was secured inexorably to mine by my hugeness – the shock seemed to have added an extra inch and I'd already been at bursting point.

And now, feeling her inner muscles, the only sign of life in her entire body, tighten terrifyingly around my cock, it suddenly occurred to me that there was a word for this. Dog-knotting. It happened to prostitutes when some fat old businessman had a heart attack and pegged out inside them and they had to go to hospital to be separated. Kind of thing you laugh about when you read it in the paper.

Well, it's not bloody funny in real life, mate, take it from me.

For a start, shock had morphed into coherent thought and I was petrified the poor girl had copped it. Surely it couldn't have been a heart attack? Aneurysm? Oh God/Whatever. I know, I know, what a way to go. But even so, I lay and sweated for what seemed an age but was probably only a few seconds whilst those slowly tensing inner muscles gradually consolidated their hold on me, and my cock, rigid with fear, buried itself deep among them like a brave but helpless ship being crushed amidst the merciless, slow-moving ice floes.

Pulse, I thought finally. I reached over with shaking fingers and picked up that limp hand. It seemed she did have a pulse, but maybe that was just my imagination, willing her to be alive.

After another century or two gripped in that dreadful vice, I had a few practical thoughts. If she was dead, I needed to move us. I had no idea how prostitutes managed to shift the body enough to make a phone call. It must be awful. Especially before mobiles. Although I supposed they'd often be in hotel rooms, where there'd be a phone on the bedside table they could reach over to. At least I was a bloke and strong enough to lift my partner up whilst I went looking for a phone. Or I would be, once my own heart attack was over and I felt okay enough to try and get up.

Just relax, it'll all be okay, I told myself. Your cock will subside and you'll be able to get out and take care of her. Which led me back to the fear that she was actually dead, or in need of help I wasn't giving her, therefore would soon be dead and it would be my fault. Or maybe it was my fault already. Could I go to prison for this? I'd only been trying to help. Oh God/Whatever! I stroked her hair and said I was sorry and felt her elusive pulse again and tried to imagine her grip on me was loosening, but that was an illusion – we were still locked together. Like Siamese twins. Were Siamese twins always of the same sex, I wondered inconsequentially.

And then, just as the sweat and palpitations were abating enough for me to think I might be able to move at some point that night, there was an almighty **BRRRRRNNNNGGG! BBBBBBBRRRRRRRNNNNGGGGGGGGGG!** and I fell back onto the cushions again with a cry of anguish, one hand pressed to my over-beating heart like a swooning Victorian maiden.

Telephone, telephone, it's only the bloody 'phone, I told myself. Well, now I knew where it was – inside my ear. And such was my state of panic and need for immediate reassurance that I'd screwed my shoulder round and picked it up from the coffee table by the sofa before remembering that I wasn't in my own home, so it was her phone I was answering and it was Bloke at the other end!

"Oh hello," he said, sounding surprised, as well he might. "Sorry, I must have dialled you by mistake . . . ." Momentary pause whilst he obviously checked his screen. "No. That's odd."

'That's odd' in a what-the-fuck? tone of voice.

"Hi, how's the wedding going?" I inquired as breezily as I could with my heart pounding so hard I thought he must be deafened by it in the south of France. "Look, I just came by to drop off a new lamp she bought the other day – it was too heavy for her to manage."

"Oh right. The wedding's fine, thanks. Listen, can you put her on?" (I did put her on, look what happened). "I haven't got long."

I gazed down at the prostrate body across mine. Tongue-tied. Tongue-tied and dog-knotted or pussy-knotted or whatever, all on the same night. Was my life really the success I'd always thought it?

"Hello? I said can you put her on, please?"

"Oh sorry mate, line's a bit dodgy . . . ."

"Are you okay? You sound odd."

Oh no! Genuine concern from genuine decent bloke and I was lying there chatting with his probably dead girlfriend fatally impaled on my Prong.

"Yeah, yeah, I'm fine thanks. That bloody lamp was heavier than I thought, that's all! Listen mate, she's just nipped out to get a takeaway and . . . ."

"Oh, you're having dinner there, then?"

Watch-glancing and lip-pursing going on at his end, no doubt. But it must only have been about 10pm – I was glad we'd started early.

"Oh just a quick bite, I have to get back to my brother – did I tell you he's going through another divorce? Tough time for him, he's come to stay at my place for a few days. But you're at a wedding, you don't want to hear all this! Enjoy yourself mate, lovely part of the world. I'll get her to give you a buzz as soon as she's . . . . free."

My strangled voice cracked on the final word, but I got it out and hung up and then gave a couple of dry sobs because this was all getting on top of me.

And she still was. On top of me. Totally inert. Locked onto me. I heard her mobile go off in the kitchen. Poor old Bloke, I'd've thought if I'd been capable of sympathy for anyone in the universe except myself at that moment. And the GC, of course.

But, I thought, pulling myself together, there was a phone within reach. I straightened her up so that we were chest to chest and I could give her her bloody cuddles, and thank God/Whatever, in that position I could definitely feel her heart softly thumping away.

And you know what? It was one of the most intimate experiences ever. Now I knew she was still alive and didn't believe she was about to die – her heartbeat was nice and steady and she had a good colour in her cheeks, though who wouldn't with all that pork rammed up them? – I abandoned myself to a sensation I suspected, and sincerely hoped actually, would never come my way again.

I'd been with a girl once who could only come on top, and she did it in about three seconds and needed to rest on my chest after each climax, which felt lovely. And this was like a massive, prolonged version of that. I felt hugely proud and at the same time impossibly touched, now that the perceived danger was over. Almost like holding the power of life and death in my arms. All man, all woman, the ultimate violence killed by the ultimate gentleness, meltdown into tenderness.

"Oh interesting," exclaimed the cheery, young-sounding male doctor they put on the phone at the local hospital, after we'd gone through the pulse and other checks. "Right, well, this is pretty rare but unless she has some medical condition we don't know about there's nothing to worry about and she should be coming round any minute now. Could be a combination of low blood pressure, not having eaten enough today, that kind of thing."

"Thank God, don't go away. Do I stay stuck, will I . . . . subside? Should I do anything? Hold on, she's beginning to move."

"Right, that should be that. Oh, and by the way, you'll both be a bit sore for a few days. We can give you something for that if you want to pop in."

Excellent service. Okay, I'd kicked up a bit of a stink about talking immediately to a doctor, but even so, I was impressed. He gave me his direct mobile number and I hung up feeling very reassured. As a matter of fact, it began to feel like a pretty interesting experience all round: incest (kind of), adultery (kind of), intense pain/pleasure peak, near-womanslaughter etc all thrown in.

The GC was stirring and muttering and whilst she took her time coming round I had a few more gulps of wine direct from the second bottle and rang my mother to let her know the loser had landed and was at my place. She said tartly she knew, and to get off the line in case he wanted to ring her. Then I savoured the strange, smug sensation on this brand new pleasure plateau, and was just thinking of fixing up Wednesday's match with BM when the GC began to push herself upright and I realised I'd been using her phone. I hoped Bloke didn't check her phone bills – you do hear of these things happening. Jealousy and stuff.

She laid a clammy palm on my chest, lifted her head with its dazed but open eyes and said,

"What happened?"

I rang the doc to say all was well and then lay stroking her cheek and thanking God/Whatever the concert pianist would be back from her East European tour next day.

I never told her any of my experiences and certainly didn't want to know about hers, but all good new things were shared physically, and anything negative seemed to get swept away in moments by the warm tides of her effortless sensuality. There was nothing we could not explore together; there was no part of her I didn't caress, tease, penetrate and delight over the decades. And though she was often inert or silent for ages after our pleasuring, she never frightened the shit out of me like the GC did that night. For which I was . . . grateful? No, I wasn't going to say that. Glad. I was profoundly glad that the CP proved the rule by being the exception.

Otherwise, life could have been too many exceptions to my rules and I would've been a tragic hero, instead of a happy one poised with the CP on Desire's glittering blade.

### Special Underbedcover Agent's Tip:-

*First Aid: I used to think this one was optional. Not saying you're going to have extreme experiences like mine, but it certainly sparks the lust light if you save her kid from choking or sew her finger back on after a slip with the veg knife or something. Oh, and do not joke about enjoying your mouth-to-mouth resuscitation classes – she'll just despise you.*

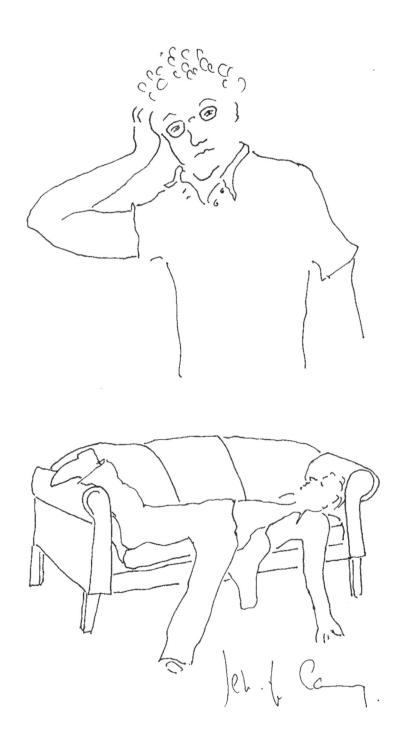

# Protocol No. 6 – Responsibility

## THE ANTI-PROTOCOL – IRRESPONSIBILITY

Responsibility: being responsible means, among other things,
being *able to take rational decisions without supervision; accountable
for one's own actions.* That's quite a burden sometimes, I really
was not expecting the outcome I got from trying to do the
good turn illustrating this Protocol, but I do believe we have a
responsibility to do our best by the people we care about.
Irresponsibility: my brother is the embodiment – you will not
believe this next stunt he pulled . . .

I READ THIS CASE once in the
paper about a boy who'd been raped.
I'd been doing quite a bit of thinking about the whole rape thing – whatever
war you've got on in the world, rape is a pretty conventional weapon, and
I was wondering how it fitted into the hi-tech conflicts – and this report
interested me because of the boy's response to his ordeal. He was, his parents
said, uncontrollably angry: kept smashing things and lashing out. And I
thought, excellent. Good on you, kid. Hasn't that got to be a much healthier
reaction than sitting blankly in your bedroom, not speaking, hearing your
parents say to all and sundry, 'Her life's been ruined' so often that you get
to believe it yourself?

I'm not belittling a horrendous experience, I'm just saying the 'male'
response of anger seemed a hell of a lot more useful than the usual – or

usually reported – 'female' one of introspection, guilt etc. The anger needed to be channelled, in the boy's case – and personally I'd say he'd've been a damn' sight better off taking up some aggressive sport (yeah, squash for example) than giving in to his parents' insistence that he see a shrink – but it was a reasonable and practical response which should have been respected more than the newspaper article implied it had been. Made me think anger expression courses would be more use than anger management. If kids learnt rational expression of anger at school, they wouldn't get road rage and stuff later in life.

But anyway, this is not to say that I've never felt anger, it just hasn't, as far as I know, hit me too often in the capped-up, sinful sense of Anger. Maybe it's because I've lived a soft and privileged lifestyle unaccompanied by the kind of danger and injustice that would have provoked Anger.

I guess what all this is leading up to is that the one time I really did do the Anger thing, it worked out fine. But that doesn't mean you should try it, I'm just the kinda guy things work out for.

\*      \*      \*

The GC had slept in late after that memorable Saturday night, and I hung around clearing up her flat whilst she had a bath. We ate the remains of the takeaway for lunch, I rang the bro to say I'd be home around 6pm, we went for a gentle walk – the doc was right, we were both sore – and then we watched another film. Yes, cuddled up on the sofa and no, absolutely not sexually. You're probably wondering if I was in love with her by then. Well, it had been an amazing experience, but no I wasn't and I never would be. Way too much power over each other and not enough control over ourselves, is what it had been, and neither of us wanted to repeat it. That took a few more weeks' conversations to sort out, but for the moment we just gazed at the box and I wondered if she'd have over-sensitivity to cuddling as well, if that's what turned her on. I mean, maybe Bloke would be better off stinting her on the cuddling if that was the case: I'd not only coped but enjoyed the experience, but that was thanks to my training and vocation – I honestly don't think a normal guy like Bloke, decent though he was, would've been able to handle it at all. Decided to ask the friendly doctor about it. I realised I had a hell of a lot more to learn about women's bodies, and that I ought to do another research course.

All cheering stuff, lots to look forward to, and the GC was well back into her usual chirpy mood when I pecked her on the cheek and took my bag of tricks back out to the car and home.

So you can imagine how I felt when I unlatched the front door, whistling cheerfully, dumped the case in the hallway and went through to the main room to find the bro slumped across the sofa with an empty bottle of pills and a disapproving cat – only one in residence at that time – beside him.

Haven't even had time to shower, I thought, going down on one knee in classic romantic pose to take his pulse etc. The GC's bathroom worked fine, that wasn't why I hadn't showered yet: it was just that after hearing I was in her flat on a Saturday evening, Bloke might be on the prowl a bit, and if he found the wrong kind of toenail clipping in the bathtub, it could go hard for her. And if it went too hard, she'd pull the fake-death stunt on him and he'd probably peg out from a heart attack.

By this time I was dialling the dog-knotting doctor of the previous night, whose number was on my phone, so he seemed like the quickest option even though he wasn't exactly around the corner.

"Me again," I said, explaining briefly. "Just got home and my brother's unconscious – looks like he's swallowed a ton of sleeping pills sometime within the past three hours. What do I do?"

"What's he swallowed?"

"20 x 10 mg Diazepam."

Beginning to feel like a real doctor.

"Can you manage him, have you got a car?"

"Yes and yes."

"Fine. I'm on duty, we'll sort him out as soon as you get here. Seat him with his head to one side so that he doesn't choke if he vomits. Quick as you can, okay?"

When I got there, they swept him away like the bit of human debris he was and the doc made me sign a few papers. Said they'd keep him in for a week or two but he'd be fine.

"Classic cry for help, by the look of it," said the doc. "We'll need to keep him in for at least a week. Any idea why he did it?"

I ran my fingers through my hair and said wearily,

"Divorce, because of the divorce I suppose. It's the second one. He's staying with me for a bit, but we hadn't really talked yet. I couldn't last night . . . . oh, you know that bit."

"Yes." He grinned cautiously, not quite sure if I was up for humour. "Busy weekend for you."

"Fuck off," I said, and he laughed. "Don't know how you manage it, my friend."

"Different when there's no emotional involvement," he pointed out. Like I was emotionally involved with my brother! Aaaargh! Or with the GC, come to that. Well, in a way maybe. "Want some of that soreness cream?"

I got home to find the cat still giving the sofa filthy looks and disgusted little sniffs. I have to say I didn't like the look of it myself any more. It had been the scene of so much pleasure – beginning with my mother's friend all those years ago, and she and I had made excellent further use of it till she went off to live with a Swiss art dealer, incidentally – that the image of a lifeless body on it, male at that, was just the biggest turn-off. On top of the previous night's near-death experience. It's as though the universe was trying to tell me something, and while the cat and I were relaxing in different armchairs – she didn't like the smell of the soreness cream either – I finally realised what it all meant. I needed a new sofa.

This one had done sterling service, and would still be fine for someone who didn't employ it as intensely as I tended to, and I'd been toying with the idea of a complete revamp for that room anyway – hence the lighting issue. A few elements were beginning to look a bit dated, despite touch-ups here and there over the years. In fact, I should re-do the whole flat, I decided. Not the kitchen, the kitchen was quality, it was wearing really well. A few new cabinet handles and the latest light fittings would fix that. There was nothing major, really – it'd be just the fun bits. Paint, colours, fabrics, shapes.

"Shopping," I told the cat, and she purred. "Need to go shopping. First thing's a new sofa; we'll think out the colour scheme, order a sofa and get cracking on paintwork before it arrives. Need to get you a friend for whilst I'm away travelling, too. Lonely for you since your brother died, isn't it? Never mind, we can organise that – plenty of abandoned cats wanting a good home. Think about colour and character, let me know what you want."

I made a to-do list while downing an entire bottle of Chilean Merlot: source new sofa and cat, pick up paint and fabric samples, check out lighting stores, oh! and bloody hell, the GC needed a new lamp! I gave her a quick buzz to remind her and we arranged to meet at John Lewis next day for a spot of browsing together. Needed to get a heavy lamp in place soon in case Bloke insisted on dropping by to see her on his way back from the wedding trip.

Then I rang BM to see if he wanted a sofa for the kids' basement: he lived up in town during the week whilst his wife ran her catering business and the family from their home in the country. He promised to nip round and pick it up in the wife's van first thing.

"Why are you in such a hurry?" he wanted to know. "Having to flee the country? Hordes of angry boyfriends after you?"

I shivered.

"Something like that. Get here by 9am or I won't be here to help, okay?"

Fleeing other people's flirtations with death, I thought, pouring out the last of the bottle and ringing the parents to cancel next day's planned family lunch.

"Oh dear," said my mother, sounding genuinely disappointed.

"Sorry Mother, but like I said, it's pretty bad food poisoning. I took him to Outpatients and they said he'll need a week or so to get over it. Let's do dinner on Tuesday the 9th instead. I'll book."

I gulped down the rest of that curvaceously-bodied wine, jotted down a few ideas for the flat revamp and went to bed.

Where's the Anger? you're wondering. The guy's being incredibly dynamic and creative, but none of it's about Anger.

Well yes, it is. There had to be a reaction at some point, didn't there? and it happened when I went to pick the bro up.

He was looking pasty and washed-up and his clothes irritated me more than ever. Even they seemed to be struggling to get away from him, straying off in different directions. And he was getting a paunch.

"Hi," he said awkwardly, getting up from the plastic chair he'd been waiting on. "They said could you go and sign something over there, I'm not sure . . . ."

"Yeah, won't be a sec. You all right? Hang on."

I signed stuff and we left.

"I'll take you for a drive," I said. "Do you good."

And I drove him out to Epping Forest and beat the shit out of him.

So that's the Anger bit. I didn't meant to do it, I really didn't. I thought we could get some fresh air and I'd have some decent scenery to look at while he dripped on about the latest gold-digger and I cheered him up a bit. But he wound me up.

"I don't want to die," he said, treading heavily on the colourful leaves. "I just don't want to live this way."

"Well, change it then."

Gawd, what's the problem? I picked up some leaves to take home and consider alongside the paint samples – my study had been a pale, pale pistachio for years but now I was straying in the direction of transforming it into a den of glowing oranges and reds and rich, thick fabrics, mainly 'cos I'd seen a couple of lights I really really liked at John Lewis that morning and was building ideas round them. Plus, the study was a nice size for pleasuring purposes. Intimate. I was having increasingly urgent visions of spanking the CP in there. She was the one who took spanking – and everything really – best, because she was excited by it but she also keyed into the pain/pleasure thing, and would encourage me to work my way round from her buttocks, punished till they were red-raw, to her entrance, and sting her there, on her shrinking, vulnerable lips. I wanted to do her in a glowing, warm study; lay her over my lap with soft music trickling between us and nothing but some shreds of Agent Provocateur to protect her from the barbed slaps. I wanted to make her cry with the delicious pain, and beg me to stop, and I wanted her to continue to weep and laugh together while I forced her down across red-raw cushions and roughly penetrated her stinging lips and thrust high and hard while I carried on slapping and she carried on begging for mercy she didn't want till she screamed and screamed in climax and her shrieks brought me noisily off at the same time. Which meant I'd be needing sound-proofing in the study too.

"It's easy for you just to say, 'change it then'," snapped my brother, sounding annoyed for some reason. "You think you know it all, don't you?"

"No, but I do try and learn from my mistakes." (This was to make him feel better: we both know I don't really make mistakes and when I do, I'm the only one who knows about them – I mean, they're not stonking great public put-it-on-the-net cock-ups like his). "And there's no reason why you can't change things."

"Oh yeah? So what's my mistake then, Mr Know-all? Mr Never-gets-depressed Successful? Mr Doesn't-need-anyone Inde-fucking-pendent?"

He kicked at the incredibly beautiful deep pink and yellow leaves I'd crouched to touch, and I stood up, stirred to anger by his contempt for beauty. He was looking pathetically belligerent. Oh God/Whatever, I thought, he really wants to know what his problem is.

"Well, you're probably not going to want to hear this, but since you ask, and since I never, *never*, NEVER want a repeat of this semi-suicide crap, here it is – you've got zero self-confidence. That means you don't wait for a good relationship, for example, you just rush into whatever second or twenty-second-best option is on offer. You don't *need* a woman, you just think you do. And you pay for that, in every way."

He was silent. Seemed to be taking it okay, no adverse reactions, so I moved on to the solution phase. Identify the problem, discuss solutions, decide on the best one and act on it. Management Manual again.

"You need to make some changes – I mean make them happen, not just let them happen to you. First of all, get through the divorce as quickly as you can – let the lawyer handle everything so that tart can't manipulate you emotionally. Tell him your bottom line, chivvy him, and don't let her take the piss any more. She's been living off you for eight years and you haven't even had any fun out of it, from what I can see."

"No, I haven't," he admitted quietly. "It's been hell. I just, oh I dunno, I just didn't want to have to start all over again, I s'pose. You have to work at things sometimes."

"Yes you do but sometimes working at it won't fix it. And it's not exactly starting all over again, it's building on the good stuff and ditching the crap. I think you ought to live on your own for a while; focus on your work and the bank balance, think about what you want next out of life. See your friends, get fit, date lots of women. Adopt some South American kids and email them. Enjoy life!"

He looked at me in the hollow way people do when they've forgotten what that means, and said,

"Live on my own?"

"Yeah, why not? Enjoy your freedom, build some confidence, get what *you* want instead of what someone else wants. Take your time finding someone new, if that's what you want."

"Of course it's what I want. That's all I ever wanted."

"Okay, but give it time."

Being patient about this no-brainer stuff was exhausting me. I bent and picked up a giant leaf whose flamboyance appealed; cushions, maybe, you couldn't have too much of that kind of flamboyance around, it detracted from the real issues.

"Time?"

"Yes! So you don't bloody cock up again!"

"So it's all my fault, then. So she's right, then. Everything's always my bleedin' fault."

"No! I'm just saying you've got a good job, you can soon recoup your financial losses 'cos you're a good salesman, and you don't need a woman to validate your existence! Make an effort, for crying out loud!" Shouting by now.

"Says Mr Commitment!" he shouted back.

I think this is where my fists clenched. It's so lonely sometimes, being misunderstood, having no-one to talk to about one's vocation. I'd learnt all that way back, but it could still hurt.

"I *am* committed!" I yelled. I could feel all the blood rushing round my head. "I am more dedicated than you can ever understand! It's just that I am committed to an abstract, to the highest there is, for me personally, on this Earth, as opposed to committed to letting all the gold-digging little tarts in Manchester line up to make me look a berk and negate my hard work and entire fucking existence!"

And I shoved him up against a tree. He shoved me right back, of course, a lot harder, so that I tripped and fell over backwards. Hurt my arse.

"You're the one who's going to end up with nothing!" he bellowed, towering over me. "Playboys get old, you know!"

And that's what did it. Playboy! All the years of study and patience and continued application of the finest pleasuring techniques I could master, in a frequently disappointing world, seemed to flash through my head like a scorch mark. He couldn't even see the nobility of my course, he'd just settled into Sloth, an apathetic acceptance of naffness in himself and in others, and now he had the nerve to criticise me for my unswerving commitment and constant endeavour, the lazy shite. Playboy! I kicked hard at his legs, he came down like a ton of bricks, and we laid into each other.

Well, we've always been fairly evenly matched, but I kept in better shape than him and he was probably a bit weakened by his 'cry for help' – though I could contend that my own weekend had been pretty debilitating, what with near-fatal shocks and lugging fake dead people about – so it soon ended with me delivering a final kick to his prostrate butt and going off to sit on a nearby log whilst he floundered about groaning and bleeding.

Finally he got up and we walked back to the car and drove home in silence.

"Where's your sofa?" he asked, coming into the main room after cleaning himself up.

"Gone."

"Wot, because . . . . because I . . . . ?"

"Because it was time for a change."

"Right."

He meandered around listlessly for a bit.

"Does anyone . . . . did you, tell anyone?"

"No. Parents think you've had food poisoning, and the gold-digger is not to have the satisfaction, okay?"

"She doesn't hate me, you know. It's not all bad. We've been together for eight years."

"Why would she hate you? What's to hate? The fact you're closing your wallet now? Don't tell her about this, just don't."

Pause.

"What are you doing?"

"I'm getting this presentation done so I can take tomorrow off and take you shopping."

"Shopping? What for?"

"For a start, clothes. Image. New life."

"Oh. Time for a change, right?"

"Right."

"I'll make the dinner then, whilst you do that."

"Yes, that would be helpful."

*       *       *

I really believe my Anger overcame his Sloth. I was livid, full of hatred about the whole thing, and the gold-digger was not entirely to blame by any stretch – he'd let her happen to him. How had the guy whose motto in his twenties was, 'If it moves shag it, if it doesn't, eat it' turned into this hopeless wreck in a couple of decades? Seemed to me ungrateful for life itself. But like I said, gratitude's a dodgy thing per se, and the way people apply/expect it is frankly off the wall. His cavalier attitude towards women used to annoy me, but even that was better than this crawling about and pretending not-good-enough behaviour was part of a normal relationship.

Apparently it happens to loads of men of that age. So the FFs told me. My conversational company was often female, and as the FFs said, women had kids or more resilience from monthly pain and/or getting paid less than men, so they didn't go into the same kind of anxiety spiral when things began to go pear-shaped. Plus they saved it for the menopause. Plus they were more fun than blokes to start with. So I hadn't noticed the male midlife crisis much. BM's marriage seemed solid, my parents had always got on pretty well, the guys at the squash club were mainly younger and still at the clubbing/having fun stage, and my other male friends seemed happy enough with their lives – not that we ever talked about it. But you never know what's going on inside someone, do you? I realised that now.

I kept thinking about how my brother had tried to top himself and it wound me up so much I had him out of bed and into town next morning first thing for Operation New Image.

My hairdresser – "*Please* Stefan, just give him a five-minute consultation, I know you're frantic, but please" – pursed his lips over the bald patch and fluffy tufts, turned him this way and that, then pronounced,

"Best move? Shave it. You've got a nice-shaped head, it'll look good. Then you'll need a very slight tan to take the dazzle off. I can do you myself tomorrow at 9am, we've just had a cancellation." He turned to me. "We can pop him in the fryer afterwards, for a touch of all-over tan, if you like? We'll give him the works. All-morning job, okay? Go away, I've got to run. See you tomorrow," he said confidently to the bro, kissed me on each cheek and hurried off.

We spent the rest of the day doing the clothes stores – not buying, just on a recce – then made the shortlist of items to be purchased over dinner. By this time, he'd accepted the idea of spending a whole morning being beautified by a poof, and I let him loose on his own next day with a clear conscience whilst I did the presentation of a lifetime to an international delegation, and saw the gleam of promotion in my visiting boss's eye. Or maybe she just fancied me, but no way. Not colleagues. Fine if you want to have a real affair or get serious, but a total waste of time for me: if I'd done one, they'd all have wanted it, and that would've damaged my reputation. They called me The Untouchable – the obnoxious sales guy had told me that once when we were downing designer beers at the lushest cocktail bar in Beirut after closing a shit-hot deal that *nobody* except he and I could've swung.

So, I was knacked but triumphant when I rocked up to meet the pirontals at a chi-chi new joint I knew they'd like, and there they were, soaking up the atmosphere and a couple of drinks at the bar, bless 'em.

"Your brother rang to say he'd be a little late," my father told me. "He had to drop the shopping off at home, he said. I'm glad to hear he's still got enough cash to go shopping. I'd've thought . . . ."

"Is he all right?" my mother chipped in hastily.

"Yeah, yeah, fine. He's over the food poisoning, the divorce should go through fast and he'll be fine. Maybe I'll be his pimp after all. Listen, tonight is *so* on me – you have to hear about . . . . hold on. Excuse me, can I get a glass of dry champagne here, please? Excuse me!"

"Look, is that . . . . ?" exclaimed my mother. "Oh!"

I turned to see what had caught her roving eye, and bugger me down dead, there was the bro sashaying over to us looking 10 years younger and a lifetime cooler thanks to Stefan's magic wand. My mother's eyes were out on stalks and there was an amazed smile on my dad's face. It was like the ballroom scene from 'My Fair Lady'. I nearly fucking cried. Stefan had given him the full works: facial, head shave, touch of tan, instant teeth-whitening, eyebrows, manicure – none of it obvious, just really, really good. And the gear was good: he'd ditched the striped shirt over a T-shirt, jeans and trainers in favour of dark brown trousers, a lightweight, round-neck brown top with a slash of orange – sleeves pushed up to the elbow – and slick, pointed shoes, which were in that season.

"You're not wearing your wedding ring," my mother commented as he pecked her on the cheek.

"Pawned it to pay for the haircut," he joked, and my dad laughed.

It stands out in my mind as one of the best family events ever – if not the best. We had a damn good laugh and covered all the ground: parents and their next big trip, me and my job, the bro and his divorce. I'd tipped one of the waitresses to give him the eye a few times and it was like catnip on a cat – I could see his interest stirring, so to speak. And you know what? I don't think I needed to do it, he was looking that cool.

"I let you down," he said to me on the way home.

"Not for the first time," I said.

"No, but it'll be the last."

Yeah. Well. Time will tell.

*     *     *

He was a good salesman, and now he'd been given the new objectives, he really went for it. Shedloads of new gear, plus he got a couple of interviews – not because he needed them, but just to negotiate his current wage up when he got offered the jobs, he said – and we spent the evenings out in bars or signing up for every internet dating service in sight. Now that wasn't something I'd tried before, and it led to lots of good stuff for me, but more of that anon. And he managed to kick the divorce and house sale along at the same time.

Two Saturdays after he landed on my doorstep, we gave a meat market party – not that we called it that – inviting about five women we'd already met via internet, plus BM and his wife, her divorced brother, the GC and Bloke with his cousin and another male friend, the FFs with a couple of male midlife crisis victims they knew, and my point-and-click salesman colleague, who brought three Brazilian dancers.

It went brilliantly. The bro and the GC got along really well, to the extent that Bloke got narked and began chatting up one of the Brazilian dancers till he realised it was another man; the food was great (BM's wife took care of that); there was tons of booze; the intrigues were fun; and I was well pleased to find myself accosted by one of the internet women when I nipped into the small bathroom en-suite to my bedroom to freshen up as the night wore on.

"Do you mind sharing?" she inquired, coyly peeking round the door.

"Come on in," I invited. So she did, locking the door.

"Your brother's nice," she said, lifting her skirt and sitting down for a pee whilst I reached for my deodorant. "But I don't fancy him. What's the deal with you? Sorry to be so upfront, but we're not teenagers, are we?"

"Absolutely fine," I replied, sharing my glass of Cabernet with her. "The deal is that I'm Mr No-Commitment, except to your pleasure. No emotional ties, no mess, no expectations, no future, just glorious, safe pleasure."

She gave me a big grin and said,

"Refreshing honesty."

Artistic type, elegant as a bone, effortless style draped over an almost aggressively lean frame, cropped hair, big earrings. After gazing at me a moment longer whilst I stood foursquare to her, she undid the belt of my trousers and looked up. My turn to grin. I reached for the condoms and she chose raspberry.

"You're huge," she commented after a fair bit of very competent tongue and handiwork.

I was being ungrateful here. I dragged the bathmat over and knelt down in front of her. She stayed seated – comfortable enough, apparently.

"Your other guests?" she murmured as we kissed, and I ran my hands up her arms and into her top.

"They won't notice we've gone," I assured her, exploring her small, hard breasts and enjoying her handling of me. "Do you want me inside you?" I asked her quietly.

"I think . . . ." she hesitated. "I think I most want to . . . . I think I'm going to shit."

I gazed at her in awe.

"Is that too gross?"

"No! I just would love to be inside you when that happens."

"Fingers," she whispered. "It's coming."

She lifted slightly so that I could manoeuvre one hand down under her and let her breath go in a grunt of satisfaction as I quickly inserted four fingers into her beautifully wet cunt. And then I could feel it too, the inevitable muscular contractions, the opening and squeezing, through the membrane separating her anus from her vagina. Abandoning all thought of my own arousal, I used the other hand and my lips and tongue all over her face, neck and tits to help her towards completion. Back arched against the cistern, she had her eyes closed and was giving audible moans under that double occupation of her intimacy. Absolutely powerless as she was moved towards inevitability, and loving it.

I had my tongue against her suddenly clenched teeth and one hand working her breasts when the other hand felt the final spasm; her vagina and her anus heaved in unison and she gave a long, gurgling cry. My hand, expelled from her cunt in a spurt of cum, went straight to my dick and under the dreamy gaze of her half-closed eyes, I brought myself off within seconds, shooting lavishly and noisily into the shower cubicle.

We spent a few minutes just sitting there amid the faint scent of raspberries and cream, recovering.

"Oh God, that was disgusting," she said finally. "I swear . . . . I have *never* done anything like that in my life. Never *imagined* doing anything like that. Oh God, I can't believe what we just did."

She was still smiling when she left.

"Hey, you missed some of the best action," the bro said when everyone had gone. "Want a cup of tea? You'll never guess what one of those Brazilian birds said to me . . . ."

*　　*　　*

My brother hadn't caused so much grief since about 25 years earlier – and funnily enough, although that incident per se was an almighty cock-up, it also led to positive results for me. Took a while though – hence the Fortitude aspect.

The whole Anger thing, quite apart from the pleasure advantages of the raspberries/cream encounter and a couple of satisfactory later spin-offs, did teach me to pay a bit more attention to my own sex. I mean, if one of the guys at work said, 'Fine' in answer to 'How's life?', I'd now sometimes try to work out if he meant it really was fine, or if he was sick to death of his partner but too weedy to get out of it, or contemplating faking his own death and starting a new life in Bangkok, or just contemplating his own death, fullstop.

Not necessary to the pleasure objectives, but quite a useful skill to have in life. Just a general sensitivity extension. And the bro had benefited from other areas of my sensitivity: if it hadn't been for me listening to the FFs and others when they banged on about the latest friend's break-up, I wouldn't have had a clue that the classic female response is to buy a new image or vamp up the old one and back off the dating scene till you're ready to go back in with all guns blazing. Which might be when the kids have grown up, or next day, or never, but the new objectives seem to get set and acted on pretty quickly. I admired that approach. It's not usually based on Anger, I don't think – we're back to the female pragmatism argument – but it acknowledges the dangers of Sloth and avoids them, doesn't it?

The blokes, now that I'd begun to take notice, seemed to sit around in denial till the whole thing went completely pear-shaped – even ones like my brother, who were effective in their professional situations – and then sit around a bit more in a bit more denial till some other female came along and picked up the bits and did what they wanted with them. Hm.

Anyway, the point is that my anger and knowledge did my brother a huge favour by getting him out of a destructive behaviour pattern. The incident in our twenties worked a bit differently.

It began one dark and stormy night . . . . Nah, only joking.

He'd just finished college and I was on my okay-but-not-great second job in London, living in some hovel, so he came to doss at my place for a few weeks whilst he was job-hunting. I was putting a lot into work, climbing the corporate ladder, looking for better openings and all that kind of thing. So I just slung the keys and a towel at him and assumed (well yeah, hoped) we wouldn't see much of each other.

Trouble was, the bro, like I said, shagged anything that stayed still long enough to let him, and where was he going to take them? Plus, he and I had very different standards when it came to judging habitats. I'd put real pleasuring efforts on hold for a few months to give myself time to change jobs and get a better place to live, but,

"Oh this is a great little pad," he'd said on entering the typical, two-up, two-down terraced house with a kitchen door leading out onto the garden. "Nice, you done nice here. Loadsa space, two bedrooms, ooh-la-la! Like the kitchen. Chic or wot?"

It wasn't chic. He doesn't know the meaning of the word. It was just clean and non-studenty.

"You can have three weeks free," I told him. "Then you're paying half the rent, and at three months, you're out."

Salesman, needs objectives.

"Bagsa time, no probs," he assured me.

Although I didn't *see* much of him, I heard him more than I needed to. It wasn't envy, it really, really wasn't. I was concentrating on finding the right place for my vocation, and being able to afford it comfortably. I had a vision – king size bed, high ceilings, bay windows, rich furnishings, minimalist kitchen, unexpected lighting etc – and I was totally focussed on achieving it asap.

It was just irritating, when I was on this visionary, monk-like jag, to be woken up at two in the morning on weekdays by slurry voices and clattering teacups downstairs, followed by giggly murmurs and then thumping and grunting from the other side of the bedroom wall. I hardly ever saw the victims, 'cos I was out of the house before he surfaced to get ready for the multiple job interviews he assured me he was getting. But there was the one standout exception to the rule.

Standout in several ways. First off, because he'd actually landed a job the day before, Friday. Secondly, I'd refused to go out on the piss with him Friday night because I had a squash match on Saturday. I was county level at that time, took it fairly seriously. And I'd invested in some earplugs and they'd done a good job – if he'd been clacking teacups and grunting the night before, I really hadn't been aware of it. Magic.

So here we were, Saturday morning. I'd got up early-ish and taken my tea and cereals and power drink back to bed to get some business reading done over the morning wank. No worries, no hurries, and I was whistling cheerfully when I emerged a couple of hours later and went down to the kitchen. The Prong had been tamed, I was feeling good about the new project at work, I would win that match, and the bro was singing in the shower, so I'd be away and clear before he got out and started yakking about how many pints he'd sunk the night before.

My first impression was that the girl in the kitchen was stark naked. Fantastic. I stopped dead and drank it in. She had her back to me and was standing on tiptoe, reaching up to open one of the cupboards. Young, nice-ish body – not the sort that would wear well, mind you, as she was already too fleshy round the hips and had zero muscle tone. Of course, I was only taking in the details because I was standing there gazing. And I'd just assimilated the fact that there was, in fact, a sliver of cotton residing in her crack and round those round hips when she said,

"I can't find the teabags," and bent over to look in the lower cupboards!

I don't know about you, but I think only one course of action was indicated. I sprang forward, said,

"Let me help," and wedged the Prong, fighting against the skimpy boxer shorts containing it, lengthwise into the bike rack.

"Oooooh! Didn't you get enough last night?" she giggled.

"No, you'll be the one who didn't get enough," I quipped, and took a couple of steps back as she turned round. "It's okay, I'm his brother. Nice to meet you. The teabags are . . . ."

Which is the moment when the morning ceased to be a thing of fun and shattered into a zillion violent fragments as a baseball bat smashed through the frosted glass pane of the door into the garden, followed by a hand fumbling for the lock on the inside.

The girl sank to her knees, crying,

"No, no, oh please no!" in a mix of screams and tears, and it was only afterwards that I realised that was the reaction of someone who'd seen it before, who knew the routine. As for me, I just froze for valuable seconds, thinking, 'What's going on?' before looking round for a weapon. Too late. You'd've thought my reflexes, as a pretty good squash player, would've been a damn' sight faster, but I have to admit I'd never been in an aggro situation like this and I was slow. Allowed valuable seconds for rational thought, and we didn't have those seconds. I dimly heard the water from the shower going off and a shout from the bro, then the intruder was in.

Big guy, firm hold on that bat – who has a baseball bat in London? It was like a bad movie; the air was full of the girl's crying and screaming and his belligerent yelling. Her face was contorted, she was clasping her hands in an imploring gesture, he stood poised over her with the bat raised, and for a split second I thought he was going to kill her and all I'd have done was see it happen and my entire life would be a failure because of it.

What he was seeing was the naked girl kneeling on the floor and a near-naked bloke with a massive hard-on standing by her.

"You filthy fucking little . . . ." he yelled, but I didn't register what else he called her, 'cos with the words, he changed direction and intention (thank God/Whatever, really) and brought the bat scything round in a vicious swipe towards the only other weapon in sight, in his eyes – i.e. the Prong. Over the screams and cries and his yelling, we all heard the almighty crack as I took it turning on the thigh and the fucker broke my leg in about six places.

"OY!" bellowed a voice from the hall doorway as I went down, and from the floor, I saw my brother from a whole new angle – stark naked in the entrance, rivulets of water trickling down his body, a bar of soap still in his hand (he didn't do gels, thought they were a bit nancy, I think), and the ugliest look I've ever seen on his face. The girl froze with her hands to her cheeks and the beefcake with the bat paused for a moment. Which was the moment he didn't have.

I've always been sportier than the bro and he'd been out on the piss half the night, but what I'd forgotten and the beefcake never knew is that the bro was star bowler for the college cricket team and he was only just out of college. He didn't waste any time on rational thought – for obvious reasons – he just pulled his right arm high and gave, hard and fast and dead on target. The big fucker went down like a stone, out cold, no time even to clap his hands to his head or make a sound as the bar of soap took him over the left eye.

"Nice ball," I croaked. "Slippery and elliptical. Nice one."

The bro strode over and picked up the baseball bat. The shivering girl began to cry and whimper again – seemed as though the sight of a bloke with a bat in his hand set her off, and who's to wonder, if this was the kind of thing she was used to? I'd probably be the same myself now, which was going to play havoc with business trips to the States, where I confidently expected to be invited to tons of top baseball games by influential, stinking rich clients.

"Where's the slick guy, the Brit?" I could hear the company president asking, against a colourful background of dinky little cheergirls, exuberant popcorn, booming horns and excited shouting. "He was here a moment ago. Oh, isn't that him there in the corner, whimpering and cowering and begging for a bar of soap?"

"Boyfriend?" the bro asked the girl.

"No, yes, no, he was," she blubbed. "We broke up, he follows me, he won't . . . . I can't . . . ."

"All right, it's all right." The bro pulled her to her feet and held her. "Okay, go upstairs and get quilts and pillows and come back down. Now!"

He pushed her towards the hall and picked up the kitchen phone, standing over the ex with the bat in his hand. I tried to recall if he'd been any good at batting, but the truth is, I'd never been interested in cricket. Too slow, I'd always thought. Too slow! Teach me. Me and my lightning reflexes, yeah yeah. Me and my superior intelligence and greater life experience.

The agony was kicking in now and I almost passed out when he carefully made me as comfortable as he could with pillows and a quilt.

There was a dull thud during the phone conversation when the ex came round and the bro gave him a tap with the bat, and I remember the girl, wrapped in another quilt, huddled and blotchy on the chair alongside.

"Right then, tea all round," said the bro, getting the cups out and re-boiling the kettle.

"Sorry," whispered the girl. "I'm so sorry, he follows me, I can't . . . ."

"Here, nip up and get me a bathrobe and some underpants, will you?"

She sniffed and nodded and left again. I just lay there, giving the odd groan, I have to admit.

"Need to get this wanker sorted," muttered my brother. "Here you are, can you drink that okay? Right. Squash club, where's the number? Don't think you'll make your game today."

He paused to give the ex another clobber.

"You'll give him brain damage," I warned.

"Don't tempt me. Scary – he must have been trailing us for days."

"Weeks, more like, if he's been waiting to catch you in bed together," I said, and just then the doorbell rang.

"And you say you knocked him out with a bar of soap, sir?" inquired a disbelieving police officer several minutes later, when the ambulance guys were also on the scene dealing with the wreckage.

"Cricket," I said feebly as the drugs began to take effect. "Star bowler. Soap, soap, saw it. Get . . . . window . . . . fix . . . ."

\*     \*     \*

Well, I spent ages in traction and it took forever to get my squash back to where it was. Plus I missed out on the promotion I'd been gunning for with that work project, and the first big international trip the company had promised to send me on. But there'd be more of all that in the future. Where the whole thing came in handy as an aid to my real life's ambition was that I used the time to develop my theoretical pleasuring skills – and there, I think it's fair to say that I showed Fortitude. It's akin to patience, isn't it? But patience sounds a bit boring and girlie, I think Fortitude has a more active ring to it. No fussing, just set new objectives according to the new circumstances and go for them. Which is, ironically, what I later learned women tend to do better than men in emotional situations, but Fortitude is still more manly to me.

In the hospital, I got the FFs to bring in loads of girlie mags and we had regular tutorials, reading and discussing the cover stories and the agony aunt letters and anything else that caught my eye or that they thought I should pay attention to. We did more role play on chat-up lines, including text messages, and I encouraged them to talk to me about their feelings. Usually fell asleep during those bits, which pissed them off but I said it was the drugs.

I also re-read all the sex manuals on the market, and made my own notes based on them and the Casanova books. Some classic stuff there to bear in mind, I tell you.

And I set myself an objective, which was to get the doctor to give me a handjob before I was sent home. Now, as you know, doctors aren't meant to get involved in any way with patients, but my argument is that I didn't want involvement, I just wanted my dick seen to. Going for a kiss or a date would've been daft. Not to mention common. Even so, you'll appreciate that it was a pretty ambitious target. I mean, she could get struck off or something, probably, and I didn't want that. It was also dead tricky in that I rarely saw her. Tons of brisk little nurses everywhere, but the doc only came round about once a week.

But I embarked on the project using my newfound knowledge, and with the FFs' words ringing in my ears. They'd giggled themselves to bits when I confided the objective to them, but eventually the FF1 said,

"Oh well, if it gives you something to think about. You need to gain her trust. Be her friend."

"I don't want to be her friend!" I exclaimed in horror. "I don't ask friends to give me handjobs! And I'm not interested in her that way!"

They looked at each other.

"No, but you see, you have to be likeable and trustworthy enough to touch," explained the FF2. "Even if it's only temporary. Most women won't touch a bloke they don't like unless they're being paid. In some way."

"Everything's a trade-off," put in the FF1. "And if you're not paying her, why on earth would she want to bring you off? What's in it for her?"

I was puzzled.

"Pleasure," I said finally, since they really did seem to expect an answer. I mean, it's obvious, innit?

There was a pause whilst they both contemplated me then looked at each other again.

"*Your* pleasure," said the FF2.

"Well, obviously it's pleasurable for me," I admitted. "But surely it's got to be good for her too? I mean, I do understand about a woman getting her pleasure first, that is the whole point – what do you think I've been studying the Koran for?"

"Calm down, we know, we know. It's just that it's different for a woman . . . ."

"I'll say! Blimey! How fucking selfish is that? What's in it for her?! The pleasure of seeing someone else take pleasure in her skills, that's what! Become helpless under your hand. That is the most incredible sensation. It's, it's . . . . intense. Joyful. Give her a break from looking into old folks' ears or dealing with OD'd junkies or battered wives! I mean, come on! Lovely big clean cock to play with and you're asking what's in it for her! I can't fucking believe this!"

More silence.

"Come on then, come on, tell me. What do you think I should do? Hm? What? What's all this friend stuff?"

"Okay, maybe friend was too strong a word," said the FF2, laying aside the magazine she'd started leafing through. "But it's true that you need to be likeable and trustworthy."

"You, the person, not you, the nice clean cock," interpolated the FF1.

"Exactly. What you may not have registered is that women get propositions the whole time – most of them don't have to take the initiative. In other words . . . ."

"In other words, they're the ones picking and choosing," I put in. "I *know* all this!"

"Right. So she'll have tons of guys fancying her or hitting on her all the time, especially in a job like this, where she's seeing people at their most vulnerable, and helping them, and . . . ."

" . . . . and enjoying easy access to their genitalia," I pointed out.

"Yes, well, anyway. The other thing is, you don't know what's going on in her life . . . ."

"I told you, I don't care! We're talking about creating a beautiful spiritual moment between two bodies, not . . . ." I broke off as the FF1 made a funny snorting noise and ran out with her scarf clapped to her face.

"Loo!" she called in a muffled voice. "Sorry!"

" . . . . not getting bogged down in all her paraphernalia."

"Nevertheless, I do think you stand more of a chance if you lead up to it gradually. Ask her things about herself, or just make some comment that shows you've noticed her as a human being, like saying she looks tired or something. Just don't do that, 'Hi, you look great, I know you've probably just worked 36 hours straight and must be aching all over as well as psychologically damaged by the five-year-old car crash victim dying in the middle of the night, but you'll feel a whole lot better if you whack me off' number."

"I wouldn't have put it like that!"

"No, I know, but you would have been thinking that because it's what you'd be feeling if you were given the opportunity. Just ask her if she has kids, or something."

"But I've told you . . . ."

"I know. You don't care." She stood up and picked up their bags. "You know, you want to be at least as careful with those three little words as with the other three."

I stared. Gem of advice. Absolute gem. I'd never used the other three and was dead respectful of them. Didn't want a bunny-boiler on my hands, and hadn't felt any urge to say them anyway. And over-stating the case then backing out is just messy. But maybe I was swinging too far the other way in some people's eyes. Hm.

"Wotcha!" called BM, looming up in the doorway and making sure he collided with the FF2. "Hello love, you're looking good. You and your friend fancy a spot of redhot lesbo action tonight, eh?"

"You bet," she replied, frotting her front against his chest and running her fingers through his hair. "But not with you around. Ta-ra!"

"Prick tease," he said resignedly, slapping her arse.

"See what I mean?" she said to me, and disappeared.

*   *   *

So, although it was an effort, because I really thought I knew all this anyway, I did some more thinking, and next time the doctor came round, I smiled politely as she checked the board at the end of the bed and said,

"You must be tired."

"No," she said, looking up in surprise. "Why, do I look tired?"

"No, no!" I assured her hastily, cursing the FFs under my breath. "I just meant, well, you know, doctors work such long hours and all that. I assumed you must be permanently exhausted."

She gave me a curt smile, rattled the curtains round us and drew back the bedclothes to look at my leg. Ostensibly. The leg was pretty much obscured by the boner, and it was hard to tell what she was peering at so intently.

"Discomfort?"

"Yeah, lots of it!" I nodded. "And my leg hurts, too."

She smiled properly that time and said,

"Oh don't worry, you'll soon be back in action. No reason why you shouldn't engage in careful sexual activity. You were lucky there wasn't damage to the testicles. You did have severe bruising in that area."

"Yes, well, I saw it coming and managed to twist a bit."

"Hm. It's all coming along fine. We'll be sending you home on Friday."

Friday! Only three days left! Action this day!

"When you say careful sexual activity, how careful do you mean?" I asked, giving the Prong a little pat.

She pulled back the clattery curtains she'd drawn round the bed and said drily,

"Common sense. You've got that, haven't you?"

I grabbed her wrist as she straightened the bedclothes, and she stopped and looked me in the eyes.

"I have got common sense, yes," I told her. "But what I'm talking about is something else. I've been here for weeks and you've all been great to me, but the hospital touch is . . . . impersonal. It's practical. And that's not . . . . what I'm, about, that's not what I am, in life. I miss real . . . . touch. That's what I yearn for." I let go her wrist and closed my eyes. "Sorry if I offended you. You probably think I'm like all the rest. I'm just not."

She left without saying anything and I just lay there for a while thinking sorrowfully that this was a lonely moment: I'd tried to get it across, but though my thoughts were softly textured and richly embroidered, they came out as thick, plain cotton when I put them into words. If only I could convey the sensations I really sought – what woman would not be charmed and melted? I didn't want what everyone else seemed to understand by a hand job; I wanted to ride the tide of pleasure, to give and take, ebb and flow, and marvel at the memory.

And this is what made me different. Was then, is now.

What good would all the studying do if I couldn't transmit this in words? I opened my eyes after a while and decided that maybe I should get to work on the poets. You know, add a few beautiful set phrases to my own repertoire, strengthen it a bit with their ideas/expressions. It'd go well with all the more practical aspects of the training. My mother had quite a few books I could dip into: I was going to stay at my parents' house for a few weeks a) 'cos they were off to Canada and needed a cat/dog-sitter anyway, and b) because it was closer to work than my own place, which the bro would be occupying. Zero imagination, that guy – he just got the window and lock fixed and carried on using it as a shagpad, whereas I never moved into a ground-floor property again. Mind you, he hadn't been attacked and hospitalised. In fact, he'd come out of the whole thing as a bit of a hero. Obviously we didn't give the parents all the details but they seemed to think I was the one who'd been messing around with some undesirable girl and provoked an attack, and they fussed over him and praised him and generally made complete pains of themselves.

Still, it was good to have a decent place to go whilst I was getting back into the full swing of things, so I had that to look forward to, and I was mentally running through my poetry plans and other targets for the next few weeks the night before my release from hospital when the door opened and closed quietly and I saw I'd been joined by the doctor!

She locked the door, switched off the lights, plunging us into delightful dimness, and approached the bed. Saying nothing, she drew the curtains quietly – God knows how she managed that, it usually sounded like a pile of saucepans collapsing – round the bed, gently lifted the bedclothes off me and then loosed her long hair and swept it slowly up and down my naked torso. I quivered all over.

Taking a tiny bottle from her pocket, she rubbed a little oil into her hands and ran them over my face, neck, arms, six-pack (now more of a three-pack after the hospital stay, but still) . . . . Drinking in that delicious sweet almond scent, I fell in love with fragrance that night and added it to the list of things to study in my lifetime and use to the full in pleasuring. Pure and fresh, seductive and convincing . . . . She was reaching up under her white coat and skirt, rubbing it into her upper thighs, and even as I realised her intention, she silenced my murmur of anticipation by climbing nimbly onto the bed and straddling my ecstatic face. Her thighs were cool and slightly sticky and I let my hands hang limply by my sides whilst I kissed her perfumed skin and entered her with gentle tongue alone.

She melted into my mouth and I explored eagerly, gratefully, immersed in shared sensations. Her hands ran over my torso and close to but not over, my dick, and the first real touch the patient Prong had received in many long weeks came from her careful lips. Groaning helplessly into her fragrant wetness, I abandoned myself to her exquisite attentions, and when she eventually brought up a hand to help, I came shamelessly early, gloriously, and as quietly as I could.

She turned then, giving me one slow kiss-taste of myself, and re-positioned herself so that she was facing the wall above my head. My hands came up and she released her first moan as a moistened finger penetrated her anus and my tongue redoubled its efforts inside her. If we hadn't been where we were, I swear she would've been slapping the wall and screaming when she came. The intensity of her internal convulsions built fast and I was wide open to drink her in when the gush came and she stopped moving, propped against the wall and breathing in gulps whilst I smeared her cum over my face with her thighs.

When the pulse rates had slowed, she cleaned up efficiently, obliterating the sweet almond scent with impersonal hospital smell while I lay marvelling over the memory. I wasn't to realise for many years that there'd be few who could respond so purely and completely to the gifts I offered.

We didn't kiss or speak, we never saw each other again. I did send flowers, though, with a note thanking her for her 'extraordinary care', and I got a text message saying, 'you're not like all the rest.'

It was my first perfect pleasure encounter.

You see, it's a lot to do with the blend of sensations, and that incident had so much going for it in a strange way: we had to be quiet and careful, I had limited movement, the Prong had not been touched for ages, the smell of hospital had been in my nostrils for so long etc etc, and who knew when she had last indulged in fulfilling a fantasy? But the main thing is we trusted each other, and took and gave everything. That really is rare. It's such a mistake to think fantasy is different from reality – it's usually just a question of making an effort. Imagination. Not a lot of that about, which is where finding someone to share it comes in. Reciprocity. It's a key difference between pleasuring and shagging, I'd say. You can teach/learn pleasuring techniques, but you can't teach/learn imagination or abandonment.

And imagination is like joie de vivre. Rare, and God/Whatever-given.

*Special Underbedcover Agent's Tip:-*

*Grooming/make-up/fragrance: This is advanced level stuff, really, but knowing that the little bit of rubber with five stumps on it in her bathroom is for separating her toes while she paints her nails (toenails) does get you more than a second glance. She'll feel a wee bit threatened if you're as familiar with the contents of her make-up bag as she is. Actually, having a semi-naked woman paint my toenails black by candlelight has always meant instant hard-on for me. Yeah, okay, semi-naked woman doing nothing at all usually means the same thing. And you need to know how to take care of your own skin, hair and nails. The guy who can exchange moisturiser tips or discuss the latest celebrity scent at a party is the one who's going to get laid. Anyway, it's fascinating. Alchemy.*

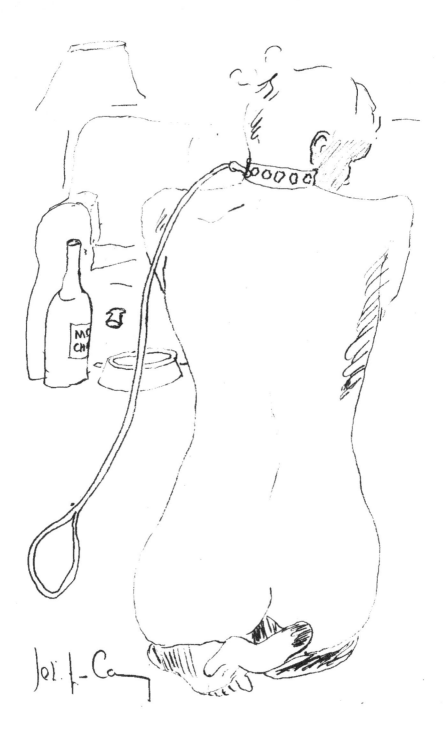

# Protocol No. 7 – Passion

## THE ANTI-PROTOCOL – JEALOUSY

Passion: my favourite definition (No 6 in the Collins) for myself
is, *an outburst expressing intense emotions.* You can probably guess
why. It's the core, it just needs to be tempered by Judgment,
Responsibility and so on, otherwise it can create a bit of a mess.
Jealousy: ooh, this one. Lots of people take issue with me on
this. I used to think it was just bollocks, absolutely pointless, but
I'm having to reassess it now. You'll see why.

WOULD I HAVE embarked
on my life's path if I'd known
how hard and lonely it could be, how misunderstood I could often feel? Oh
yeah, things get hard and lonely anyway, from what I've seen, without the
satisfaction I've had.

Anyway, anyone who, like me, is at the top of their game, has had to
work bloody hard. And never stop learning. Genius? Not sure what that
means – I often suspect it's just someone talented but ultra-selfish who
pays so little attention to other people that that in itself attracts attention. I
couldn't get away with that – it'd be against my calling. Maybe we should
just call it immense talent.

The calling is the starting-point. Acknowledging the vocation and
committing to it. No retreat baby, no surrender.

Look at the bro and me – now that's the difference between sex and pleasuring. Pleasuring involves awareness, dedication, sensitivity and skill. Sex is sex. Can be anything from great to instantly forgettable. In the bro's case, always great for him and instantly forgettable for her, probably.

But you don't need to be my level, you don't need to be a genius, to get huge benefits from the art of Pleasuring and avoid being like the bro.

I was coming away from the Reina Sofia Museum in Madrid one fine spring day recently after trying to make my mind up about Dali once and for all and then deciding not to bother, when I saw the most amazing piece of living, plastic, sexually arousing sculpture.

It was a young, very young man lying on his back on a stone bench by the Botanical Gardens, licking a vanilla ice-cream with his eyes closed. It stopped me in my tracks and I stood to stare. In colour terms, Madrid is pretty much pale beige, with lime-green trees in spring and a hard blue shell over everything in summer. But on this day, the shell was a paler, kinder blue oozing a few clouds, the lime green of the trees was arresting, and the warmth of the sun was gently promising.

It was also not so hot that you couldn't eat an ice-cream on your back without it melting all over your face within about ten seconds.

He was savouring it as though it was his final suckjob. It was as though, after years of practice, he knew just how to keep the luscious target from his full lips and probing tongue, holding off those moments when he'd part his lips fully and embrace the whole thing. Yet there was no lack of eagerness, no desire had been lost in all the years of practice a kid like him had had no time to acquire.

Eyes closed against outside distractions, all his senses were focussed on the creamy, welcoming, irresistible and finite cornet of pleasure he held between careful fingers.

I watched while he ran his tongue eagerly up the slowly surrendering sides, then probed a tiny dent in the top, once, twice, his head reaching up just enough to make that precious contact before sinking back to savour, but the third time the cock raised his eager young throat to crow in creamy pleasure, I turned my back on him and breathed Botanical Gardens till I knew he'd be gone and there'd be only the traffic.

He was my disciple. It was either turn away or go and sit on his face.

\*     \*     \*

Right then, the basics are talent and dedication. Talent doesn't mean having a huge one. Necessarily. I'd say it helps, but then I would, wouldn't I? Don't be daunted – you've got to put the training in, that's the dedication bit. It's worth it, whether you're in training for the vocation or just for improving your Saturday night session after the kids have gone to bed.

Right, on to the Pleasure Pantheon. My Pleasure Pantheon.
**Desire is the deity.**
And since we've been talking about Sins and Virtues, my Pleasure Pantheon is peopled with its own. They sometimes move around a bit, because some of them are like Pride and Envy – a little of them is fine, only bad when it gets out of control. So Jealousy, for example, which is like Envy only directed towards people not objects or characteristics, can be fine for some people because it keeps them careful of their partner.

I did have a near-Jealousy experience once.

It's difficult to admit that, 'cos Jealousy was always something I'd observed in others but not really registered in myself at all. And yes, I suppose I was a bit contemptuous of it. It was the kind of thing the bro and other losers got mixed up in. But you see I give it the respect of capping it up – not because it's one of The Deadly Sins but because it's one of My Deadly Sins, i.e. an Anti-Protocol. I only came to realise that it had a place in the Pleasure Pantheon – ie could be a virtue up to a point – after a weird incident involving the Stepkid. Not mine, no!

A few years after his second divorce, my brother met and actually managed to hold onto a really great lady who gave him more fun out of life than the miserable git had any right to hope for. When you found out that her husband had been a violent drunk and her only daughter had hanged herself at the age of 19, you thought, now there's someone who could be forgiven for being in and out of the shrink's.

But no. She had the heartiest laugh I've ever heard, listened to everyone as though she just expected them to be hilarious, and had a permanent air of being about to clap her hands and burst into a roar of laughter – which she often did. She ran her own clothing boutique on Ibiza during the summer months and spent chunks of the rest of the year travelling to India – where one of her sons lived – Thailand etc to buy new stock for the sun-hungry, cash-heavy tourists.

The other son lived in London and he and I got on really well and often hung out together. He had the kind of energy that lasts a lifetime, not just the illusion of energy that usually comes with youth, which was the sort my brother had had. Sort most people have, from what I've seen – if they've got any to start with.

But anyway, that's all off at a tangent. And to be fair, although I'd lost all respect for him after his 'cry for help', the bro wasn't such a miserable git and he did get some of the old zest back after the second divorce. Truth is, he liked the simple things in life, and HL – the Hearty Laugher – had learnt to be one of them.

Stepkid was a sinewy young man – round 30 when the incident happened – with a really expressive face and a wicked sense of humour. Not too cruel – as Arnold Bennett said, all good humour involves compassion, and Stepkid was mature enough to be learning that – but quick to spot other people's inadequacies. He gave the impression of being pretty sorted, but then lots of 30-year-olds do, don't they? The danger zone seems to be 35-45. If you can reassess then and learn how to move forward, you should be okay. I only say this with hindsight, looking back on the bro and others. Frankly, I didn't have a whole lot to reassess, or else reassessment has always been so much a part of my life that it was spread out rather than concentrated. Bit like adolescence – I never really did that either.

Anyway, I'd almost tripled the size of the Pleasure Palace by buying the flat upstairs, which had a great roof terrace, and I gave a monster house-warming party.

A work colleague had once said that I didn't get out enough, and he was right – most of my activities were indoor, though I had taken up jogging. And made sure I got in more outdoor pleasuring, which was great but difficult to arrange and frequently uncomfortable.

So now I had the ground floor, let out, with the upper two floors and roof terrace for myself, which was magic, 'cos nothing overlooked the terrace, so I was all set for outdoor pleasuring opportunities with all the comforts of home attached! The renovation took a couple of years and I gave away tons of stuff in the process – it was almost like I'd died. The en-suite bathroom to the main bedroom wasn't everyone's cup of tea – tiny turquoise and gold mosaic tiling floor to ceiling against a chocolate brown ground, with a fabulously vulgar gold bathtub and turquoise and brown towels – but it always drew gasps. It just glowered with confidence. It was secret and blatant and totally unafraid of its own extravagance. Very me.

I did lots of entertaining and made good use of the extra space. I'd put the study upstairs, and done it in all the orange/copper/red hues I'd fantasised about, and the CP – who was the only one allowed in the house before the launch party – had lent herself enthusiastically to fulfilling my other study fantasy. More than once, ach'ly. She too carried on opening up more than ever. Great stuff.

You might be thinking it was all CP, CP, CP at this stage, but that's not really the case. It's just that she's the best, so she was/is a constant. Her amazing appetite makes us perfect pleasure partners, and she particularly enjoys combining the joys of eating and pleasuring. I should have realised on spit-roast night with my brother the significance of her eagerness to please as many of her orifices as possible at the same time.

When I was doing my cookery course (this is another great way to go if you're serious about training for pleasuring, or if you just want good lays, actually), I used to take the more manageable results round to her place and we'd arrange them on, and eat them off, each other.

And one standout Christmas I gave her a beautiful scarlet leather dog leash with diamanté studs and a long, gold chain. Held my breath a bit on that one, I have to admit, but her witchlike smile broke over her face as she lifted it out of the box. Without a word, she disappeared and returned stark naked except for the leash, heavy dark eye make-up, and a scarlet tanga I'd given her a couple of years earlier.

I whistled her over and she came. My God/Whatever, how she came! We broke our own records that night. First, I put down a bowl of champagne for her in front of the log fire and she lapped some up on all fours while I just sat and admired. Then she gave me tongue while I stung her a few times with the leash's leather handle.

I know, I know, you're thinking back to Miss Pussy and Mr Vet and how I hate role play. But the CP's different. Nothing ever seems contrived or false with her, she just optimises everything within her reach, and that includes me.

When I finally entered her with the Prong, after aeons of delicious all-fours-play, her cunt was hot and oozing wet and I teased her for ages with the tip, smacking her buttocks raw and jerking on the leash for punishment when she tried to push back onto the whole rod.

She came eight times in all, the first three in variations on doggie-style by the fire, with me filling her ears and anus with my fingers and feeding her chunks of chocolate from the palm of my hand during each climax, and her lapping champagne thirstily from her bowl afterwards.

And when she finally stopped, sated, I laid her down on her back on the hearth rug, removed the leash and, ignoring her unprecedented murmurs of 'I don't think I can take any more', prised apart her resisting thighs and plunged in up to the hilt. Her upper body convulsed upwards, I caught her slack and exhausted torso and supported her while I thrust long and slow and deep, and gradually her head lolled back and her beautiful dark eyes melted all down the sides of her face as I ploughed towards her centre.

She was still weeping when I eased out centuries later. Knowing that I wouldn't be able to touch her till her raw nerve endings settled, I reached up for a rug from the sofa and covered her cooling flesh, tracing her tears with butterfly kisses.

Desire is the ache to be reunited with a missing part of ourselves. Orgasm reminds us that in the achieving lies the leaving. Death, where is thy sting? All over her pale body; I kissed the wicked little marks left by the lashes of the leash and at last she turned her head towards me and smiled, and we bathed our naked kisses in the laughing pool of champagne.

\*       \*       \*

But on top of the ongoing encounters with the CP, there was the usual pleasure research going on round the time of the Pleasure Palace house-warming party, not to mention a couple of more bizarre, related incidents, such as BM's 19-year-old daughter coming along and asking me to teach her how to give good hand/blowjobs 'cos she'd met a boy she really liked and wanted to blow him away. And you know what? I just thought back to the BM all those years ago, pontificating down the phone after the Ferrari Challenge about how I should stop acting like Little Lord Fauntleroy, admit the joke was on me and call my brother, and I said, 'Come on in, love.'

I did warn her that she wasn't going to find the new boyfriend as well endowed as me, and she nodded intelligently, taking it all in. All I said, I mean. The lesson went really well. It was fascinating to instil knowledge and confidence in someone whose naked body I'd only ever seen at bathtime a couple of decades before. Obviously there was no question of anyone taking their clothes off now, or me touching her or trying to shag her or anything. I wasn't some desperate, dirty old man taking advantage of her innocence. She wanted to learn a specific skill and I was willing to teach her. I did feel a bit weird when I sat back in the armchair and let her unstud my trousers, though. Letting her see the Prong, then touch it, her fine fair hair falling over her hands and an intent look in her eyes.

I told her not to get discouraged if there weren't instant results – the Prong had always had lots of staying power, whereas the new bloke'd probably shoot his wad within 30 seconds of her closing her flowery fingers over his knob. "I know!" she laughed, in a tone that indicated the guy was unloading before he even got the thing out of his trousers. I asked her if that was the case, and she laughed again and admitted it was – he was younger than her, 16 – so while she ran her tongue up and down my stem, glancing up occasionally for approval, I suggested a few techniques that might help him hang on till they'd got some action together, 'cos if he was that nervous he was probably really keen on her. And I could see how he might find her intimidating: she wasn't staggeringly beautiful or clever or anything, but she dressed in an edgy way and had that I-can-take-care-of-myself expression flashing out from under the jaggedly-cut hair.

Then I got her hand-pumping while lick-sucking, and I caressed her still-round cheeks and remembered to tell her that if a guy didn't stroke her hair or touch her or murmur thanks/appreciation during a blowjob, he was a selfish turd and deserved to be left mid-blow. I was being a really good teacher, in fact. I was just thinking I ought to try and come quickly so as to build her confidence, though the temptation was to let her soft young lips and brittle wrists carry on trying, when the doorbell rang and I froze. She raised her head, glanced at her huge orange watch and said,

"Oh, that'll be Dad. He said he'd pick me up."

"What!" I hissed. "You told him you were here?"

"Yes, sure I did. Came to borrow your book on Egypt for my Fine Arts course, didn't I? Can I come back round the same time on Thursday?"

"He's got his own key, you know!"

"Blimey! Has he? Why?"

"In case anything happens to me, you silly little tart," I snapped, thrusting the protesting Prong back into my trousers as the bell rang twice more. "I've got his keys too."

"Makes sense," she nodded, obviously thinking it was a good idea for the old folk to look out for each other.

"Tell him I'm with someone, tell him I'm having a shower, tell him anything. Give him some tea. I can't see him like this, he'd kill me!"

She giggled and went to open the door while I lugged the Prong into my en-suite bathroom and slammed the door, sweating. Gawd! Teenagers! Didn't know their own daftness.

When I emerged several minutes later, they were supping tea in the kitchen.

"Hello mate!" exclaimed BM. "Thanks for lending her the book – she needs it for her coursework, doncha love? They're all out in her library and it'd cost a fortune to buy."

"Yes, I hadn't realised how *huge* it'd be," she said, grinning at me with her back to her father. "Good job Dad could pick me up."

"Yep, well, my pleasure, no probs," I managed to say. "I'll leave you to it, though – got company, mate!"

I jerked a hand towards my bedroom and winked at BM. He gave me a thumbs-up and winked and leered back at me, and I disappeared till they'd buggered off.

The girl did come back on Thursday and we had time to take it easy. When she managed to bring me off and I clutched her hair and cried out in the moments of release, she lifted her eyes in innocent amazement and gazed at her dad's best friend, fully clothed yet totally naked before her. I smiled, touched her cheek, said 'Thanks'.

"Wow," she said, no hint of a naughty grin. "That's . . . . awesome. That's different from other times I've tried. That's how it should be, isn't it?"

"Yes it is," I assured her. "You're learning. You'll be able to blow your trouser-stainer away, no problem."

Well, that was that: all very nice but she was the single-minded sort who'd learnt what she set out to and I was a busy guy, so we didn't need any more sessions, and I was left with the pleasant sensation of having spread my knowledge on fertile ground.

I did begin to feel as though my Charity was being taken advantage of, though, when BM's wife rang me a couple of weeks later – *surely* the kid hadn't told her mum? – and asked if she could come round for tea and sex. I laughed and said of course, assuming it was a joke. Well, you would, wouldn't you?

Turned out she was divorcing BM and was dead serious about the sex! I was blown away.

"But, divorce?" I exclaimed. "You can't mean it! He hasn't said anything to me. He thinks the world of you!"

She gave me a no-point-trying-to-make-me-feel-better smile and said,

"He's told you that, has he? No, thought not. He hasn't told me he loves me once in the past ten years . . . ."

"Ten years!"

". . . . and we haven't had sex for six. We sleep in separate bedrooms. The kids are grown up, I've stuck it out for them, he's a great father. But I'm sick of him looking at other women . . . ."

"He only looks!"

"I know, it's almost worse. No excuse for kicking him out. I'm just tired of financing the whole family, and he's lied to me for years. Sorry, I know he's your best friend. I thought you of all people would know how it was – he's borrowed money off most of his friends, they don't come round or call any more."

"No sex for six years!"

"Well, I don't know about him, but I've been all right for that. Can I have some more tea?"

"What?"

"More tea."

"No, you know what I mean!"

Well, turned out she'd been banging the gardener! Not some tea-guzzling old Percy who whacked off in the rose bushes, either, but a muscular, genial bloke I'd chatted to myself several times! Used to be in IT, then he re-trained and went into landscape gardening etc. Mainly the etc, by the looks of it. Talk about a handyman round the place. And they were going to get married and move to Corfu and run a hotel together. Well, she had the dosh and she'd earned it, but of course I felt bad for BM.

"I can't believe it!" I kept muttering.

She held out her cup for more tea and added the tragic clincher, the lesson I'd learned decades before:

"I wouldn't have minded, I could've handled it, I honestly could – not everyone's good with money – but he *lied* to me. For years. I can't live with that."

BM didn't want to talk about it when I asked him what was going on in the pub a few nights later. I could see her point: he evaded issues.

"Yeah, divorce, that's what she wants. Shame, but I'll still get to see the kids same as always, that's the main thing."

Hm, right. His kids were almost-adults, burning along the highway to ecstasy, his choices nothing but a blur in their rear-view.

"Anyway, it was bound to happen," he said, shrugging. "Never did understand what a smart girl like her saw in me. No education, no brain. She was a stock-broker, remember? Smart girl. Couldn't believe it when she said yes. Wasn't hard to see this coming, was it?"

He sniffed hard and went to the bog, and I thought, bugger me, talk about self-fulfilling prophecy! Made me see him in a whole new light. A dim one. After 30 years of waiting for disaster, he was now doomed to winking and belching at barmaids down the local over a pint of the usual for the next 30. Sloth, anyone?

"Yeah, but it's not too late yet, is it?" I said when he came back from the Gents. "I mean, you just need to cut this new berk out of the equation by giving her a third option."

"Third option?"

"Yeah, the new you! You know, do an intensive massage course and take her away for a few days and give her the works. Make her think a bit."

He gave me a really foul look and said,

"You've always got some fucking trite little solution up your sleeve, haven't you? Massage course! She's leaving me – don't you get it? She doesn't want me. Doesn't want me, that's all there is to it."

"Well, yeah, that's why I'm saying change yourself a bit, then she might want . . ."

"Shut up! Shut the fuck up! Never even had a proper girlfriend, let alone a marriage! You do not know what you're talking about!"

I know, I know. Like my brother – hurtful. Easier to lash out than to think about what someone's saying to you. But he was my mate, so I let it rest for a few minutes then tried again.

"Cooking course, then?"

"She's a Cordon Bleu! She's been running her own catering business for 20 years!"

"Oh right, yeah, you're right."

I wracked my brains while he glumly sank the rest of his pint and gestured for another, and then I went a bit wrong – although I honestly was just trying to help, I was a bit flustered, that's all – 'cos I said (and you'll recognise this from earlier);

"Well, you know, mate, gardening isn't the Percy game it used to be. You're right, you don't want to try and compete in the kitchen, but how about doing a gardening . . ."

Which is the point where I realised what I'd just said and shut up as requested, though not soon enough to stop him punching me in the face and walking out.

You probably want to know if I went to bed with his wife. Oh come on! That's a no-brainer, innit?

*   *   *

Although he didn't show up for the Pleasure Palace house-warming, which did upset me a bit 'cos we'd been mates forever and it wasn't my fault gardening conversation was suddenly taboo, BM's daughter brought the new boyfriend and a gaggle of skimpily-clad young things along, and gave me a thumbs-up when I raised enquiring eyebrows at her and the foetus fatale boyfriend.

"Who's that?" asked Stepkid, who was meeting most of these people for the first time, and had turned up surrounded by several sharp whizzkids – probably all impotent at 30 from yapping at stocks 'n' shares boards all morning, but decorative nonetheless. When seen in a group.

He poured more wine into my glass while I explained and then caught his breath, looking over my shoulder.

"What?" I said, turning. The CP had just arrived, I noticed. "What is it?"

"Nothing," he replied vaguely, so I went off to greet her.

It was only later, when I saw them chatting, that I connected her entrance with his gasp of admiration, and I began to keep an eye on them. And I confess I was worried. There must've been at least 25 years between them, but I'd always thought of her in terms of 'Age cannot wither her, nor custom stale her infinite variety', so it didn't exactly surprise me that he should be attracted to her humorous serenity. They were both, perhaps, a little wicked. And I'm not. I realised that. I'm basically conservative – that doesn't mean repressed or boring or hung-up, obviously, it just means I can be shocked.

And when I saw the tempting/tempted lilt at the corner of her mouth, the enticing response in her eyes when he murmured something into her hair, I lost it. He was going to have her! He could! He wanted her. Fine. But, and this was the shocker – I suddenly saw that *she* wanted *him*!

It was like seeing all the gods and goddesses in my private Pleasure Pantheon turn and stare as Temptation, clad in everyone's favourite gear, holographically gorgeous, slid unchecked through the locked gates and sauntered among them.

And Desire herself was just stepping down off her pedestal when I reached her side, put my arm round her waist – the kind of thing I never did 'cos people start making all those dumb 'couple' cracks – and kissed her lips, open in laughter at what he'd just said.

"Don't you dare!" I whispered into her ear. "Don't you dare!"

She laughed softly and tilted her head to look beyond me at Stepkid. There was a tense, three-way pause and I just kept thinking of that Orbison song about the girl's old lover reappearing and him yodelling, 'Which one would it beeeee?' higher and higher before she 'turned away and walked awaaaaaaay with meeeeeeeeeeeeeeeeeeeeeeeeeeee!' Not before she said it had been lovely talking to him and he'd given her his card. I knew she might call him – fair enough.

"Just didn't want to see it, okay?"

"Fine," she replied serenely.

It had always been our pact. No details, no diseases.

Stepkid was still there on the fringes, toying with his canapé and apparently unable to stop giving her the eye, when his mother appeared and said,

"You two always seem to be together, but you're not . . . . a couple, are you?"

The CP turned laughing eyes towards me and said,

"No, we're just . . . . always."

"Always and forever," I agreed, touching her fingertips with mine.

Her smile came up to meet my lips and Stepkid just disappeared, carried away by the flood of our warm passion, his mother's awed 'Wow' swept back to and around us in ever-diminishing ripples under the requited rainbow of Desire.

When I opened my eyes after that kiss, the CP had slipped away in her magically elusive way, and I was looking at my mother. Well, she was looking at me. With curiosity, I think.

"When you were a teenager, you were very mature," she remarked.

"Yes, I know," I put in.

Didn't want the old duck highlighting her senility by chuntering on about my childhood in front of the guests. Not that anyone seemed to be listening, but I'm a person with rights as well, and I just didn't want to hear it. Looked round for another drink.

"Everyone used to comment on it," she continued. "I didn't know why all my friends complained about adolescence until your brother hit his teens."

"Well, that wasn't adolescence, Mother, the man's a problem person and that's all there's ever been to it. Good thing he hasn't had kids, if you ask me. It's probably hard for . . . ."

"But just now, when I saw you kiss her, you looked like the teenager you never were."

There was a silence. I thought I was way too old to be getting this kind of talk from her. I had just bought myself a Maserati, for heaven's sake. Metallic blueberry, packed to the topless with gadgets.

"Or have always been?" I challenged, and she smiled.

"Or have always been. But I didn't mean it as a criticism. And she's the same, isn't she?"

"Yes, she's the same."

"Never to lose one's illusions," murmured my mother. "You are luckier than you know."

She turned as if to drift off, but I grabbed her arm angrily and her surprised gaze switched back to my face at once.

"You're wrong there," I told her. "I have always known how lucky I am, and how dedicated you need to be to get lucky sometimes. Believe me, I do not let a single moment of 'luck' slide by unperceived. I take every, tiny drop of enjoyment on my naked skin. And I *feel* it. I feel it in a way no-one else seems to. Except her."

For a few seconds I held her gaze, angered by her clichéd dismissal of my vocation. Not that she knew about it, of course. Illusions have to be maintained. But they are real, they exist, they cannot be 'lost'. To lose sight of them might be possible, I wouldn't know, but to lose them altogether? No. People get tired of looking after them, that's all.

My mother was still gazing at me and I realised I was still holding her arm, and after a few more moments I understood what her look meant. For the first time, she'd experienced me as a man, not as her son.

"Don't you *ever* have doubts?" she said finally, in a soft, wondering tone.

"Doubts!" I exclaimed scornfully. "Did Jesus Christ have doubts? Did . . . ."

"Yes, he did. He suffered horribly because of his doubts. He . . . ."

"Oh all right, all right. But he got over it, didn't he? Made the right call in the end. A bit of doubt's okay, but it's usually like embarrassment or regret – a total waste of time. People spin these things out to avoid taking action or making changes."

"I see," said my mother. "So you think Christ was spinning it out to avoid taking action?"

(I'd only picked on him because I thought it would strike a chord with her, by the way).

"Yeah, 'course he was. Wouldn't you? He knew what he had to do – get crucified. Just wriggling around a bit to see if there was a way out of it. So would I. Who wants to be crucified?"

"But you were comparing yourself to him just now because neither of you had any doubts, apparently," said my mother, swinging into cross-examination mode.

"I was just trying to say we both had conviction, that's all!" I snapped. To hell with the Management Techniques Handbook. "He had a tougher option, that's all. Or maybe he was just less decisive than me. Don't you get it?"

"Ah, interesting!" she remarked. "Now you're being like a teenager again, but not in a good sense."

"Look, if you're judging me by him," I said, jerking my head towards my brother, "there never is going to be a good sense. You don't seem to get that either. Can't you see the difference? Can't you . . . . ?"

I suppose I must have raised my voice. The FFs stopped chatting up BM's daughter and were glancing over. The CP materialised at my side like a warm glow and my mother said,

"We very much enjoyed the CD you gave us of your most recent work. It must require so much dedication, what you do."

"Yes," agreed the CP, her fingertips lightly suggestive against the back of my trousers. "But it goes with the territory. No effort, no reward."

"Didn't you ever have any doubts about your career?" inquired my mother slyly.

"Oh no," was the serene reply.

She smiled up at me and my puzzled, defeated mother muttered, 'Teenagers!' and moved away. You'll be glad to hear that she and I made it up over … yep, tea at Selfridges a couple of days later, 'cos a week after that, she and Dad copped it in a speedboat accident at Monte Carlo. I know – stylish or wot? And they were in their 80s and it was quick and they went together. That's what I call a good end to a good life. Never did find out who let them have a speedboat, though. Madness. They could've killed someone.

"Thank you," I whispered against the CP's cheek.

"Mm, but I need a favour in return."

Now I smiled. She had never asked for anything I didn't want to give her. But then, I'm a very generous guy.

"I have a tasty little canapé inside me, and I need help extracting it."

"I see," I murmured, riveting her to my side with one arm and gathering up a bottle with the other hand on our way to my room. Champagne never tasted so sweet as when served from her cunt. "I can help with that. But we mustn't be long."

"You two are disgusting," commented my brother as we passed him. "Always snogging like teenagers."

"Envy is the root of all evil," I retorted.

Behind him I caught a glimpse of Stepkid, a slight frown marring his expressive and – yeah, okay – handsome face.

In love with the abstracts of Pleasure and Music, how could we tire of each other's restless imaginations? Later that night, when everyone else had gone, I played her deep into the harmonious core of our shared universe, eloquent and silent as a tongue.

\*    \*    \*

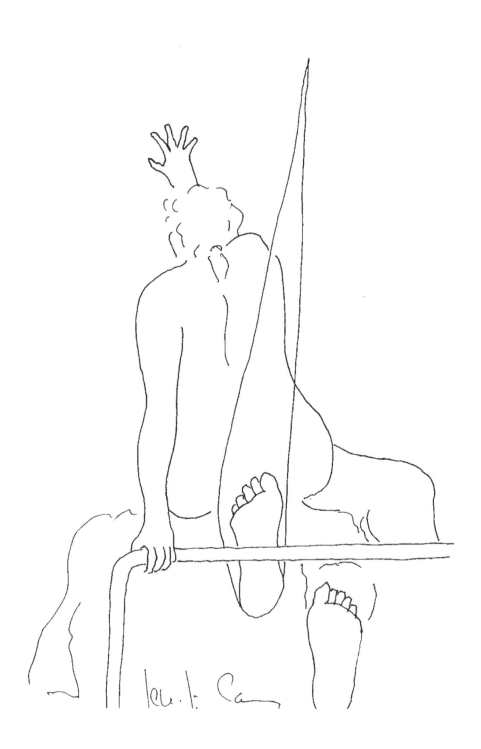

# Appendage

YOU'RE PROBABLY THINKING well, good on you mate, that's nice, chapeau and all that, but what's in this for me? Like I said at the beginning, you should by now have the Golden Rules of Pleasuring at your fingertips. The Protocols. And a handy list of Anti-Protocols.

But let's have a summing-up, save you flipping back through the book, all right?

Desire is the deity in the Pleasure Pantheon. You've really got to want to do it, and do it right. Yeah, bit of effort involved. Desire is not just about fancying someone's knobs off.

I've identified seven Protocols and Anti-Protocols, like the Sins and Virtues – and the Disciplines. The Disciplines are what my mother would've called vain: they move from mirror to mirror in my Pleasure Pantheon, not, as she would assume, to admire themselves, but rather to assess themselves and work on improvement. They may rest between workouts after each assessment, but they soon get up and start another circuit.

And then you've got Luck, which has its place in the Pantheon – like the colourful, deformed little court jester, it will do more harm out than in. Don't forget, Luck swings both ways . . . .

So the full line-up is:-

# DESIRE

## *PROTOCOLS*

- **GENEROSITY** (Of spirit, not just wallet)
- **PASSION** (Go for all the positive sorts – that plonker with the baseball bat tried to get off with a crime of passion argument! It didn't fly, but you'd be surprised how often it does)
- **OPENNESS** (Includes telling the truth. Well, the bits they can handle)
- **JUDGMENT** (99.9% of people have an agenda, they are incapable of hearing what you are really saying, they will chop you into mincemeat and call it love, just to get what they want. I know, I know, that sounds bitter, but remember what happened to me when I lost my judgment temporarily?)
- **FAITH** (You *can* do it! Well, I can do it, so you may be able to if you're paying attention to all this)
- **FUN** (Can take a bit of negotiating. Farting in bed may be fun for you but not for the rest of us)
- **RESPONSIBILITY** (Don't reach out for things you don't want. I'm proud to say I've always nipped it in the bud when someone looks like falling in love with me – I don't do STDs)

## *ANTI-PROTOCOLS*

- **DULLNESS** (Being boring/humourless/unimaginative, especially in bed)
- **WASTE** (Not making best use of your talents or hers, especially in bed)
- **IMPATIENCE** (Especially in bed)
- **FEAR** (Usually a waste of time, or an excuse for being inadequate)
- **IRRESPONSIBILITY** (Hurting people deliberately or unnecessarily is really crap, just Plonkerville)
- **DISHONESTY** (Anything from faking orgasm to maintaining an unhealthy relationship)
- **JEALOUSY** (Hm, yeah, well, feel free to contact me about your own experiences with that one – jury's still out for me)

## *DISCIPLINES*

- **Awareness** (Yes, of your own actions and . . . . what's that thing I've heard about? Shortcomings. Yes, look out for your shortcomings and correct them)
- **Dedication** (Pleasure is a decision)
- **Acceptance** (Other people are often plonkers, including in bed: you can't expect them to be up to your level. At least, you probably can, but I can't)

## *LUCK'S BACKING GROUP*

- **Imagination**
- **Abandonment**
- **Reciprocity**
- **Joie de vivre**

If you ain't got the last lot, you can't learn or buy them. Sorry about that, mate. But you can still have a lot of success. Just won't be as much fun. G'luck!

## *END*

Printed in Great Britain
by Amazon

59162372R00098